"*The Promise of the Pelican* is Hoffman at his best: Adventurous, soulful, perceptive, tender, gutsy and wise."
—Dewey English, *Alabama Media Group, Huntsville Times, Birmingham News, Mobile Press-Register*

"Roy Hoffman secures his place alongside the great American writers from the Deep South."
—Michael J. Gerhardt, distinguished professor University of North Carolina at Chapel Hill School of Law, and author of *Lincoln's Mentors: The Education of a Leader.*

"Filled with heart-stopping events and complicated characters . . . Good and evil, right and wrong are interwoven in this memorable novel from the New South."
—Lee Smith, author of *The Last Girls*

"A thrilling novel, with characters as memorable as those of Shakespearean tragedy . . . I could not put it down."
—Sena Jeter Naslund, author of *Ahab's Wife, Four Spirits*

"Hoffman is at the height of his powers, his language vigorous and transportive . . . This mystery, drama, literary marvel swept me up and would not let me go."
—Elaine Neil Orr, award-winning author of *Swimming Between Worlds*

"*The Promise of the Pelican* is a masterpiece of oral and visual creation, a dramatic and searching tale about immigration and assimilation."
—Sabe Fink, *Fairhope Living*

"Though a murder is at the center of this masterly novel, Hoffman is most interested in writing about people, the best of us and the worst of us."
—Charles Salzberg, Shamus-nominated author of *Man on the Run*

"Hoffman's narrative is a contemporary nod to the Harper Lee classic, *To Kill a Mockingbird* . . . The ending is beautifully moving."
—Heidi Slowinski, *Jewish Book Carnival, Association of Jewish Libraries*

"Roy Hoffman has become one of Alabama's best storytellers."
—Don Noble, *Alabama Public Radio, Tuscaloosa News, Yahoo News*

"Powerful."
—*Walter Edgar's Journal, South Carolina Public Radio*

"A fast-paced and mesmerizing novel."
—*Mystery Tribune*

"Hits the sweet spot for me because it's a murder mystery . . . quite well written."
—Cynthia Tucker, Pulitzer-Prize winning journalist, *11 Best Books for Summer*

"A character-driven page turner."
—Frye Gaillard, *Mobile Bay Magazine*

"Hoffman masterfully weaves in Hank's own lingering childhood trauma to show the source of his empathy for the oppressed."
—Laura Platas Scott, *Alabama Writers Forum*

"The one thing we know about a Roy Hoffman novel is that it's full of love and hope and generosity and spirit."
—Susan Larson, *The Reading Life,* WWNO, New Orleans

THE PROMISE OF THE PELICAN

A Novel

ROY HOFFMAN

ARCADE
CrimeWise

An Arcade CrimeWise Book

Novels by Roy Hoffman:
Almost Family (1983)
Chicken Dreaming Corn (2004)
Come Landfall (2014)

Nonfiction:
Back Home: Journeys Through Mobile (2001)
Alabama Afternoons: Profiles and Conversations (2011)

Arcade CrimeWise Paperback Edition 2024

Arcade Publishing books may be purchased in bulk at special discounts for sales promotion, corporate gifts, fund-raising, or educational purposes. Special editions can also be created to specifications. For details, contact the Special Sales Department, Arcade Publishing, 307 West 36th Street, 11th Floor, New York, NY 10018 or arcade@skyhorsepublishing.com.

Arcade Publishing® and CrimeWise® are registered trademarks of Skyhorse Publishing, Inc.®, a Delaware corporation.

Visit our website at www.arcadepub.com.
Please follow our publisher Tony Lyons on Instagram @tonylyonsisuncertain

10 9 8 7 6 5 4 3 2 1

Library of Congress Cataloging-in-Publication Data is available on file.

ISBN: 978-1-956763-91-1
Ebook ISBN: 978-1-956763-09-6

Cover design by Erin Seaward-Hiatt
Cover photo by JD Crowe

Printed in the United States of America

With love and gratitude to my wife, Nancy,
Our daughter, Meredith,
And the memory of
My mother, Evelyn, and father, Charles,
Who was Alabama's oldest practicing attorney
At age ninety-seven

AUTHOR'S NOTE

The promise of the pelican, by legend, is that the great bird, in dire times, will pierce its breast for blood to feed the starving chicks. From medieval bestiaries to heraldry, religion to literature—"the kind life-rend'ring pelican" Shakespeare wrote in *Hamlet*—the soaring creature evokes sacrifice, devotion, protection of the young and the vulnerable.

A Pelican Feeding Her Young 1278–1300, unknown illuminator, Franco-Flemish. Tempera colors, pen and ink, gold leaf, and gold paint on parchment, The J. Paul Getty Museum.

PART I

1
DUTCH

IN FIRST LIGHT, ON THE vast bed he was not yet accustomed to inhabiting alone, Hank lay awake listening to Roger's breathing where his grandson slumbered on the nearby sofa. In and out, in out, steady, no congestion, thank the Lord.

He is four and I am eighty-two and when he's my age I'll be 160.

He will have to be Methuselah, he knows, if his daughter keeps up her reckless ways. Somebody has to care for the child.

The luminous clock on the nightstand showed 5:30 a.m. Fran starting up the grill at Jewel's Café for the old-timers, the changing of police shifts in the somnolent station, the Brown brothers on the pier with their arsenal of rods and reels in position—Hank's mind clicked through morning rituals of the little town. Somewhere a couple were rolling toward each other in half-drowse (how often he and Margery had done so when their bodies were electric and he was not yet preoccupied with his criminal law demands for the day) enfolding each other like new lovers again. But she was fading no matter how he tried to hold on.

He heard a scrabbling at the front door. "Lupita?" He got up, padded into the living room and pulled back the curtain and thumped the window: beneath his pecan tree squirrels scurried off with their bounty. He opened the door. The October air of coastal Alabama was finally fresh and cool, like September along the Prinsengracht Canal in his boyhood Amsterdam. He whispered the *Shehecheyanu* prayer welcoming the new season.

Lupita had never been this late: five forty-five. He went back in to the bedroom. On the sofa, made up with blankets and pillow, Roger stirred.

What his grandson saw and heard he could not tell. The boy understood more than he could express and sometimes laughed when nothing seemed funny or cried when startled by what seemed like no big deal. Did he make up for it in his dreams? Maybe there he was like any other four-year-old running across the playground and scampering up the jungle gym without falling, or casting a line and reeling it in, fine motor skills smoothly developing.

He envisioned the road leading down to the pier, and could smell the mullet.

It was now 6 a.m. "Lupita be damned," he said. "C'mon, Roger." He bent down and tousled his hair. The boy blinked up at him. "Gradee," he said.

"I'm your Gradee, right, c'mon now. It's time I taught you something useful."

He helped the child dress, fixed him breakfast, and snugged him into a Crimson Tide sweatshirt.

"Know that when we get where we're going you'll have to stay put," he said. "I'm too old to be jumping into the bay after you. OK?"

"O," Roger said, and a moment later, grasping Hank's hand, "K."

"Thatta boy. You can help me pull the wagon."

He went out to the net hanging dry after he'd run the garden hose over it yesterday to rinse off the brackish bay water, lifted it off its peg, and coiled it onto the red wagon. He filled a Styrofoam chest with ice and set it in next to the net. He grabbed the handle of the wagon with one hand and Roger's hand with the other. They started off.

Down the lane where magnolias canopied creole cottages, by the porch where the rocker sat empty of his late friend, Judge Nikos, toward the bay peeking through the pines where a bar pilot navigated a freighter to port, they made their way. They passed the seafood restaurant where his firm held his retirement party—how he'd prayed that Margery would rally and they'd enjoy his new free time together—but that retirement, now in its lonesome fourth year after her rapid decline, seemed to stretch behind him for decades.

If it hadn't been for going to speak to the judge a couple of months ago about his daughter's dangerous repeat DUIs, he wouldn't have been inside a courtroom at all. An attorney herself who should have known better, Vanessa reacted like the air had been knocked out of her when given an alternative sentence at the Beacon Home for Women, but he'd felt satisfied. Her firm put her on medical leave, a damn good deal, too, he told her, and with Lupita's help he could handle Roger. He'd gone home and kissed Margery's picture, changed clothes, and headed out to the pier.

Behind them as they walked, Roger's little legs moving in a lopsided gait, the wagon bumped and rattled. He should have brought a radio—that would keep Roger occupied if he wanted to wander, any kind of music would.

Hank glanced behind him, imagining Lupita hurrying to his door, always showing up on the dot to help take care of Roger through the long day. "Don't keep her on," one of his neighbors had said. "Those people pick up and move in the middle of the night. Immigration police come snooping around and they're gone."

"Do you live in my house?" he'd said. "Mind your own damn business."

Through the trees he caught his first glimpse of the pier stretching out a quarter mile into the water. There was a skein of light over the bay.

"There it is, Roger, look. Fairhope Pier! We're gonna catch some fish."

"Fih."

"Yes, Fih. And plenty of them if we hurry."

During his years practicing law, he and Margery had been rooted in Mobile across the bay, picking up a weekend cottage in this waterfront village. When Vanessa went off to college they'd expanded the cottage, making it their full-time home, Hank commuting the half hour into Mobile, handling cases on the Fairhope side of the bay, too. He'd spent his first hours drinking coffee with Margery and reading the news, checking the weather in the Netherlands and the price of air travel though he hadn't set foot there in the decades since his escape. But he was too busy to venture down that dark path again. During his career the glimpse of old men languishing on a pier on a workday morning made him shake his head at the thought of folks whose productive lives were over.

Now he could not get to his spot fast enough, his heart leaping with the sight of every mullet net spinning out in a golden circle.

They arrived at the top of the bluff, the sidewalk leading down to the pier in a long curve. The water was slick.

Pelicans swooped and plummeted to scoop up shiny menhaden before flapping aloft again. "What a show!" he exclaimed to Roger. "They fly together, a family, just like us." He started to tell him of the legend that a pelican, if her chicks were starving, would pierce her own breast to feed them her blood. But he didn't want to scare him. "They'll do anything for the babies, like I will, like your Mommy. She loves you."

"Mommy."

Down by the marker for the founding of the single tax colony in 1894, past the rose garden fountain they made their way.

At the pier's start he saw the Flounder King and the retired butcher nicknamed Cap'n and the man who spoke through a hole in his throat called Ol' Fella and the Rev. Jonathan Blue, forever mourning his son, all focused on their endeavors. Roger was captivated by the Flounder King in his straw hat. Even as they kept walking down the pier, Roger was turning his head to watch the lean old-timer walking along the railing dragging his line.

"Look here," said Hank. He saw Roger gazing back over his shoulder. "No matter. You'll come around."

They got toward the end of the pier, to a spot the regulars knew was Hank's, and settled in. "You sit here." Hank lifted out the ice chest and set it down and patted the lid. Roger took his position.

"Now," Hank said, "we prepare."

How he loved the swirl of the netting rising over his arm, its folds like Margery's skirt slipped off, bunched against the sofa.

He lengthened out part of it, shook out the kinks, making sure the weights on the hem hung free, and trained his gaze on the bay.

Roger, on the edge of the ice chest, was a very good boy.

"Know what I'm looking for?"

Roger sat motionless, staring out, then turned his eyes to Gradee.

"Look there, son."

Even though the sky was cloudless, a patch of darkness moved swiftly over the water as if a fragment of cloud blown across the sky were casting a shadow.

"It's a spirit breathing on the water."

The spirit raced toward them and Hank rocked back then forward, letting the net fly.

The orb of light on the Prinsengracht Canal from his childhood window, the turn in the Alabama River at Selma when he was a teen, the full moon rising across the woods from the bay —all the patterns of his life blending into this near perfect "o" of netting that turned straight down and lassoed the bay.

There was a shimmer of silver beneath the surface. "Look, Roger!"

Hank pulled on the cord attached to the net and the glimmers showed themselves as the rounded heads of fish. The net became a loose sack brought high over the water until Hank drew it all the way up, gave it a yank, and the bag came over the railing and plopped down on the wharf.

Roger got up cautiously, bending to the creatures, holding one hand out, a tiny finger pointing at the eye of the biggest mullet, the fish lying still as if paralyzed by the light, Roger's finger getting closer until Hank said, "Don't poke his eye now, that'd be mean," the fish sighing, already resigned, it seemed, to whatever bizarre fate it had encountered on what had begun as a sunstruck, swimmable morning.

The mullet gave one violent spasm, flopping up as if a flying fish and Roger was off, his little legs churning, no longer the tyke lollygagging on the walk but a four-year-old making a dash for the railing, up and over it now.

Arms and legs flailing, he was airborne for a long moment as Hank gasped and raised his hands as if to cup Roger's head in a Sabbath blessing—"God bless you and keep you"—the boy seeing who knows what sunlight, bay, twirling nets, sailboat masts, looping gulls all far from the evil eye of the fish. Then he dropped straight down.

That Hank's heart might give out was of no concern only that he go flying over the railing too.

But then he saw a small agile form beating him there, the woman's leg over the railing in a seamless move like a hurdle jumper, and Lupita was in the air, thick black hair flying upward as she plummeted down and, by the time Hank got to the spot, bobbing up with the boy in her arms.

"Oh, Lupita, Lupita, thank you." Hank felt the tears streaming down his face. "Lord, thank you." He tasted their salt, the bitter herbs of an old man's neglect.

"Lo siento, lo siento."

I am sorry, Lupita kept repeating, soon able to stand in the shallows, carting Roger along.

A small crowd quickly gathered, the Flounder King, the all-night sitters, the Brown brothers and Ol' Fella, all pushing around.

Lupita came ashore holding Roger, squeezing him tight, then setting him down. The boy uttered nothing, but pressed up against her.

Hank squatted until he was eye to eye with his grandson, reaching out to him. The child looked at him shyly, then went to him.

"It was because of Julio," said Lupita. "My brother."

Hank nodded, not understanding her reference, but happy just to be holding Roger who relaxed against him now.

"The police came to my house, *buscándole*. Looking for him. *Oh, Mr. Hank. Necesito su ayuda.*"

Ayuda. Help.

"Anything for you, Lupita. You saved my boy's life."

"Julio, *la policía*, the police, they say they are looking for the man who did a killing last night."

2
JULIO

On the dirt lane behind the small house, he moved through the lifting darkness, the blue light of the sheriff's car cutting swathes through the misty dawn. The light from Lupita's room shone like a fading beacon behind him. He had gone there long enough to change his bloody shirt, grab a jacket against the October chill, and somehow lie down and sleep a fitful hour or two, the violence on the seventeenth green—the golfer's white polo shirt turning red with blood, the man's hand twisting toward him, cash spilling onto the ground—surreal in his head, a grotesque dream that had taken him over and not let go. Why had he thought they wouldn't look for him here?

It had been a late afternoon like any other, knocking off at 5 p.m. from his day on the grounds crew at the resort hotel, taking the short cut by the lush camellia garden that looked out to the sweeping fairways of the hotel's golf course, the big oaks casting long shadows like ghosts stalking the last players scooting by in their carts. He was behind his usual schedule, though, having lingered to visit with a Honduran newcomer, typically home by five thirty in the dormitory at the resort perimeter if not traversing the four miles to his sister's for a hot meal and falling asleep in front of the TV watching her telenovelas. Rather than go by the work shed to leave off his serrated garden knife he carried it on his belt, sheathed and ready for the next morning. The boys in the Tulane sweatshirts—he'd seen them the day before, too. *"Hola, amigo,"* one had shouted and waved him over as they stopped their golf cart on their way back to the clubhouse. *"¿Cómo se llama usted?* My Spanish is pretty damn good, huh?"

"My name is Julio," he answered in his rudimentary English.

"¿Usted de Méjico?"

"Honduras," he had answered.

"We love Roatan," they chimed, stopping the cart. "Good ganja, too. You want?"

He knew "ganja," from the Jamaicans who worked in the kitchen.

He'd looked around to make sure no supervisors were watching and stepped closer to them. He'd overstayed his work visa, but no one would bother him unless he was picked up for smoking pot, or another infraction. He was too valuable, he knew, in his cheap but tireless toil.

He sucked on the joint, passing it back and forth to the college boys still seated in the cart who went on about how good the fishing was off the coast of his country. One held out his cell phone for a group selfie, motioned for him to lean in tight, saying, "Peace, Julio," and all three made the peace sign. "Keep the faith, hombre," they yelled as the cart zoomed off. He'd continued on, the sinsemilla already setting him atilt.

"Help me!"

In the encroaching dusk the words had been low and plaintive, coming from the course, and he'd hurried to see who called out. The golfer alone on the green, holding onto the pin, wavered before Julio, the pot turning the fairway into liquid green that he stepped across, faster now.

There was no one else on the fairways, only the arcing shapes of the trees, wraiths spilling over the sand trap, onto the clipped grasses.

"Help me."

The golfer's white polo shirt was turning deep red, the blood soaking the fabric, his red pants like the bright flash of a cardinal that came from the nearby woods.

Julio thought to yell out, but the man seemed to utter his name, and crumpled bills spilled from his pockets, a ball of fifties and hundreds in his grip. It was as though he were handing it all to Julio.

He smelled sweat and grass and the unmistakable stench of whiskey, too, and the man, uttered, "Take it," he thought—could it be?—dropping the bills, and reaching out to grab him.

He felt himself in the crush of the golfer's embrace—beefy, hot, the man beginning to sag—and it was as though he were being pulled down into the earth, the clipped golf course a maw sucking them both in.

He heard a voice inside, "Run," and was holding a stranger sinking down, his face so familiar now, like other golfers he'd seen liquored up, lit with booze and betting.

Run.

A wooziness overtook Julio and the golfer falling to the ground, blood seeping into the green around him, seemed unreal, and he watched his own hand grabbing at the cash, sensing he might need it for the long haul ahead. Had the golfer said "Take it?" Had he said, "Run?"

He looked around frantically. With no phone he thought to reach into the golfer's pocket and find his, calling 911, or just shouting for help. But then he saw a distant figure, another worker, who'd emerged from a distant sand trap and was yelling at him. From his right, a flash of red again—a hurtling redbird?—and his feet were in motion.

Through the gloom he raced, into a construction area where the hotel was building condos, into a partially built residence, its walls sheltering him against prying eyes. In the far distance he was aware of the whoop of sirens and then it stilled, like the night, the dampness circling him round.

When there was no movement anywhere, no sound, he found himself leaning back against a wall and closing his eyes before the golfer loomed before him. Only the wads of cash crumpled up in his pocket made him realize what had happened. The stench of sweat and whiskey, the man's oily skin and pomade of his hair, his chunky arms clutching him, holding tight, then grip loosening—the kaleidoscope of sensations coursed through him.

"Lupita," he said, and started toward her home, past stately houses at the perimeter of the resort, through shadows beyond the reach of streetlights, farther into the county where red brick ranch houses stood on clearings and a barbecue smokehouse was dark and shuttered. He turned into the woods to follow a back path to Lupita's, the hooting of barred owls and racket of crickets his company. When he got caught in a tangle of vines he pulled out his knife, its sheath covered in the golfer's blood. Ripping at the vines he sliced his finger, his blood spooling onto the knife. He wiped the blade on the sheath and hurled it into the overgrowth, slipping the sheath off his belt and pitching it into a watery ditch.

Arriving at a clearing the stars revolved overhead like he was walking to his house in San Pedro Sula, his mother in the kitchen awaiting him, a lunch bag packed like he was heading off to school instead of the US, where his grandfather had found him work with a chain of resort hotels. He knew what his mother would say: *"La policía. Vete a la policía,"* go to the police, but he would answer, *"No me fío de la poli,"* I don't trust the cops. How could he when so many were on the take? Some controlled by the very gangs they were battling?

Lupita had told him it was otherwise in the US, that here the police could help you, too.

"Ten fe en Dios," Mama's words reverberated. Have faith in God. He would go to the police right away and tell them what had happened.

He did not want to arrive there soaked in death.

At his sister's, he stripped off his shirt and changed into other clothes he kept there and thought to rouse her. But he felt an enormous fatigue, like the marijuana lassoing him in its own net, and lay down for a few minutes. The darkness covered him like a cowl, safe, warm, secure.

He woke with a start as the blue lights flickered through the air and knew that if he were picked up he'd have no story they'd believe and he'd be thrown into an Alabama jail, or worse, sent home for judgment, his work papers expired, where the Scorpions gang would hunt him down as they had vowed.

If he could just make it as far as New Orleans.

Heading out from Lupita's, her house trailer next to open land, he went from stand to stand of trees, racing across a field where a boy in pajamas on his porch like a red-haired goblin shouted, "There's a man playing chase in the yard." Julio veered away toward the road, glancing behind to see the boy inside the house with his mother looking out from parted curtains. The sun rose and he stayed an hour in a barn, then took off down another road where the turf farms stretched to both sides, Latino men rolling up the grass like coils of carpet. Here is where Immigration and Customs Enforcement looked the other way he knew, ICE authorities downing beer and boiled shrimp with the landowners at the seafood joints, their kids dating each other in high school. It was not until the word came from above that it was time to crack down, candidates for office decrying the crime of illegal immigration, local authorities pushed by the feds—*tolerancia cero,* zero tolerance, was the new mandate—that the white cars with ICE logos would roar up, sending the Mexicans and Guatemalans and Salvadorans and Hondurans scooting off into the fields. Then the tension eased off, it always seemed, and Spanish voices rose again bending, cutting, picking over the lush, coastal terrain.

Which way to the skiff he and Paco had bought for a pittance from a Colombian being deported? They'd tied it up in a tributary leading to Fish River then out to the bay. He'd recently filled the gas canisters for the 25 hp outboard, enough juice to get him across the bay to the Mississippi Sound where he could refuel before heading to Louisiana. Being waterborne, hugging the barrier islands— Dauphin, Horn, Petit Bois, Cat, Ship Island—was his best way to hide.

He came to a crossroads near a gas station where a sheriff's car sat idling. Was it a sign? His mother had spoken to him, as they'd walked home from church, how Jesus set out signs to heed, like street signals, she'd said, showing the way. *"Solo necesitas leerlos,"* she explained. All you need to do is read them.

"My name is Julio Blanco. I work at the Bayfront Resort and Golf Club. Last night I found a man on the golf course stabbed in the chest, bleeding, crying for anyone, dying. I went to help him. He grabbed me, held me in his arms. I was afraid. I ran. God sent me to him, I now know, for a purpose. I am here to tell you what happened, to tell you the truth."

As a pickup truck zoomed by at breakneck speed the sheriff set off his siren, though, and peeled off behind, disappearing around a far bend.

That was the sign.

Julio cut across fields now, stepping through stalks stripped of their corn, to the back of a barnyard where chickens clucked and scattered and a man appeared on his back porch, shotgun in hand, demanding, "What you want round here?"

"I want to work," Julio lied in his best English.

"No work here. Git!"

Julio backed away, walked at a steady pace to the road, and soon recognized the path by the cotton field leading to the creek. He saw the sheriff's patrol car returning from its chase.

He ducked into the cotton field, surrounded by hip-high stalks, and moved through it crouching down for cover. The siren whooped. Another car came from a second direction.

He was a fugitive now, leaving the scene of a murder he did not commit but fleeing like he had. How had God, the protector who watched out for them all, his mother claimed, set him on this path that had taken him to the dark circle ruled by Satan, he now believed, where he'd felt a man's last breath against his neck, sensed the life draining out of him like water shaken from a net?

He found his way back to the path to the creek, locating the skiff. He jumped in, untied the line, squeezed the priming bulb to gas up the motor, and pulled the starter cord. The engine blasted on. He opened the throttle and coursed toward the river, knowing he'd soon find the salvation of the wide-open bay.

3
VANESSA

At the Beacon Home for Women, Vanessa ran her mop in "S" patterns down the hallway, pushing the wet tangle by the cafeteria and toward the common room. "I need to update my CV," she said to herself. "Salutatorian, Andrew Jackson High. Honors graduate, Vassar College. JD, NYU Law. Inmate, Beacon Home for Druggies and Drunks."

Residents of the center for substance and alcohol abuse were called "clients," which made no distinction between those who'd checked in on their own—stressed-out PTA moms, unhappy young marrieds, grandmothers who couldn't stand one more day of pretend—and those, like Vanessa, sent to the Beacon as an alternative to doing time. "Inmate" was more accurate for her, she knew. Two DUIs, the second resulting in the near crash of a motorist who careened off the road when Vanessa had swerved into the oncoming lane—that was enough, in addition to her onerous fine, for a sentence up to a year, most likely at Tutwiler, the women's prison upstate. It had been humiliating but essential to turn to her eighty-two-year old father for help, making her feel like a child again. Putting away his fisherman clothes and donning his old seersucker suit, he'd escorted her to the courtroom and asked for leniency. The judge had admonished Vanessa, "You have a son to raise, a great education, and so much to contribute to our community. This behavior has got to stop." He'd directed her to a long stint at the Beacon, where work and chapel, along with group therapy sessions, was a mandate.

That she had given over care of Roger to her father, with the help of Lupita, had caused her to weep uncontrollably the first night at the clinic, but she also knew—and said in the group circle—that Gradee, as Roger called him, was a monumental figure in the boy's life. And Lupita, in her employ since Roger's birth, was like his big sister and second mother. Any chance Mack would get custody was out of the question. The same demons that had taken her down had destroyed her ex, too, bourbon his vice, vodka hers. Bloody Marys at lunch, martinis at happy hour, vodka tonics to herald sunset near Fairhope Pier. Alcohol heightened Mardi Gras, Fourth of July, college football kickoffs, any occasion a good reason for pouring a libation.

"The nightcaps," she told her group. "It got to the point that without them we couldn't even be intimate."

"What was really going on?" the facilitator asked.

"You're asking if that's what we had in common?" Vanessa questioned aloud. "Our fuel?"

"Only you know the answer."

She had begun to wonder, indeed, what the answer was to the question put to her by other residents—why did you throw it all away? "The vodka," she'd say.

But they pressed her, "It's just a symptom, not a cause."

She'd fallen for Mack on a trip home one winter break during her senior year of college, she told them, captivated by his radiant smile, his easy athleticism, his buoyant way of heading off for a jog or leaping headlong into the bay for a half-mile swim. That he'd mostly sat on the bench as a third-string quarterback for the Crimson Tide made no difference to his being a hometown hero, a big-time stockbroker on the local scene his first year out of school. He'd invited her to a Mardi Gras ball and she found herself in a circle of socialites she'd only known from a distance growing up.

With Mack there was no mournful casting back to the grimness of the concentration camps, no sadness, like a ship's wave, washing over them every time a mention of Amsterdam came about. She'd grown up in lower Alabama but had not really felt part of it, eager to go north to college, never thinking she'd return home for good until meeting him. It had been fun to share with her roommates in Poughkeepsie tales of her lark with a hometown boy. Then when she was in law school at NYU he'd come to see her in the city and had waxed eloquent before a Rembrandt at the Met—he'd done his homework on the Dutch masters of her father's native land—and she felt carried away. He sketched, too, quick renderings of joggers in Central Park and tourists at Times Square and replications, while standing before them, of his beloved Rembrandts and Vermeers.

"You didn't see that sensitivity right at first," she told the group. "He kind of kept it tucked away, for me. It was pretty amazing."

When they'd married he'd yearned for a son, and when Roger was born his baby gifts were "Roll Tide" onesies and a football signed by Mack's famous coach.

She told of a night, a few years earlier, after a booze-flowing dinner party, when their friends started talking about the first moment little Eddie or Bobby had held his head up without help, or discovered his feet, or taken a first step. Beautiful but all-too-quiescent Roger was already so far behind. She and Mack had gone into his room after the party and leaned over the crib, watching him sleep, and Mack had burst into tears. She'd tried to comfort him, but he turned away.

At two years old when Roger could hardly throw a ball, two and a half when he could not keep up with other toddlers racing across the yard, Mack grew more distant still.

"He said to me," she told the group, "he said, 'When you were expecting, you were fucking'—I hate this word, and I hate him saying it—'trashed.' Was it my fault? Is that what he was telling me!?

"I cursed him. He backed off. I couldn't admit to my father, who was grieving my mom, how Mack was treating me. I was their future. I tried harder, but something had changed.

"I got pregnant again. But after seven weeks"—she shook her head—"it wasn't meant to be. Mack didn't say a word. Every evening after work I'd read Mother Goose to Roger then start into my Grey Goose. By now Mack would rather spend time with Jack Daniel's than with me."

She'd found comfort in telling these stories to the other residents and didn't mind when they said they were praying for her—she was used to that expression having grown up in the Deep South—but the "Righteous Path of Jesus," part of the Beacon's stated mission, didn't sit well with her either. It made her envision a twelve-step program to heaven, even though the director, nicknamed Crazy Betty when they first met in high school, said the clinic respected all faiths. "Not Christian but Christ-centered," Betty said. "Just think of His teachings."

A heathen among the believers—that's always what she would be as the lone Jew, she knew. Why did she ever imagine it would be otherwise? That the clients were joined in their bad behavior, their folly wrecking marriages and careers, made for a higher calling, though. Sin provided a stronger bond than virtue.

Having mopped as far as the dorm rooms she looked up to see Crazy Betty hurrying toward her, announcing, "Phone call!"

"It's not phone hours, is it?"

"Your father. You can take it in the office."

She felt herself crumpling, the fear she lived with, a young woman's dread, an old dad's looming mortality, descending over her again. The story oft told by the family of how Vanessa had been the best forty-eighth birthday gift of all to Hank from her mom, a miraculous forty-one, brought smiles to everyone but her. She'd been named Vanessa for both her paternal grandmothers—the one she never knew, Vida, murdered at Auschwitz, and Violet, who welcomed her with big hugs and sweet iced tea in Selma, at the house where her dad was raised. Vanessa's was the weird family tree in eighth grade, the multiple grandparents, the vanished uncles, aunts, and cousins, all listed at her father's insistence. At high school graduation her friends asked which grandfather Hank was, and she blushed when saying he was her dad. Seventy-six when she married Mack, the look on his face when he gave her away—that softest kiss on her cheek, his warm hug—made her wish he was young again. That he could still knock heads in court then, facing off prosecutors two generations younger, gave her heart, though, that he would be with her and her son for a very long time.

"Daddy, what is it?"

"I need you to know something."

"What's wrong?"

"It's OK now."

"Are you sick? Is it your heart?"

"It's not about me."

"Tell me then!"

"This morning I took Roger to the pier with me."

"Oh, God."

"He's fine now."

"Why did you take him!"

"Lupita was late."

"Couldn't have you waited for her? You and your damn fishing."

"Roger loves going with me."

"What happened, Daddy?" She was shaking.

"Lupita got there, to the pier. I just didn't want you to hear it from somebody else."

"Did something happen to my boy?"

"He got startled, you know how he can be. He started running from me."

She had a picture in her mind, his little legs churning, his face stricken with fear. *He needs his mother. He needs his mother.*

"Before I knew it—I tried to stop him—he grabbed hold of the railing, he's so small, I didn't think he could get over, he grabbed hold of the railing."

"He *jumped?*"

The walls of the Beacon closed in on her, the confines no respectable parent should have to feel, no decent mother should have pressing closer still, keeping her from her child.

"He didn't hurt himself."

"He can't *swim!*"

"And then Lupita was there. Jumping in too, grabbing hold of him, bringing him to the beach."

"Could he breathe OK?"

"Breathe, yes, he thought it was an adventure!"

"I need to get out of here, Daddy."

"You know what Judge Myron ordered."

"Get me out of here. *Please.* I can't stand it."

She heard him say that the woman she'd forced into a ditch with her drunken recklessness was now complaining about shoulder and neck pain but held off suing knowing that Vanessa was in what she called, "a good Christian rehab. It makes it easier to forgive her."

"I need out!"

"Vanessa, *mijn schatje*," he said, his Dutch endearment, my loved one. "It could be so much worse. So very much."

"Always be worse, you're a broken record, but this is pretty damn bad, too."

He put Roger on the phone and she repeated, "I love you, I love you, I love you."

"Mommy bye."

Crazy Betty came to the door and tapped her watch.

She started back with her mop, only a short while until the day's first meeting. At the end of the hallway was a door to the wide world beyond. WARNING. DO NOT OPEN. ALARM WILL SOUND.

She cleaned up to its edge, then hearkened to the clinic's bell. She stowed her cleaning supplies and, insides churning, so much new to share, headed to group session.

4
STRANGERS' FACES

AFTER PARKING ON MAIN STREET, as Hank headed to Jewel's Café, he felt menace roiling the air. The victim's name, Beau Shepherd, spun the atmosphere like a hurricane bearing down. As a criminal lawyer Hank had immersed himself in the details of destructive acts, witnessing families, whole communities, ripped apart by violence. Whatever happened—a shooting, a beating, a fatal car crash—the world of those caught up in it, no matter the judicial outcome, was never the same. His serene village, with its verdant bluff above the glittering bay, its police blotter a usual litany of petty crimes, was in shock—Beau Shepherd, a local contractor and former state legislator, had met a gruesome fate on a tranquil October day.

On the phone to Vanessa he had said nothing of Julio—why should he throw her into a panic about Lupita's family?—hoping, as he told Lupita, "they're just following all the leads." Why had Julio disappeared, though? *"Sus papeles,"* Lupita said. "His papers." He'd urged her to head home to wait for word, but she wanted to stay at his house, caring for Roger. She would leave early to get to five o'clock Mass.

In the café he recognized Beau's full, ruddy face in the photo of the Tuesday regulars near the cash register. Riley, the longtime waitress, showed him to a booth.

"Poor Mister Beau," Riley said. "Whoever did this"—she poured him coffee—"look at me, I'm shaking, will damn sure pay."

A mounted TV showed Shepherd shaking hands with the governor in Montgomery, then a loop of the plane crash in Africa that had almost claimed his life four years ago.

Hank knew the Africa tragedy well. At the pier, over and again, the Rev. Jonathan Blue—Pastor Blue to his fishing buddies—had recounted the accident that ripped away his son.

Pastor Blue's church, Bay Jubilation, had set out for Uganda on an annual mission trip, headquartered in Kampala. With Pastor Blue unable to make the African journey, Zach Blue, his son, was teamed up with Beau Shepherd, a board member, and two other congregants, to explore new destinations to carry the word of Christ. On a small plane chartered from Kampala they set out to far-flung areas, scouting for future mission homes. The Piper Cherokee plummeted into a remote mountainside.

After two days, at the crash site in dense jungle, the bodies of the pilot and other members of the church team were recovered. But Zach disappeared. That Shepherd, dehydrated and near starved, had found his way back to a village after three days, became the stuff of legend. He said his prayers for a miracle had been answered. "I never saw Zach after we crashed," Shepherd said.

But Blue was convinced his son had survived. "God spoke to me," the pastor said.

Sometimes, with Hank, he'd lean against the pier railing and look out at the sun saturating the horizon with its deep colors at end of day. "I feel he's out there, still, somewhere."

The pastor had traveled twice to Uganda on his own since the crash, to no avail. No trace of his son. No word.

Blue's marriage had fallen apart, he'd stepped down from his pulpit at Bay Jubilation and started spending time on the pier about the same time as Hank. Their connection had deepened when Hank told him how often he imagined his parents were alive. Somewhere. His last image of them was in front of the deportation center for Jews in Amsterdam as they embraced him with fervor, the guards taking him and other children for incarceration in the school across the street. The youths, too, were soon sent on to the camps in Germany and Poland, except those, like Hank, who escaped. He'd repeated the story often to Blue how he'd never seen his mother and father again. But even when he was on a ship to America, soon with new parents in this strange place called Alabama, he imagined they were coming for him. "I am over eighty and I sometimes wake thinking I am a boy and they are coming in my door."

Riley broke his reverie. "Fried chicken today, Mr. Hank?"

"Just the coffee, thank you."

"I don't blame you. Who can eat with all this going on? I can just see Mr. Beau sitting there at his favorite corner table, big, friendly, proud of being sober. He wasn't ashamed. He took up drinking after that Africa thing, then went cold turkey."

"I'll be."

It was one of those Southern expressions like "I declare" or "bless your heart" Hank had mastered in Selma, a polite invitation for the speaker to keep on.

"I used to bring him sweet tea, adding extra sugar, he needed something to get him going, but last time I saw him, poor thing"— Riley made a motion like tilting a glass—"he was backsliding. You could smell the bourbon on him from here to Biloxi. Rest his sweet soul."

Had Beau been inebriated on the seventeenth green? Hank made a mental note of it. That Julio might be a suspect was still a possibility. The cops would cast their net wide, especially if it involved what they called "illegals." The politicians got too much traction out of it.

He finished up and departed Jewel's, driving to the water.

On the pier he found the men clumped in a small group, talking. Even the Brown brothers, whose attention was always focused on the water, had joined the gab.

"Cash. Lots of it. That sucker loved to bet."

Hank heard the words and moved in closer.

"He fucked me over once, I'll tell you."

"Somebody got back at him."

"Whoever it was is a dumb motherfucker, out on a golf course. Broad daylight. Had to be a stranger, one of the Spanish guys works there. They like that"—T. Brown made a lunging motion—"blade work."

"Hey, Dutch."

He wasn't aware they'd noticed him. Over the years he'd been retired each man had turned to him with a legal question about some daily drama—a son's divorce, a title dispute, a threatened home foreclosure. It was a long sight from defending a man indicted for capital murder to dispensing advice about child support or work-men's comp, but what he gave them, he knew, was often all they got. "The way I see it," he'd begin, ending with, "but you need to consult an attorney in that field." Few did.

The only one he counted as a true friend was Pastor Blue, whose absence seemed odd today. If Hank was the pier lawyer, Blue was its faith leader, listening to the confessions while angling for speckled trout and redfish, of an array of broken and regretful retirees. A savage murder would rattle the old-timers, striking fear, stoking anger. They needed Blue's calming spirit.

"Let 'em come out here on our pier with anything they want," said Cooter Clark, whose specialty was catching flounder. "I'm ready."

The men gathered closer, Hank leaning in to see, as Cooter unsnapped his tackle box to reveal a black Ruger. The handgun was nestled in the lures.

"Anybody seen Blue?" Hank asked.

"Probably at church with Shepherd's people," B. Brown said.

"Don't none of Shepherd's folks go there no more," Cooter said, snapping his box shut.

"Blue might be there by himself," T. Brown said, "just thinking about his boy. Shepherd survived the jungles of Africa then gets cut down playing golf at the hotel. Probably brings it all back even worse to Blue."

"He could use church," B. Brown said.

"Out here is Blue's church," said Cooter, holding his arms wide.

"All ours," T. Brown added.

Hank nodded in agreement.

The wind picked up, the water got choppy, and not a mullet was to be seen. Along the pier were commemorative benches, and Hank walked to the one inscribed: "To MARGERY, THE LOVE OF MY LIFE. YOU ARE WITH ME ALWAYS." He sat a spell, imagining her next to him in the place they'd enjoyed sunsets, sipping wine, rubbing the kinks out of each other's shoulders, heralding God's glory in radiant clouds while saying hello to dusk amblers.

"Vanessa and I had a lousy talk on the phone this morning," he said, confiding his heart to the empty place alongside. "She gets so mad at me. I'm doing what I can."

"You're doing great, sweetheart. Our daughter's an intense young woman, she's just finding her way."

"At thirty-four?"

"She needs you to be there for her. No one else is. Stay strong."

He closed his eyes and leaned into his palm. An image of Beau Shepherd took over, a face twisting in agony. Margery would be aghast.

"They're chasing somebody now." It was Cooter's voice.

Hank looked up. Cooter's son held up a big smartphone with a headline: "Suspect in Golf Course Homicide."

Scanning the news, "Hispanic male, 20s," Hank stood up and went to his truck in the parking lot.

He started up the narrow streets home but decided to detour to the golf course. He followed the road to the clubhouse then turned onto the lane by the spacious homes fronting the fairways, to the camellia garden at a juncture. He pulled onto the pine straw and looked over the fence to see yellow tape cordoning off part of the turf. A police car was parked on the cart path.

The police had gone to Lupita's house asking for Julio, which meant the suspect might be affiliated with the hotel. How many Latinos now worked there? Who had given the cops a lead?

In earlier years when he'd played tennis with Margery at the resort complex there had been few Spanish speakers, either as guests or workers. Employees had been black or white from the local community, or Eastern European, Russian, or Caribbean—each group revolving through in a round-robin labor pool. Unlike Texas or Florida, Hank's stretch of the coast was only now becoming more international. But the shift was slow.

At a bar association retreat at Bay Resort in early 2000 he'd welcomed his friend from law school days, Jaime Montero, who told him that the National Hispanic Bar Association was hoping to make inroads in Alabama with a new generation of attorneys. "Times will change," Hank said, "but like much else here, slowly." He told Jaime there had been only a handful of Jewish attorneys when he'd opened up his office in the 1960s.

Back home he found Lupita on the couch transfixed by TV news, Roger curled next to her.

"Julio!" she screamed.

Lean, scruffy, as doe-eyed as a sleepy teen, her brother's photo filled the screen. "The suspect may be armed and dangerous," the news anchor reported. "A manhunt is underway." A tip hotline flashed.

Lupita jumped up and yelled at the broadcaster: "*¡Mentiroso!* Liar!"

She whirled toward Hank. "Help him! Please!"

"He needs to turn himself in. Now."

"He has hurt nobody."

"If you can get him a message, tell him, 'Go to the police. A man on the run looks guilty.'"

"It's a lie."

"Armed, you know what that means? They think he has a weapon. That puts him in danger, too."

"He did not do this. You must help him."

"I'll find you somebody. I'm out of it, Lupita."

"*Toda la gente*, everybody. The fishermen. At the store. My church. They say you are a man who helps."

"I can hardly help myself anymore."

"*El judío sabio*, they say. The wise Jew."

The distress in her eyes, the anxiety in her voice, was a state he'd seen many times—the loved ones of the accused. Even the guiltiest were believed innocent at first by those who loved them, no matter how wretched their histories, the mind reeling to catch up with the jolt of what happened, not unlike the reaction of a victim.

He wanted to know more about Julio. Had he gotten into trouble in the past? Was there any reason someone else might want to point a finger at him? But he would refrain from asking. He had to help Lupita, yes, but also stay strong—that was the word Margery had used—for Vanessa and Roger. The stress of a criminal proceeding would be too great. Defend a man accused of murdering a local celebrity? The pressure would mount. It was no longer for him.

He took Roger's hand, so small inside his own—he squeezed it tightly, seeing him going again over the pier—and they went outside.

"We'll see the harvest moon tonight if a storm doesn't come." Cirrus clouds brushed the sky. They grew tinged with darkness.

"Mommy," said Roger.

"Mommy will be home soon."

Cumulus clouds began to build on the horizon. Pelicans soared further inland.

Looking up, Roger held out his arms and began to turn. He wheeled and wobbled, stumbled toward the clothesline—the dryer was on the fritz—grabbing at garments and falling to the ground, rolling gleefully.

Hank scooped up the child and the clothes in one big jumble.

"I brought these in for you," he said to Lupita. "Roger made hash of 'em."

He looked down at a piece of fabric in his hands—a pale work shirt with a deep brown stain mapping it. "God damn," he said.

"It's dirt. Bring it here. To wash again is no good. Here"—she pulled the garbage can from under the sink—"I am putting in the trash."

"I know what it is. You can't get rid of blood. Whose is it?"

"I try." Lupita looked down, face crumpling. "I try."

He waited until she collected herself and faced him again, anguished.

"The last thing you want to be doing is tampering with evidence."

"I always wash for Julio."

"Lord knows, child. Don't get mixed up in this, too."

"Por favor."

5
HUNGER

JULIO'S SKIFF SLIPPED DOWN THE river, the water's reflection like the fairway shifting beneath his feet as he'd made his way to the golfer, the crickets' hum rising like in the woods along the course, louder, beating at his ears. He bent low to obscure his face as he passed houses where residents on their docks relaxed grilling shrimp and waving to the last anglers and jet skiers of the day. He breathed in deeply, trying to hold the scent of the brackish water and pine woods in his nostrils, but the stink of the dying man, the sweat and liquor, kept returning. He rubbed his cheek, trying to wipe away the stranger's jowls pressing against him.

"Paco," he said to the wind streaming over the bow, seeing the lights of the Fish House and its sign—GOOD FOOD, GOOD TIMES—winking through the trees at a far bend of the river. Not a mile farther was the bay. There was a risk in stopping but, as he made his way toward the open expanse he felt he could expire from lack of food. All he'd eaten in twenty-four hours were a handful of croutons, a hunk of cheese, and two dinner rolls he'd kept smashed in his pocket, scant leftovers from the resort kitchen the day before. Paco, a dishwasher at the Fish House, always did much better, rounding up crab claws and boiled shrimp before they hit the wastebasket, bundling it all up to bring by Julio's where they feasted like patricians.

But was Paco even working today?

Scrabbling at the window, showing his face, asking for Paco—it could be his death sentence if he'd been publicly identified yet as a suspect. He'd seen how suspects in high-profile crimes were judged guilty by the public once their pictures were splashed across the local news. Anything for money. He'd lingered himself in the post office by the posters of scowling men under the banner, WANTED, REWARD, and imagined cashing in by recognizing a fugitive in plain sight at the Bay Resort drinking by the pool or drifting down a road trying to hide his visage like Julio did now.

Two monster outboards growled closer, like big, black dogs nosing forward the shore patrol's sleek bowrider. The patrolman nodded at Julio, coming within feet of his prow, glancing at the registration stickers—fortunately, Paco kept it up to date—saying, "Howdy, everything OK?"

His English was good enough to answer the all-purpose "Yes sir."

The patrol boat's radio crackled. The patrolman looked hard at Julio, who considered his 25 hp Evinrude alongside the twin 200 hp Mercury outboards and realized he couldn't outgun him.

"I need you off the water"—Julio's breath quickened—"right away."

"Yes sir." He turned the throttle and the skiff purred ahead. The open water of the bay was getting near.

The shore patrol zoomed right up on him, the officer's voice rising. Julio could not make out the words. Now the patrolman was heading him off at the point where the Fish House stood, at the juncture between the river and the bay.

Julio slowed, puttering nearly to a standstill.

The patrolman spoke through a megaphone now, his warning, "Storm, turn back," filling the air.

Ah, *storm*.

Julio's breathing became regular again. He turned his bow toward the restaurant. The shore patrol gunned his engine and took off after a catamaran crammed with partying teens.

With relief he glimpsed Paco in the kitchen window, bending over the sink. His boyish face, round as a moon, a sliver of moustache, close-cropped hair, reminded him of the first time they'd met, as little kids in the displaced persons camp. When the big boys had surrounded Julio to steal his rations, Paco had stepped in to help him fight them off. After the bullies knocked them both down and kicked them, they became friends forever.

Paco's way of breaking into a smile when he saw Julio, like the moon alit, was not the case now when he tapped at the kitchen window. Paco's eyes opened wide and he motioned with his hand for Julio to crouch out of sight in the bushes. A moment later the kitchen door opened and Paco casually lit a cigarette as if on a smoke break, then ducked into the cluster of branches.

"*¿Qué hiciste?*" What did you do!?

"*Nada.*"

"*La policía . . .*"

He'd found the man dying, he told Paco quickly, went to help, ran. "*Comida. Necesito comida.*" I need food.

"*No corras más.*" Do not run anymore.

"*Tengo hambre.*" I'm hungry.

"Shhh." His friend glanced at his watch, leapt away, and returned in seconds with a small red cooler, shoved it at Julio, clasped him in a hug, then disappeared back to the kitchen.

Julio opened it to a mess of fried fish and shrimp and reached for a mouthful but two cars screamed into the parking lot—he glanced from the bushes to see the squad cars—fastened the cooler back up and toted it like a football down to the skiff, skittering toward roiling skies.

The river opened into the wide expanse of the bay and a gust of wind caught him and pushed him forward. *"Pon tu fe en Dios"* his mother had said when he climbed on the bus heading north, put your faith in God. That had been her mantra after Hurricane Mitch's rains had washed their village down the mountainside, the land beneath them like the water beneath the skiff, like the deep green grass sliding under his feet as he'd run from the collapsing golfer. That they had survived at all—the flowing of shacks and trees, churches and animals, the schoolhouse, the general store, their hands up, cries piercing the churning clouds—had made stronger than ever his mother's conviction that Jesus Christ, in his hands, held them like fragile robin eggs.

But Julio knew better. It was the absence of God that let all the demonic forces of the universe come whirling in like furies that brought the hurricane, washed away their mountainside, sent them to the displaced persons camp where they'd lived waiting a cinder-block dwelling, brought him to America, where the allure of a good job as a groundskeeper at a playland for *los ricos*, the rich folks, had put him on a murderer's path to Satan in a blood-soaked white shirt, set his bow on a course he could not alter.

As his boat took a wave, rising, falling, rising again, he opened the cooler and grabbed at the victuals. A wave splashed over the gunnel and sloshed over him as he tore into the fried fish. He took out boiled shrimp, tried to peel them with one hand, the other on the throttle, the boat climbing the whitecaps then plunging down.

He looked around. There was no shore patrol. No Coast Guard rescue. No freighter making its way from the gulf into the channel. He was the only craft on a crazy sea, hidden in the wide open.

Freedom.

6
STILL WORKING ON ME

THE RISING WIND SEEMED TO make the Beacon clients drop their defenses even more. Vanessa had come to learn each rehab sister's tale of woe, the mean father, the abusive husband, the ungrateful daughter or son, a downfall beginning with an innocent puff of dope with a feverish date in a pickup truck, or a jolt of whiskey to loosen up for a stressful holiday. There was so much more to tell.

MaryLynn, from Citronelle, confessed to snorting coke with her supervisor at the paper mill when they took rides downriver, furtive lovers. When he dropped her after a few months and she ratted him out to his wife, she got fired. "I went right on down, no job, no money, but I scrounged. Anything I could do to get high," she said. "And kept right on at it."

A former teacher from Bay Minette, named Dixie, said the long illness of her husband had driven her to become "a pothead," puffing weed with friends off-hours in empty stadium bleachers. A student had snapped their photo with a cell phone and texted it to the principal. "That little suck-up," she said. "I told 'em they can't prove anything. They made me pee in a jar. I took cleaning jobs to pay for my husband's meds. You scrub somebody else's toilet, you want to be high."

One of the phrases Vanessa heard repeated was "getting my GED," as residents told of struggling to obtain their high school equivalency diplomas, ten, even twenty years out from graduation day. A two-year associate's degree, or, in some cases, a prized four-year bachelors, was a Holy Grail. A law degree from a fancy university way up north? Unimaginable.

The sliding scale for resident fees, given church support and fundraisers, meant that no one was excluded. But anyone who had the wherewithal, Vanessa knew, opted for a private facility like River Run, with its plush sofas and soft mood music, its full-time chef and dietician. At the direction of the court she'd had no choice.

She tried to downplay her pedigree, hinting at "hard times," but she looked out to see skepticism on the part of the others.

"How'd you afford all that schooling?" one asked.

"Scholarships," she said, not mentioning they were for academic achievement, not need.

"I know who your daddy is," Rhonda, from Chickasaw, leveled at her in the circle. "My husband paid him two thousand goddamn dollars to keep him from going to jail after some peckerwood lied he'd seen my Henry robbing that store. He's sitting up in Atmore now, cursing your daddy every day. We wished we had that money back. I guess it was sending you to school."

"This is a safe space," Loretta, the facilitator, broke in. "No personal attacks."

"I ain't attacking, just telling the truth."

"Did he take the money?" Vanessa asked.

"What did you say, prom queen?"

"Did Henry steal the money?" She glared at the woman

"Not enough to pay your goddamn daddy what he screwed him over for."

"Time out!" Loretta said.

During the break Vanessa sidled down the hallway, breathed deeply, looked out the windows at the rain lashing the pines. Was her little boy afraid? He could be so skittish. On family visiting day at the Beacon he'd clung to Lupita, crying out when one of the women walking by patted him on the arm saying, "What a handsome boy," and he drew back when Vanessa tried to lift him. She knew how he would curl into her at home on the couch when it thundered, a small creature mystified by the elements, trying to hide from the cymbal crash of the skies, from all that felt unsafe. Gradee would console him, she knew, putting on mellow music to lull him to a calm.

She saw Rhonda walk by, head down, and wondered how Daddy had handled her husband's defense, most likely having gotten him a better deal than anybody else could. If he hadn't, she knew, he'd beat himself up over it, committed to helping the poor and disenfranchised, the school dropouts turned twentysomething criminals, the kids with rap sheets turned violent grown-ups covering their faces against TV intrusion as they were led to jail. Vanessa preferred her law to be about numbers, paperwork for major clients in button-down shirts her idea of the good fight, the clean fight. Otherwise she'd spend her career with folks just like the ones she was residing with at the Beacon, those struggling from the start.

"Hey." It was Rhonda who'd spoken.

She turned to see the woman, sheepish. "You didn't do nothing. It's all me. Henry deserved what he got."

"Don't worry about it."

Back in the circle as Vanessa spoke Rhonda nodded visibly, her biggest champion now.

"The first time I tasted alcohol was Mogen David wine, really sweet, at a Seder at my grandmother's house in Selma. The Seder is like the Last Supper."

"On Good Friday we have one at our church," Dixie put in.

"And sometimes, when I got a little older and would visit her, she'd give me a sip of mint julep on her porch. Bourbon, sweet syrup, crushed ice, mint—it really brings her back.

"I wasn't prone to getting drunk. Not until Mack brought out that part of me. It was so freeing. At first."

She glanced up at the clock. Roger's bedtime. Was Gradee reading him a story?

"I worry about my son," she said suddenly. "He needs me."

Nodding all around.

"I've got to stay sober."

"Yes, Lord," came in whispers.

"I can. I know I can."

A neurologist had told her Roger might not ever be able to read. She'd called the doctor "a dumb sonofabitch," and threatened to sue him for malpractice.

"Can you believe Mack suggested it was because of me! Because I'd been drinking?" All her stories of alcohol abuse bent toward this moment, the heartlessness, the outrage of his attack.

"But what if he was right?"

Acting nonjudgment was the rule of groups but in a chorus the other women chimed, "no, no," Rhonda's voice loudest of all.

"I've read everything I could get my hands on about it. It's not me. Not Roger! It was nothing I did! I didn't have a baby with fetal alcohol syndrome any more than I had a crack baby."

The women fell silent. Rhonda was turned away.

"Thank you, Vanessa," Loretta said in her calmest facilitator's voice.

"They said my baby was." Rhonda's meek confession shook the room.

"I didn't mean," began Vanessa, but Loretta cut in, "Let's hear from Rhonda now."

After the session, as the women were heading to their bunk room, Crazy Betty stopped Vanessa in the hallway and pulled her into the office.

"I hear there was some tension in your group," Betty began.

"We were telling our stories."

"Don't stick your nose in the air, Vanessa. You're not better than the others."

"Betty? Is that a professional thing to say to a client like me?"

"Oh, cut it out. We've known each other since high school. You always had this superiority complex, smarter, more interesting, more . . . exotic."

"I'm doing my time here, you're my jailer, so just leave me alone."

"I'm not your jailer, but I am in charge. You don't behave and I'll bounce you out of here quick. Make havoc with my other clients, the decent ones, and you'll find yourself up in Wetumpka. Tutwiler's got plenty of room for you."

"You've done well for yourself, Betty. Finally found a place you can be paid to be a bully."

The final bell rang and Vanessa hurried down the hall and joined the other women who made a circle as Betty followed a moment later, freshly lipsticked, pretentiously in charge, to lead them in evening devotion.

As Betty spun out blessings from Jesus, Vanessa bowed her head. Her Vassar friends visiting her home in Alabama, even Christian ones, had blanched when they heard an invocation at a local football game ending with "in Jesus's name we pray," but she'd long taken it in stride, like the Lord's Prayer, which she'd recited as a child in public school and as a grown-up at AA meetings. It was still omnipresent in the South, though sometimes, like now, she went deeper inside and said her own blessing, the "Sh'ma," the "watchword of our faith" the rabbi had taught her the very first week of Sunday school. She'd repeated it with Roger at bedtime, who uttered, "sh sh," which was enough to give her heart. God, if he truly existed, would understand.

No one else doubted his presence; it was the key to their recovery.

It was Rhonda's turn to lead the nightly pep rally. She took her place up front and began to clap a rhythm. The others joined in, their hands smacking out a percussive beat as they sang:

God's still working on me
To make me what I ought to be
Faster clapping now.
It took him just a week to make the moon and the stars
Earth and sea, Jupiter and Mars
What a wonderful blessing I've received
For God's still working on me.

As on cue a lightning flash and thunderbolt rocked the Beacon and the electricity was snuffed out. Vanessa stood near the exit and laid her hand on the bar warning, ALARM WILL SOUND, and pushed, the only noise in the dark the excited voices and laughter of the women. The wind whipping in the crack of the door pulled her forward and she slipped outside and in the blowing rain set off to see her son.

7
TOLLING BELL

As THE SKIFF SMASHED DOWN into the waves before struggling upward, topping a whitecap and dropping down again, Julio held tight to the throttle, wedging the cooler between his feet to keep it from washing away. If he could make it as far as the Sand Island lighthouse he could tie up, curl under a rock for the night, and head westward when it calmed, running the Mississippi Sound toward New Orleans. Not even the ghost of the golfer could find him there. He would hide in the streets of surrounding parishes where some neighborhoods felt transplanted from his Central American home.

In 2005, after Katrina blew through New Orleans, the need had been acute for laborers in rebuilding the city. He'd been too young to join the exodus of Hondurans making their way to the Crescent City with the prospect of work, many with relatives there already. Contractors were desperate; immigration officials looked aside. For many the city devastated by Katrina offered opportunities where few had existed in his own country ravaged by Mitch in 1998 and reeling for years to come.

If he could leave and go north and work in New Orleans, he'd realized even as a boy, he could be outside the reach of Barrio 18 and Mara Salvatrucha (MS-13), and other gangs starting to dominate blocks in the cinder-block city built by Samaritan's Purse for the countless displaced by Mitch. He could wire money back to his mother, always desperate for funds to cover the household budget and pay the gangs who patrolled her candy kiosk a "war tax." But he would have to wait. Lupita, two years older, went ahead of him, getting a work visa to help in a school in New Orleans with an abundance of Spanish speakers. By the time he was ready there was a demand to fill positions in a chain of resorts. With his grandfather's help he applied for a work visa in the tourist industry and was placed first at a luxury hotel at Hilton Head, South Carolina, then a wooded complex on Sea Island, Georgia, now the coastal golf club and hotel on Mobile Bay.

In the American seaside places he'd worked there had been torrential weather, but it fazed him little. It was as though Mitch, washing away the mountainside where he'd been little, had baptized him against the fear of maelstroms. Nothing could be worse than the screams of his friends reaching out to grab hold of the teacher, clutching their chairs, the schoolhouse collapsing, homes whisked away in a mudslide.

But he had never been out in a skiff bucking and catching waves sideways, rocking and tipping. He thought to turn back but the wind kept him southward. He envisioned Papi, who had died in this same gulf where it curled onto the Honduran shore. Abuelo, his grandfather, had been a gardener for a resort in La Ceiba, and found restaurant work for Papi at the hotel. But his father quit to join the commercial fishermen and had fallen overboard and drowned. "You must be strong in the water," Abuelo had told Julio when he taught him to swim in salty surf. Could he negotiate these gargantuan waves if he fell in?

When Abuelo had told him the story of Jonah he'd tossed all night, not knowing if it was worse to cause a sea storm by terrible conduct or tumble into the belly of a whale. "Abuelo," he said now to the old man howling in the wind. "*¿Soy Jonás?*"

"*Sí, sí,*" whistled back the wind.

The skiff's bow went skyward and came down with a bang that shook Julio to his bones. A massive wave nearly washed the cooler overboard and he undid the boat line from its cleat, tied it in a circle to the cooler handle and looped the line over his shoulder, across his chest, cinching the plastic container against him. He could not afford to lose the food!

In the driving darkness that wrapped him round a strip of clearing opened on the horizon—was there a full moon?—and looked like a human figure, sprawled out, dead to the world. Was he seeing a mirage, as though the golfer bleeding to death on the green had imprinted himself on his eyeballs and become an image repeating itself like the aftershock of a camera flash?

Night stitched closed the opening but still Julio saw him. Looking down, wreaking havoc. It was not a mirage at all.

A far-off gong sounded, the school bell that Doña Patricia had rung as Mitch's winds shook the barnyards and corrals, the locomotive of wind curving down the mountainside. Over and over, *clang-clang*, the windows blowing out, the glass scattering like frantic birds, the only solace the tolling of that bell, and when the teacher linked arms with students another woman in the village took over, and when she couldn't stand upright in the wind a man took over, then two. It was a signal to the villagers on the next hillside, and the next. Mitch spun out tornadoes as it advanced, then engulfed them all.

The tolling of the bell got closer.

He *was* Jonah, he now knew, bringing this tempest onto his own little vessel. There was no crew to save—he was alone—but there was his soul. There was no propulsion, no steering. The skiff rose higher. The rain stung his face and the wind howled. He gave himself up to whatever might come. He had not murdered the man but neither had he tried to save him by stooping to press his hand against his wound and yelling for help, holding him back if he could from his last breath.

The bell tolled at his shoulder and the skiff leapt and came crashing down on an iron cage wildly bobbing, and as Julio came to his senses he tried to hold onto what he realized was a bell buoy bucking and turning, clappers ferociously knocking, his vessel taking on water up to his knees, his hips, disappearing beneath him as he lunged for the iron platform to make the buoy his refuge. It swung back and forth catching him on the head, and the noise of the wind and waves was no longer outside him but inside and he fell into the roiling waters, swept away by the unforgiving night.

8

TO SHORE

As THE STORM ABATED AND next day's first light peeled through the blinds, Hank knew what a glorious morning it would be at Fairhope Pier, fishing lines zinging, mullet popping, pelicans coasting the thermals beneath washed blue. Packing his fishing clothes for later, he donned tan slacks and brown blazer for his first-period talk at Maxwell Middle School. If he hadn't been scheduled long in advance he'd have bowed out, letting Lupita have the morning off. But she'd shown up, long-faced, eyes red still, with no word about her brother. She'd asked him again for his help, but he repeated that it was a job for a younger man. He'd make the contacts when the time came.

Once a month since retirement, at the behest of the Gulf Coast Holocaust Education Center, he'd visit a classroom to tell of his childhood in Amsterdam, his rescue and journey. "I don't have the experiences of Alma Fisher, Agnes Tennenbaum, or Harry Zaremba," he told the directors, among them a Jewish educator, a Catholic nun, and a Baptist scholar. "They were in the concentration camps," he said of other survivors in the area. "They truly suffered." The directors told him, "You're a survivor too with an important and

moving story to tell. You help make it all come alive and can speak
to the issue of bigotry." By now, he had outlived most of the others.
It was his duty.

He'd see the astonishment, the incredulity, of the students
when he appeared in their class, the walking embodiment of a time
they'd read about in history books. He'd begin with an overview
of his birth country: "The Netherlands is a small country, only
16,000 square miles. Alabama is 52,000 square miles. Before World
War II the Netherlands was home to 140,000 Jews. In Alabama
there are 9,000 Jews. So you have an idea of just how many of us
thrived there, with more than half of us, 75,000 Jews, in the city of
Amsterdam, like my family.

"My father was a businessman, my mother a homemaker. We
lived in a canal house—not like houses here with porches and yards,
but narrow and tall—and we were happy. I was only four or five and
remember one day, after the German soldiers came, my family, all
the Jews, had to wear a yellow star. I thought it was pretty. My older
brother, Benyamin, hated his and said he would rip it off. My father
told Benyamin to do as we were told. It was 1941, and the Nazis
were in charge.

"By 1945, when the war ended, nearly three out of every four of
us, think of that"—he pointed to three students, then a fourth—"had
been deported to the concentration camps of Germany and Poland,
including my mother and father, Vida and Reuven, and my sister and
brother, Shayna and Benyamin. Hitler and his killing machine murdered six million Jews from throughout Europe, as well as Gypsies,
Poles, gay people, people who were physically and mentally disabled.
Hitler wanted to create a master race. We were seen as flawed, as
'other,' as subhuman. Who could believe that but a madman?"

The students looked terrified.

"Yet so many followed that madman.

"Before I tell you my own story let us have a moment of silence to remember the victims of genocide."

In the profound quiet he gazed out at them, heads bowed, innocent and protected. *"God bless you all,"* he said in his silence. Benyamin and Shayna could have been among them.

The third floor of the row house where his window overlooked the Prinsengracht Canal, not far from at the edge of the Jodenbuurt, the Jewish quarter; flower boxes bright in the morning sun, barges sliding by; the ancient crone by the canal, her cape like a pelican's wings, singing at the top of her voice; bounding down the stairs to the smell of warm bread in the kitchen, *moeder* and *vader* greeting him at the table, grasping his satchel in one hand, father's hand with the other, as they headed to his school; exploring the gardens of the Plantage then passing by the Hollandsche Schouwburg, the Dutch Theater, until the Nazis came with their high boots and semiautomatics and it became the Joodsche Schouwburg, the Jewish Theater, where the deportations took place; the horror on his father's face, his mother's deep dark eyes, the cries of neighbors when their names were called; the relief of those passed over until a later day—new details pressed forward each time he told it.

"First were the Jewish stars, then the raids—Nazis pulled up in front of Jewish homes and forced families out, holding guns, using truncheons, like big clubs. Our family was still safe, though. Some Dutch citizens in support of the Jews protested, had a strike. The Nazis retaliated, and also had different strategies.

"They began to use us against ourselves. Members of the Dutch Jewish Council were enlisted to provide the names of other Jews to be sent to Westerbork, a transit camp in the north of the country, where they were sent on to Germany and Poland. A merchant in the margarine business, a Jew named Walter Süskind—my father knew him through the Unilever Company—was put in charge at the Jewish Theater where the deportations took place. He made a pact with the devil.

"'We need your Jews for the labor camps,' the Nazis told him, 'to help the war effort of the Fatherland. One hundred today, two hundred next week, three hundred the following. We need the numbers. You give us the names.' Did Süskind believe them? My parents knew better. Their friends knew better.

"Süskind had saved his own neck—in exchange for sacrificing thousands of others. Who could live with that?"

A boy said, "Not me."

Others chorused they could not either.

"If we have the choice between good and evil, will we always choose good? If it means risking our own lives?"

A girl's hand shot up. "Like the family that hid Anne Frank! They chose to do good."

He nodded.

"My family was ordered to report to the deportation center. My father said we would be dignified. We walked there with our belongings. Ultimately, nothing would happen to us, he said, if we did what we were told. By then I was six. To me it was like a weekend excursion.

"Across from the Jewish Theater was a Protestant religious seminary run by a man named Johan van Hulst—*Hervormde Kweekskool* was written across the front of the building, I can still see it—and next to it, on the other side of a garden wall, a nursery and daycare. I soon discovered the terror of what was to occur.

"With the Nazis in charge, Jewish children under thirteen—Benyamin and Shayna were ten and twelve—were separated from their parents and made to stay there. Shayna and Benyamin went before me. They disappeared forever.

"One morning Mama, Papa, hugged me and kissed me goodbye and said that I should call myself Hans, but never forget, deep down inside, who I really was, my name was Haim, and that they loved me forever." He hesitated. "And ever." He took a deep breath. "There we were, a room of children, kindergarteners, first graders, in long rows of beds, nice lady teachers in charge of us. Standing guard were Germans. I would toss and turn, aching for my mama and papa, so close they were, and sometimes I'd hear other children being rousted up by the Germans, given coats, led out to who knows where. The crying. I can hear it now. You see my old man's face? Remembering this makes me feel like I am a little boy again, heartsick, homesick, in that room.

"Süskind's conscience began to eat at his soul. He devised ways for children to be rescued, handed off, over the garden wall to the seminary if they were small enough, or along secret passages, out back doors, some blocked from view for a moment when the trolley ran by on the street called Plantage Middenlaan, on to the Dutch Underground, friends risking their lives to get us to safety. It wasn't long before the Nazis found Süskind out. They put him on a train to a concentration camp, too.

"So what happened to me, you want to know?"

A room of silent, blinking eyes, was before him.

"To keep us healthy our teacher, Juffrouw Greta, a sweet conspirator, led us on walks around the block, telling us to take deep breaths of fresh air. I can still hear the guard counting us, in German, *'Eins, zwei, drei, vier, fünf, sechs, sieben . . .'* And next thing I knew a blanket went over my head, around my whole body, and I was grabbed up and pushed into the back of a motorcar and my escape began. Why me? Luck? A blessing? Where I happened to be in line?"

Juffrouw Greta with her goldspun hair; the priest at Mozes en Aäronkerk, the Moses and Aaron church, with its celestial ceiling, brooding saints, and back corridor; the farmer in rural Friesland cloaking him in his barn; the nuns at the abbey in Haarlem, hiding him in the root cellar with other children; the winter passing with its harsh winds and stinging rain; and then the summer with a sky painted purple and a great white pelican, like an image of God, soaring overhead on the Dutch coastline; the boat at 3 a.m. into the rough North Sea; waking to look out the porthole, calling out, "Mama, Papa," burying his head to cry in the pillow—he told it all plainly, narrating another man's long ago life.

"In New York City a kind couple met me. An organization called 'the Workmen's Circle' had contacted them. They had no children of their own. 'Would you like to go home with us to a nice, cozy place and live with us until your mama and papa return?' I was cold; I had a hungry belly. They told me they had a warm puppy waiting to lick my face and sleep next to me in the bed."

He heard sniffles in the classroom, saw a girl take out a box of Kleenex, pass them to her friends.

"What do you think I answered?"

Softly, together, the students answered: "Yes."

"They brought me to Selma, Alabama, and I went by the name Hank. Mama and Papa, so far away from me, thousands of miles by the map, as far away, to my little heart, as the moon, could never come for me." He paused, knowing how the words would wrench the hearts of the beautiful youths held rapt before him. But he owed them the truth. "They died in a Nazi gas chamber."

He hung his head, the sadness welling up. *This is my last school presentation. I can't do this anymore.*

He looked back up.

"Don't let anyone who is different from you in any way—their color, their religious belief, the language they speak, how they look or act or love—give rise to hatred in you. Hatred shattered my world, orphaned me, destroyed millions. But it takes more courage to love than to hate. It was love—the risk by Jews and Christians to hide me, the open arms of an American couple to adopt me, the heart of a beautiful wife and daughter to help make me who I am, the path of goodness to guide me—that is my salvation. I am a Jew who says a *brucha*, that means a prayer, every morning on waking, and every night before going to sleep.

"We must be grateful for our blessings and open our hearts to others. And we must never forget."

After the class expressed their thanks, he headed back to his truck, slipping into his pier clothes. He wanted to lose himself in the whorls of his net, letting the anguish of his parents telling him goodbye stream off him like fog off the bay.

Fatigue set into his shoulders—the tension of retelling his story—and he thought just to sit on Margery's bench. Sometimes like Roger, he realized, he could not bear even to look at the helpless eyes of the fish.

Parking and starting to the pier's entrance he heard shouts. His gang was way out on the end, clustered at the railing. He ran toward them—they were pointing and yelling—and he knew someone had hooked an enormous redfish, battling it with light tackle as onlookers cheered, or maybe a sand shark or cavalla.

Halfway to them he saw Pastor Blue stripping down to his T-shirt and boxer shorts and climbing over the rail. *My God, someone has fallen in!*

Then Blue was airborne like Roger had been, arms up, legs bent, a kid leaping from a high dive. His heart banged. *He must be rescuing a child!*

He arrived to see Blue churning wildly toward a figure floating fifty yards away, a creature Hank imagined at first to be a manatee, like one he'd seen on a trip to the Florida Keys with Margery, chewed up by a boat propeller, bloated and drifting. Now he made out the shape of a man, shirt billowing, line around his neck, flotation device like a big red cork as Blue reached him, treading water as he threw off the line and pushed away the float, a small cooler, and turned him on his back, cupping his hand under his chin as he backstroked toward the shore. "He's breathing," Blue gasped out, "praise God!"

As EMS sirens screamed down the hill, police roaring behind, Hank and his pack hurried up the pier and on to the shore as medics splashed in with a stretcher, taking over from Blue, bringing in the man borne by the bay, dead to the world.

Up close the strange voyager looked shell-shocked by the storm, gash on his forehead, mouth twisted. The medics pored over him clapping on oxygen, sitting him up as he coughed out water, gagging and spitting, taking oxygen again.

From the man's pocket a police officer extracted a wad of wet, crumpled bills, and an ID card that Hank, pressing closer, recognized from the Bayfront Resort.

"Mr. Julio Blanco?" the officer said.

The medics helped him sit up again. He gazed out blearily.

"Sí."

"Yes, you are Mr. Julio Blanco, employed at the Bayfront Resort and Golf Club?"

"Yes." A spasm racked him and more bay water gushed from his mouth. Then he grew settled, looking up at the sky, then the officer.

"You're under arrest for murder. You have the right to remain silent."

"Yes."

"You have the right to a lawyer and to have one present while you are questioned."

As the officer read out the Miranda rights, a familiar ire rose up in Hank, a rankling to see a poor son of a bitch, wrung out by the fates, helpless on his own. He felt a twinge in his hip from scurrying up and down the pier, and wondered how many years, or months, he might even be good for.

But he could still be of use now.

He pushed forward, and, as the medics prepared their patient for transport to Thomas Hospital, announced: "My name is Hank Weinberg. You can talk to me. I'm Mr. Blanco's attorney."

9

PANCAKES

FIVE MINUTES AFTER ESCAPING THE Beacon, as Vanessa had cowered beneath an oak to keep from getting soaked, the electricity burst on and she could see the women making their way to the dormitory. That she was gone they might not notice; if they did, they'd let the director know. If she returned contritely to ring the door buzzer Crazy Betty would make good on her threat. And if she went to her own house in Daphne, Alabama, fifteen minutes from her father's in Fairhope, she might find a cop car waiting for her already. Either way, by morning she'd be on a van heading upstate. She had violated her judicial order. "Good job, Vanessa," she said to herself sarcastically.

Impulsiveness had been her strength but also her bane. In high school she'd been put on probation for a shouting match when another student in homeroom told her Jews were "Christ killers" and "they're all going to Hell." She'd been suspended for leaping up in history class and calling a teacher racist who argued that the Civil War was not really about slavery but about states' rights. If being a quick-tongued liberal down south got her in trouble, in New York, like a dyed-in-the-wool conservative, she nearly turned over a table at a dinner party in a rage when the host lambasted Southerners as "rednecks." "Keep a steady head and use your writing, your logic, to argue the opposite," her father had advised, grooming her for the courtroom even when she was young. "That will deliver a bigger punch. When you're hot, think twice—even three times—before you say or act."

She forgot then remembered his advice the first time after impetuously walking out on Mack, even before Roger was born, and the second, when they were arguing about Roger's developmental lag at four months old and she bolted out the door. "Walk out again and it's for good," Mack had warned, and when she did it was like leaving the Beacon. "I can't go," she told herself, realizing without an exit strategy she was going from bad to worse. "But goddamn I can't stay."

As a Beacon guard had stepped out, flashlight beam bouncing around the yard, she hid behind the oak until it was safe to run to the road. A moment later she'd hitched a ride as far as Walmart. Beacon residents had been allowed to keep on them a billfold with ID, family photos and debit card, but cell phones were stashed in lockers. She purchased a go-phone with 100 minutes and punched in a number she knew well. Douglas, her law firm buddy, answered.

"It's me," she said.

"Good Lord, aren't you in . . . Are you OK?"

"I've got a day off. I'm going to see my son, but it's too late tonight."

"You want to come by?"

"Can you come get me?"

"At the clinic?"

"No, I'm at Walmart."

In cosmetics she bought lipstick, freshened up in the ladies' room, and was out front when Douglas rolled up in his sports car, hopped out with an umbrella and escorted her into his lair of leather seats and XM radio jazz.

"You look . . ." he began.

"Like hell," she completed.

"How'd you get here? I know you can't be driving."

"I'd love a drink," she said.

"Are you kidding?"

"I mean hot tea or something."

Together, before her leave, they'd worked on the buyout of a community bank by a regional one, paperwork stacked high on their desks, traveling back and forth to headquarters in Charlotte until one evening, with adjacent hotel rooms, they unlocked the connecting doors and fell into her luxurious king bed. He was the only man she'd slept with since splitting with Mack, and his cool, artful sexuality was exciting and uncomplicated.

Arriving at his house she asked about Polly—"or was it Molly?" she said—and he answered: "Ran its course."

"You're the last Peter Pan."

"Tell me what's going on."

"You never saw me, OK?"

He nodded.

"Let me hear you say it," she insisted.

"I never saw you. P.S. But damn you look good."

"You're so sweet, Dougie. Sorry I'm not in the mood tonight."

"Understandably."

She felt herself exhale, as though she'd been holding her breath since her conversation with Hank about Roger and the pier. The group sessions, Crazy Betty, the judicial order—it flowed out and away, like a yoga meditation.

Douglas gave her his bed while he took the couch. In the middle of the night, the storm beating the tin roof, he tiptoed through her room to make sure the jalousie windows were cranked tight, then started back out. Aware of him, she lifted up her hand to take his when he passed by.

"You sure?" he said.

She gave a gentle tug.

The comfort of his presence as he climbed in next to her, the heat of his body as they stripped down, his slender, hairless torso in contrast to Mack's pumped, simian chest—she drifted with him, transported, restored.

In the morning, when she had him drop her off a block from her father's house, relieved to see the truck gone as she approached, Roger seemed to know just when to come to the window. His little face pressed against the glass, his sudden grin and hand patting the window, was gift enough in exchange for the consequences she'd face for being AWOL.

"My precious boy," she said as Lupita opened the door and he ran out and into her arms.

Vanessa told Lupita she'd gotten the day off for a surprise visit. Lupita's phone rang—it flashed Hank's number and Vanessa said, "Don't say I'm here." Lupita answered and listened intently. The moment she hung up, she shouted, "*¡Esta bien, mi hermano esta seguro y bien!* My brother," she went on breathlessly, "is alive, he's OK, in the hospital" and she recounted the saga.

Hugging her, Vanessa realized how dependent her own world was on this young woman now.

"I'll drop you off at the hospital," Vanessa said, "while Roger and I celebrate with pancakes."

In a kitchen drawer, she found the keys to her mother's sky-blue sport utility vehicle Hank kept gassed and gleaming in the garage, as if Margery might reappear.

In her old bedroom she kept clothes and shoes in the closet from her undergrad and law school years. She changed out of the tired brown dress she'd worn repeatedly at the Beacon, put on black jeans—they still fit!—yellow blouse and sandals from college days, and stuffed a tote bag with other clothes and essentials. She grabbed her purse, containing her wallet and passport, that she'd secured in a dresser rather than in the lockbox at the Beacon.

"Let's go!" she called out.

With Lupita in the back seat and Roger in front bouncing and chanting "pa-cake," she drove first to the hospital where Lupita got out, then set off with Roger for a big boy breakfast.

10
ABUELO

"Abuelo, yo intenté a nadar. Siento que me ahogué."

Coming up out of the pain medication in the hospital bed, head pounding, Julio felt like a man trying to emerge from water.

"Grandfather, I tried to swim." He heard his Spanish translated. "I am sorry that I drowned."

But his grandfather was standing over him, and he realized this must be the heaven his mother liked to talk about, that she promised for them all at the end of their days. Jesus had not convinced him; the priest had not persuaded him. But now Abuelo, dead for three months, was there holding out his hand.

He recognized his tall, strong frame, his large hands, his curly silver hair and a way of leaning down to him as a boy, speaking close: "Julio."

But it was not Abuelo's voice.

"Has cambiado."

A nurse acted as an impromptu translator.

"No, I have not changed."

"Dónde estoy?"

"You're in the hospital. You almost drowned. Your sister, Lupita, asked me to represent you. I'm a lawyer. 'Abogado.' Do you understand?"

A second face appeared alongside, speaking prayers. Was it his father, forever engulfed by the Honduran waters?

"Papi," he uttered.

"No," the voice said.

"Can you sit up?" It was the third voice, speaking in Spanish, the nurse, who put a firm hand behind his back, to help him sit up. Fluorescent light flooded his eyes. Strangers in white coats looked on.

Like a wave cresting over the skiff the last hours curled and broke over him—the golfer drenched in blood, the green turf moving away beneath his feet, the little boat into the angry sea, the men pulling him in, his clarity on the stretcher before tumbling downward again.

The old man identified himself as Hank Weinberg. "Do not speak to anyone else about your case except me. And this is Pastor Blue, a preacher. He brought you in to shore."

"I can go?" He knew those English words.

Hank shook his head. "You'll be here a while. A policeman is in a chair outside the door. They will transport you to the jail. Pastor Blue is here for spiritual counseling. He offered to come. The nurses and doctors are here for your medical help. But let me repeat, talk only to me about the charges against you."

Julio spoke to the nurse, who translated for Hank, "He says, 'I did not kill the man.'"

"Do not speak of this now," Hank said. "Tell him that. And that I will come see him again very soon."

Julio knew it was Abuelo, not in heaven but in the old man's way of turning his head, instructing him.

"I have been defending clients for over a long, long time," Abuelo said as the nurse interpreted. "Your sister, Lupita, loves you very much and works for my daughter, taking care of my grandson. I am doing this as a favor to her. Is that your wish, too?"

"OK."

"Let us pray," said Blue.

Julio felt the man of God's hands fold over his and heard the words in English: "Dear Lord, bless our fellow man, this journeyer through the darkness, help him find again the light. Let Julio Blanco know the power of you, the grace of you, the forgiveness of you, and let him be strong in spirit for the difficult days to come. Fill him with the holy ghost and guide his footsteps forward. And bless my friend and brother, Hank Weinberg, one of the chosen, who will help guide him, too. In Jesus's name, amen."

"Amen," said Julio.

"I found you in the water," said the pastor. "God led me to you."

"Can I go?" Julio repeated.

"You're under arrest," said Abuelo. "Do you remember what happened?

Julio envisioned two paths, one leading back to the beaten-down blocks near San Pedro Sula where gaunt dogs roamed through hollowed-out facades, blood from gang violence staining the street corner, the other on to the cold cell of an Alabama jail where he could not breathe fresh air or feel warming sun but inmates pressed in from all sides, taunting, threatening, like the Scorpions all over again.

"I wish I had drowned," he said.

Hank opened the door and Lupita peeked in, speaking to the lawyer and entering. As she covered Julio with her embrace, the old man headed out and Julio whispered to his sister, *"No digas nada a Mamá,"* imploring her not to tell their mother anything at all.

11
THINK TWICE

THE CLUE "PANCAKES" FROM LUPITA was all Hank needed to guess their destination—Southern Folks, an old-timey themed diner on the edge of town. Pulling into the parking lot he saw them by the window, sitting next to each other in a booth. He started to go in and rail at Vanessa—unable to heed his own advice to "think twice" when in a lather—but stopped. The blue SUV next to him was his wife's. He caught a reflection in its window. "Margery?"

It was only a passerby. "Of course," he said.

He knew too many friends sinking into confusion, seeing, for real, their late spouses or parents. He was prone to reverie—drowsy afternoons on the pier gave rise to it—but knew the phantoms were of his making, whether Margery's arms around him in ardor or his mother's desperate last embrace. The old men at the shul, the *alter cockers*, debated whether it was better to go head or body first. "I'll keep my brain," Hank had said. "With a shot of scotch I can deal with the rest."

When he talked aloud to Margery on her bench at the pier, he realized, passersby figured he was already demented. His fishermen friends thought nothing of it, though. Each had their ghosts, like

Blue, who asked his vanished son whether he thought a spoon or plug was the right lure, or implored him to whisper his whereabouts in Africa. All the men spoke to Jesus when they needed a miracle—Blue had shouted "praise God" to the heavens as he'd swum in with Julio—and Hank voiced his prayers, too, as instructed from boyhood. But he knew the line between what was actual and fantastical. He felt octogenarian pride in still being able to discern the difference.

"Hank," Margery answered back. Her voice was startling—tender, immediate. "Be gentle."

He got out of the car and, unseen, watched Vanessa bend toward Roger, cutting his pancakes. Roger lifted up the syrup dispenser, letting it pour. Vanessa reached up and set it aside.

"Doesn't she understand," he said to Margery, marveling at their beauty, "the happiness in her reach?"

Vanessa looked up and caught his gaze.

He entered to Roger's exaltations, "Gradee! Gradee!"

"*Mijn geliefden kinderen.*" He scooted into the other side of the booth.

"My beautiful children," Vanessa translated to Roger, eyeing her father warily.

"I love you both, dearly," he said, waiting for her to acknowledge the outrageous fact—she was defying the court order. "Poor child, Lupita," he went on. "Her brother!"

"Lupe," said Roger, not looking up from his pancake feast.

"She was beside herself when I got to the house," said Vanessa.

"I'm glad to be able to help."

"What do you mean?"

"She didn't tell you?"

"You found a lawyer for Julio already?" Her face brightened.

"I'm going to do it."

"What do you mean?"

"I'm taking his case."

"Isn't it a little late in the game for heroics?"

"I thought you'd be pleased. The way you've championed her. She asked for help."

"But you, Daddy? After all this time?"

It was a familiar game. No matter how he started off with patience she tested it. "You don't think I can handle it."

"Haven't you played Atticus Finch enough by now?"

He could not contain himself. "Why did you skip out!?"

"I'll call Douglas at my firm. His brother does criminal defense. I'll finance it."

"You're not listening."

"*You're* not listening."

"The Beacon called. The police called. You just bolted! You were all set—all you had to do was follow the program—not run out the goddamn door!"

"Well, maybe I wouldn't have been there to start with if you'd done a better job arguing on my behalf."

"No, you might be in a prison cell somewhere, God help us."

"Why not a suspended sentence, community service? You know that's what I wanted."

"You wanted special treatment, you mean, and after a repeat offense, lawyers above the law."

"Don't moralize to me."

"The judge could have revoked your license for a year. I think the ninety-day suspension was pretty good treatment, and time at the Beacon, and you blew it."

"Then let me just enjoy these pancakes with my son!"

"Pa-cakes," Roger said, drawing his index finger over the plate and licking it.

He remembered Margery's counsel. "What's going on, Vanessa?" he asked with softened tone.

She dabbed a napkin in his glass of water and started rubbing it on Roger's syrupy hands.

"You've got a wonderful life," he said with quiet intensity. "So you married a jerk? It happens. But the best schools, a big income, a handsome boy. He has difficulties, but happy? He's happy. Look"— Roger grinned at Gradee now—"what a smile."

"It's not that simple."

"It is that simple."

"You always try to make it seem that way."

"One word, one sign, one moment and it could all be yanked away. My parents, they clutched me one last time, then *gone*. Exterminated."

"I hate that word."

"You don't like the truth."

"This is not about the truth, it's about punishing me because you think I've got this perfect world except I keep screwing everything up. I'm so sorry that Oma and Opa and Benyamin and Shayna died like they did, so sorry for all of them, and so grateful that you escaped and came here and with Mama made me but that's not my life now. This is."

"'Doesn't she understand the happiness in her reach?' your mother said."

"When did she say that?"

"A few minutes ago."

"Oh, Daddy. And you're really going to do a murder trial?"

"I'm fine," he said, knocking his fist on the table as other diners turned to look.

Roger began to cry.

"We're heading to the beach," she said, grabbing up the check and sliding out, taking her son by the hand.

"Violating a court order, driving without a license—if you're going to throw away your future, go right ahead, but don't drag him along."

As she paid and exited, hoisting Roger onto her hip like he was a two-year-old, Hank followed right behind.

"I'll take you back to the Beacon," he exhorted. "I'll cover for you. I'll say it was my heart, that I needed you—they'll remember that I called—and you were scared for me so you took off."

"I don't belong there!"

"Belong? What do you mean? You're there for recovery, Vanessa. For addiction. It's exactly where you belong!"

When she loaded Roger into her mother's car and hopped behind the wheel, Hank stood his ground in front of the hood. She started the ignition and rolled down the window. "Move, dammit! Let me take my son!"

Hank's leg shook, a tremble he'd felt when standing up in court too long the months before retirement. He took a step to the side and a stone threw him off balance, sending him down against the black-top, banging his right forearm and hip. He gasped for air, watching the car door open and Vanessa's sandals clipping toward him—"Oh, Daddy, you'll kill yourself"—and Roger bounded closer.

"I'm fine!" With her help he climbed back to his feet, body throbbing.

"I'll take you home."

"I can get home on my own," he snapped. "Drive yourself to the Beacon."

She got back in the SUV alone, while Roger clung to Hank's leg. Vanessa's image wavered on the windshield, images of mother and daughter flickering together. "Guide her," Hank whispered to Margery. "If you can."

"Gradee, fih," said Roger.

"Not now," Hank answered, as he climbed with difficulty into the cab of his truck, his pier buddy perching next to him. "We've got work to do."

12
FLOWER CHILD

HIGHWAY 90 THROUGH RURAL ALABAMA paralleled the railroad tracks, the slow way to Mississippi and on to New Orleans, and Vanessa found solace in the back-road anonymity. The Beacon, receding on the other side of the bay, sat like a crystal prison in her mind. The morning with Roger had reassured her—he was doing OK. His little arms squeezing her neck, the smell of aloe soap Lupita used on his sensitive skin, his fragmented words that were music to her ears—how he revitalized her spirit. She imagined Roger before her and said to his big brown eyes: "Just one day."

A good night's deep sleep, twenty-four hours of calm, that was the therapy she ached for.

She mapped out her strategy. Once refreshed, she could accept her father's offer of help, one last time. Betty, indeed, might accept her mea culpas if Mr. Weinberg, respected father and lawyer, escorted her in the door. And if her law firm got word she'd broken the court order, she'd rely on Douglas to smooth it over when time came to resume work.

She passed the Church of God and Church of Christ and Baptist and Methodist churches tucked away in the pines and took a detour to see the Bodhisattvas of the Buddhist Temple on property owned by the Lao community. Her firm had helped orchestrate the real estate deal, which involved a gargantuan cash payment from the Buddhist community, bags of five- to twenty-dollar bills reeking of seafood that Alabama Coastal Bank was skeptical of at first.

It was a South she hadn't known growing up, still largely invisible to her friends up north—the Southeast Asians and Caribbean islanders and Hispanics like Lupita and Julio who wanted to make the newest "New South" their own. There was a West African social club in the west of town, a storefront mosque in the historic district, and a sign outside a Presbyterian church announcing times for services in Korean. She sensed their yearning for a new home and unease, too. As a child she'd felt like the outlander, the daughter of a Holocaust survivor in what Flannery O'Connor called "the Christ-haunted South." Daddy never let her forget that, even today at the restaurant stand-off.

She wondered if others of diverse backgrounds felt rooted in the landscape while also displaced, folks for whom Robert E. Lee and Stonewall Jackson were figures from a statuary as foreign as ancient Crete. Had they struggled too with what it meant to honor the stories of their families while partying as teens to Lynyrd Skynyrd's "Sweet Home Alabama?"

She remembered the first time she had. At sixteen she and friends had piled into a car and driven this same highway in Alabama, where the drinking age was twenty-one, across the state line to Mississippi, drinking age eighteen, to the Red Barn where most nights no one was carded. They bought two-dollar pitchers of Dixie beer, soon woozy, and when their home state's anthem came on the jukebox they sang along, punctuating "sweet home, Alabama," with "Roll Tide Roll," at the appropriate times. As college boys in Southern

Mississippi University T-shirts started ribbing them and flirting, they ran out laughing. A mile down the road they realized they'd left one of their group behind, finding her sloppy drunk, making out with a rangy boy. It was Crazy Betty. When it fell to Vanessa to lay a hand on her shoulder and urge, "Come on, we've got to get home," Betty had turned, striking out, "You little bitch." All piling into the car for the return to Alabama, Betty had sat fuming while the others joined in to radio hits.

Passing the site of the Red Barn now—replaced by a Dollar General—Vanessa realized it had been a moment she felt she belonged, was one of the pack. Like with Mack, drinking was the sacrament.

How long since she had touched a drop?

It had been five weeks and three days since she had escaped the bottle. She glanced at herself in the rearview mirror. Her eyes weren't bloodshot anymore, but dark circles were beneath them, her face no longer puffy but faint creases whispered at their corners. Her mind was clearer, her body more resilient, save the tiredness that fell over her like a cowl. She could have mastered addiction on her own, she believed, and felt rested, at least. Fighting with Mack, worrying about Roger, enduring Hank's lectures, and now trying to sleep on a bunk bed with stone mattresses in a constantly buzzing rehab center—exhaustion had become her fate.

Beyond Pascagoula she saw the distant cranes of Ingalls Shipbuilding, drove by fast-food restaurants and strip malls through Gautier. The creeping shadows of live oaks and power poles created a latticework over the highway.

The blue SUV around her made her remember how steady Mom had been, always there for her, at every stage. Margery would not have dreamed of her taking off on her own for a solitary evening, much less a whole night.

She reached the bridge over Ocean Springs, demolished by Hurricane Katrina and rebuilt, and the casinos of Biloxi appeared, a glittering Oz of tacky glamour where fishnet-stockinged hostesses poured free liquor to high-stakes Texans and elders chanced Social Security checks on dreams of fortune.

She pulled into the garage of the casino-hotel where she and Mack had spent a weekend during her pregnancy and found herself by the swimming pool looking to the Mississippi Sound. Though the October dusk was chilly, guests lounged in the heated pool clutching plastic cups brimming with cocktails. She remembered the kick of a Bloody Mary—"extra Tabasco," she always requested—and the sun warming her big belly, Mack leaning to listen in to their son.

"Hear anything?" she'd asked.

"He's saying, 'hup one, hup two, hike!'" Mack had said.

She ordered a ginger ale and sank back in a lounge chair and imagined herself back at that juncture—shining young couple, baby on the way—wondering how she'd veered off to here and now. In another moment she sensed welcome sleep coming around her, then a nudge on her shoulder—an attendant saying it was 9 p.m. and the pool was closed. Blearily she went into the lobby and booked a room, went upstairs, and lost herself in the sumptuous bedding, then realized Hank didn't have the number of her prepaid phone.

She texted: **Hi, Daddy, how are you? I hope your body's not too sore! How is my precious boy? I pray he's not still upset. I love you both so much. I'm so sorry I left like I did, I just needed some space for myself, a mental health day, I know you don't believe in that kind of thing, but in order to be a better mother, a better daughter, I needed to unplug. Just for a bit. I'll explain it to Betty, maybe she'll understand. I'll be back tomorrow and responsible again.**

She'd sunk into blissful sleep when his text pinged: **I hope to God.**

The next morning the front desk woke her at checkout time. Deliciously refreshed, she decided to drive farther west, to New Orleans for lunch—how she missed rich food after weeks of cafeteria nothingness—and return home in time to tuck Roger into bed. Lupita could stay with him while Daddy returned her to the Beacon.

She stopped in Gulfport on the way, taking a vigorous walk on the beach, uplifted by boundless sky. When she returned to her SUV a police cruiser pulled up next to her in the parking bay. She froze. The officer nodded, got out and stretched. His radio crackled. He took off.

"Be careful," she said to herself, driving on.

By the time she got to New Orleans, lunch hour was over and restaurants were starting happy hour. She drove to the French Quarter, parking on Royal Street in front of an antique store whose owner, with thick, wavy hair and pencil-thin moustache, looked her up and down through his shop window as she got out of her car and hit the street. She felt breezy, sexy all of a sudden. Maybe she would give Douglas a call.

She found an establishment her father would call "classy," where a bartender in crisp white shirt at a teakwood counter was pouring libations. She took a stool, ordered a Perrier with a twist of lime. Looking over the cocktail menu just for fun, a drink called "Flower Child" caught her eye. She laughed, thinking how her mother had once called herself that as she reminisced about dancing barefoot at a rock concert in the 1960s. It mixed Absolut pear vodka with Pearl cucumber vodka. What would it taste like?

"Fix you something, ma'am?" the bartender asked.

"I was intrigued with Flower Child. St. Germaine?"

"A liqueur," he said, "with the scent of elderflowers. It's added to the pear and cucumber vodkas, along with a splash of lemon and lime juice—very refreshing."

"I'll stick with my fizzy water."

A few minutes later the bartender returned with a Flower Child. "It's from the gentlemen at the end of the bar."

Two young men in pinstripe suits, neckties loosened, gave her a wave. The couple next to her departed and the men moved to their slots.

They introduced themselves: Mike and Michael, first year practicing law, maritime specialty.

"I'm Doris," she fabricated. "I'm a writer."

"Wow. Cool. I'd like to write," said Mike.

"He thinks he's Hemingway," said Michael.

"Thank you for the drink, but I'm abstaining."

"Gotcha," said Mike. "So what have you written?"

She began to spin out a story of a first novel about a woman marooned on an island who falls for a glider pilot who survives a crash landing, and her second, in progress, about a female musician "looking for love in all the wrong places, as the song goes."

"Is that what you're doing?" asked Michael.

"I've done my share of research." She circled the swizzle stick in the glass.

"I'd like to write about an ordinary guy, say, a lawyer," put in Mike, "who's really a superhero."

"And practices in New Orleans?" she asked.

"How did you know!"

She laughed, warming to these puppyish guys.

Michael signaled the bartender and he poured the men another round, asking Vanessa if she wanted something else. She shook her head and touched the glass to her lips.

It was unthinking, like kissing an old boyfriend in a forgetful moment whose romance she had forever sworn off. The vodka blends trickled down her throat, and she sipped again.

A warmth began to move through her, like a strand of DNA marked conviviality unfurling with subsequent sips. The lawyers seemed funnier, telling their first-year associates' stories of harumph-ing senior partners and back-office politics. The literary one, Mike, seemed cuter too. She'd forgotten, too quickly, how alcohol lubri-cated desire. Note to self: do call Doug.

"On the house," said the bartender, setting another Flower Child before her. She was about to decline when a band started up from the adjacent restaurant, New Orleans blues.

"Can we buy you dinner?" Michael asked, leaning in.

"No," she said, standing. She downed her drink. "Every lawyer for themselves."

They did not catch the slipup and moved their party to a table surrounded by diners relishing Creole fare. They ordered vodka mar-tinis and oysters Bienville, chardonnay to accompany the flounder topped with crabmeat, and she felt alive, her every pore humming, not minding when Mike leaned over and kissed her on the cheek and thinking it comic when Michael, from the other side, did the same.

"You need a scene like this in your new novel," said Michael, who nuzzled her neck.

She brushed him away playfully. "Let's dance," she said.

The three of them joined the partiers on the small dance floor, jouncing around, free-form, until Michael disappeared and returned with a Stoli on the rocks for Vanessa, and when she knocked it back she knew she was a goner.

The French Quarter streets were funhouse mirrors they stepped through, finding themselves in the lobby of a big hotel where the M's announced they were getting a room and before she could beg off Hank's text flashed on her phone: **Roger was waiting. Asleep now.**

She texted back: **Tomorrow.**

Response text: **Shame on you.**

Her blood curdled.

"We're ordering champagne," Michael said.

"Don't you guys have wives or something?"

"So, who's Roger?" Mike asked.

"You looked at my phone!"

"You were standing right there!"

She took out a photograph and shoved it in their faces. "My little boy. Twice the man you are already."

"Hey, hey, calm down," said Michael.

"Fuck you."

She heard their coarse guffawing behind her as she headed out of the lobby onto the street. Endless strange faces elongated before her, like an early Mardi Gras, each visage a mask taunting her, Mikes, Michaels, fakers, con guys, screwballs, her mood plummeting further as she found her car, but a linen truck had blocked her in. She got in, leaned on the horn, then chanced to ease out an opening between the truck and the car ahead. No luck. She backed up, banged the car behind her and its alarm blared. She stepped on the pedal, felt a thump, setting off the alarm in front.

She tried the opening again, getting wedged between the truck and the car ahead, then put it into reverse to extricate herself and smashed the pedal, her mother's beautiful sky-blue SUV bounding backward, over the curb, into the window of the antique store now closed, glass shattering, alarm blaring.

The driver of the linen truck appeared and scooted away. As she heard a police siren turning the block, she put the gear in forward and peeled off, catching the first light, taking a right near Jackson

Square, slapping Roger's picture back on the dash, repeating, "I can't let this happen," finding her way to the bridge over the Mississippi River and crossing it, pulling into the first truck stop she found, waiting until the coast was clear and continuing west, asphalt blurry and shifting, to who knows where.

13

ENCLOSURES

IN THE OPEN HE FELT he could survive, even in a hurricane, a mud-slide, a tiny boat on a big sea. But not in a cell.

Released from the hospital, in custody in the back of the police car, Julio looked out at the approaching county jail. He saw the long, flat building, a warren of enclosures, on a barren field like a space ship marooned on a lunar scape. He remembered as a boy riding by Danli prison in Honduras with his Abuelo, who warned him, *"Los que entran aquí nunca salen."*

Those who enter here never leave.

"¿Por qué?"

Inside it is dangerous. You cannot hide. You cannot run. *"Siempre es más seguro quedarse afuera. Ser libre."* It is always safer to stay outside. To be free.

It was all that had comforted him when his father drowned, the recognition that he had been outdoors, under God's blue heavens, like he had been on the skiff before being saved by the cooler. But had he been saved at all? "I wish that I had drowned," he had said to the old man in the hospital, the one that Lupita said could help make him free. But after several days in recovery he was not free at all but inside a cinder-block room being fingerprinted, the clothes he'd changed in to at the hospital, brought clean by Lupita, stripped off him in exchange for navy pants and shirt with COUNTY JAIL on the back, his black leather shoes from Lupita bagged and stored, exchanged for a pair of flip-flops. He shuddered, like an old man himself with a fever down into his bones, as he was led through the complex by the guard unlocking doors, counting off the pods, each pod with multiple cells—parole violators, misdemeanors, felons—through the racket of men shouting through bars as he passed, the noise an enclosure itself pressing in, beating against his skull.

The din was like the gymnasium's, too, echoes reverberating through the floorboards, the rank and chaotic shelter where he and Mama and Lupita had ended up after Mitch had swept away their hillside home. *"Los damnificados,"* they were called, "the damaged ones," who were moved into the shelter fashioned from the gym where the boys and girls at first thought it a playground and the elders a refuge safe and clean, churches and charitable groups sending boxes packed with canned green beans and yams, jars of peanut butter, cereal, powdered milk, and caps, shirts, and blue jeans. But the numbers of Mitch refugees inside the gymnasium grew too fast, families spilling out the door, into the beaten-down dirt yard, down a hillside, on the slopes leading to a drainage ditch.

Julio's mother kept watch over their place inside like a lioness guarding her cubs. She'd fashioned their lair in a corner near the grandstands—a curtain hung on a clothesline, mattresses against the wall, their mishmash of clothes in the corner. Outside of the gymnasium, where so many lived in a tent city of their making, he played *fútbol* with Paco and the scores of other children, chasing the lumpy ball around the dusty field, and under the Central American skies long clear of storms he felt free, even when the big boys bullied them. It was inside, like now, moving through the confines of space, that he felt he could not breathe, in the recycled air a thousand men's exhalations choking him. Like drowning. Indoors.

"No puedo," he said. "I cannot."

The jail guard said nothing, merely opened a cell, gestured for him to enter. Julio did not budge. The guard nudged him with his club.

Inside was another man, said his name was Smoke, charged with armed robbery, didn't do it, he said, a fuckin' railroad job, waiting on his jailhouse lawyer sent by a judge, some pissant don't know shit, he said. "You Mexican?"

Julio said nothing as the door closed behind him. He sat on the edge of a bunk, squeezed his eyes shut, saw the fairway beneath his feet again, heard the golfer.

"You got a girlfriend? Wife?"

Julio shook his head.

"You queer?"

"Leave me alone."

"I ain't telling nobody nothing either. They use it against you. But we in this together, coonass. Fuckin' lawyers, they're spies is what they is."

Julio looked at Smoke, his brow the color of chalk, a crease across it like scar, his eyes dull green marbles.

"I seen an angel, too, right in that window." Smoke pointed at the barred window where light leaked through a dirty pane. "Killer angel. Watch out for yourself."

In the commissary he sat hunched over his food, trying not to make eye contact. He heard Spanish, looked down a long table. Two men leaned over, nodded his way. He turned back to his plate.

I do not belong here.

The next morning the guard's voice was outside his cell. "Julio Blanco? Your lawyer is here."

After snaking through the corridors to a warren of small rooms he saw Abuelo waiting for him at a table, along with a thin woman in wire-rim glasses. The old man asked him to take a seat as the guard stepped outside the door.

"Hello, Julio," Hank said in English.

"Hola, Julio," the woman repeated.

"This is Grace Juarez, a translator. Anything you say is between us, confidential."

The woman said the words in Spanish.

Hank told him again how Lupita had retained him to represent Julio in the court proceedings.

"Yes, OK," Julio said. The attorney was as hoary as a prophet but Lupita had assured him his services were free.

"You're lucky to have such a wonderful big sister. I had a big sister, too. How are you feeling?"

"Better."

"That's good to hear."

The old man, his eyes deep-set, his lids heavy, said he had been a criminal defense attorney for a very long time, and that he would do everything in his power to have Julio exonerated.

"Exonerado," the translator said.

"The prosecution has filed initial charges against you. Later this week you will have an arraignment, where the charges are read in court—capital murder, the most serious of felonies. The state will argue that, in the act of robbing a man, you committed homicide—you stabbed him to death. The judge will ask for your plea. Guilty? Not guilty? 'Nolo contendere,' meaning no contest, you accept the charges."

"I did not kill the man."

"You will have a court-appointed translator. You will plead not guilty."

"I did not rob the man. I was walking home from work. I found the man stabbed, bleeding. I went to him. I picked up some of his money to give back to him. I got scared. I ran."

Abuelo had set a yellow pad before him and was taking notes. Julio had not seen someone writing with a pencil since he was a boy.

He recounted his story: end of the workday, heading to his lodging, the cry from the golf course. He didn't mention smoking the joint with the college boys, fearing it would hurt his case and even get him deported.

"That was Beau Shepherd, correct?"

"I didn't know who he was."

"Beau Shepherd," Hank said.

Julio felt the victim close, his sweat and blood, but anonymous until now. In the hospital he had refrained from watching the news.

"You did not know him?" Hank asked, scribbling. "Had never met him?"

They merged together, the tubby men at the resort with their sunburned white faces, shirts bright as parrots, lording over the manicured grasses. Had he?

"No," he answered.

His memory was a haze. Had the golfer whispered "Julio?" Had his voice exhorted, "run?" He said nothing of that. He wanted to leave this place. He saw himself on the couch at Lupita's, drinking a beer and eating *carne asada*, relishing how she grilled the flank steak with flavors of home, as he cheered on the Honduras nationals. With Paco he'd chipped in for Lupita to rent satellite TV just for the soccer. If he told the lawyer too much, about the pot, about the money, what might happen? "They're spies," Smoke had said.

"The police report describes the knife wounds," Hank said. "Did you have a knife?"

He answered that he'd carried a garden knife, issued by work, in a sheath on his belt. "I never took it out until later, to cut through some vines. I hurt myself and dropped it, it's gone, I don't know where."

"Did you see anything else at all?"

The hurtling of a red bird in the woods, to his stoned brain like the bloodied wing of an angel, or *el diablo's* brow creased like his cellmate's. Or was it how it seemed looking back? None of that was worth repeating.

"There's a report of a witness, another resort employee, who says he was working at the sixteenth hole and saw the incident taking place at the seventeenth. He says he shouted at you and called his supervisor. There's a record of that call. The prosecution will depend a great deal on his statement. Did you hear anything?"

The groundskeeper's voice striking out like a blade hurled through the chill air. "I don't know."

"We'll get that exact distance measured. It's pretty far away. The prosecution will gather its facts. I'll also do some investigating."

"I want to go home," Julio said.

"I want you to go free."

"Lupita can take care of me, at her house."

"Julio, I'm not an immigration lawyer, but if you're not a US citizen and you're charged with a felony, even if you're found not guilty on all charges, you may face deportation."

"I cannot go back to Honduras."

"I will contact an immigration lawyer here, a woman born in El Salvador. The political situation is very hot, once you're out of the shadows it's nearly impossible to duck back in."

"Lupita said you can help me."

"It's a different court, another proceeding. For a long time I've been afraid of where I was born, too. I lost people there that I loved.

And I was only a very little boy. I also swore I would never go back. But what if I had to? I would."

"*Nunca,*" said Julio, and translated himself: "Never."

"Isn't your mother there? Doesn't she need you?"

"I send her money from my work. She has to pay."

"For her food, for her house," Hank said. "I understand."

"She has to pay the men."

"What men?"

The youths in their sleeveless T-shirts, tattoos curling over their biceps, gaining on him as he ran through the streets, doors slamming shut except his mother's, wide open, a machete in hand she kept in the doorway as she readied to protect him, her precious son. "*Cuánto, cuánto?*" she shouted at the pack. How much? Every month since then she had given them money, the only reason they left her alone. It was him they still wanted, but until then his money would do. His work visa had been his liberation.

"No men," Julio said, realizing he'd already said too much. "Nobody."

"It is still better than an Alabama prison. Or death row."

"If I go home, I die."

Why had he let himself be captured at all? Had he angled his skiff toward the shore he could have weathered the storm, found shelter until it had passed, made his way to New Orleans, losing himself in Little Honduras. He cupped his hands over his face. "*Lo siento,*" he said into his palms.

"We've done enough work for now," Abuelo said. "Have faith. My friend Pastor Blue can visit, if you want. You have family who love and support you. Be strong."

"*Lo siento, Mamá.*"

Heading back to his cell, not even Smoke, jabbering at him about snitches and conspiracies, could distract him. There was an hour scheduled for recreation, the weight room or the jail yard with the basketball hoop, but he did not want to mingle with those broken men.

He lay down in his bunk and drifted into the shallows, deeper water still, soon submerged where he yearned to be.

14
BLUE MORNINGS

HANK MADE UP THE MULLET net, draping it over his arm while keeping an eye on Roger perched on Margery's bench, trying not to think of the police report from New Orleans: "Malicious Destruction of Property. Leaving the Scene of an Accident." A security camera had picked up Vanessa's license plate, tracing the car to him. And Julio as alleged assailant had been repeatedly in the news, in light of the funeral of Beau Shepherd that weekend, throngs paying last respects to the man praised for his public service and devotion to church and family.

A week earlier Hank had been a blithe octogenarian, fishing and dawdling through timeless afternoons. Now he was an anxious father worrying about a daughter acting more like a wild teen than a working mom, and a reborn attorney, however creaky—the arthritis in his hands had even flared up as he took notes at the jail interview—defending a "monster," as a relative of Beau's had reviled Julio in the press.

"Gradee," said Roger, looking out where the mullet leapt.

Yes, he thought, *pay attention to the fish*.

His concentration off, his throw fell lopsided and he hauled up only a twisting eel, a somnolent crab, and a few wriggling baby flounder. He shook out the spoils over the bay, ready to try again.

Blue appeared alongside.

"How was it?" Hank asked of Beau's funeral.

"Lived as a sinner," Blue said, "eulogized as a saint."

Hank looked at him quizzically. "Doesn't sound like a preacher talking."

"A father."

Beau's story, with Zach Blue part of it, had been replayed again to the public. The Uganda mission trip, the plane crash, the three bodies recovered, Beau walking into that village three days later, bedraggled and dehydrated, and Zach nowhere to be seen.

"He knew about my boy."

"I'm so sorry," Hank said.

"Everybody else accounted for, but not my son. No trace of him in the wreckage . . ."

"I know," Hank interjected.

". . . and you mean to say Beau never saw him again?"

Cooter Clark arrived, leaning in, listening to Blue, then T. and B. Brown came up, their small forest of rods and reels rising in their roll cart.

"Suppose they started out together," Blue said, "dense jungle, Zach could be struggling, it was brutally hot that day. Did they have any water with them at all to start? Did they share it?"

"We'll never know now," said Cooter.

"Shut up!" Blue said. "We do know. I could see it in Beau's face. He got back here and became famous 'cause of that crash, would have gone all the way to Washington like a wounded war hero if he hadn't gone on one damn long bender."

The Brown brothers were nodding.

"And my son . . ."

Hank felt the ache deep in his friend, as if he had just been to Zach's funeral, not Beau Shepherd's.

"It's hard when one loss brings back another," Hank consoled him.

"No wonder I don't have a church," Blue said, contrite now. "Listen to me. God rest Beau's soul."

Mullet were arcing out of the water like they meant to grow wings. Roger stood and started hopping up and down, waving at them.

"You've been mercifully kind to Julio," Hank said.

"He's lost in a jungle, too, isn't he?"

The pelicans were wheeling.

"You think he's got a chance?" Blue asked.

"That's my job."

His stance was hardly as steady as when he'd been younger—his fall in the parking lot had reminded him of that—but he was regaining his footing in a world he knew. Where he had a purpose. A role. *The wrong man doesn't hang on my watch* was his unspoken motto. He felt a surge of strength in his arms and readied the net and, to Roger's cry of delight, sent it far up and out.

The hoop earrings that Vanessa wore at college graduation, the chocolate cake Margery baked him for his seventieth birthday, the brim of his father's top hat as he looked down on his parents strolling to the Dutch National Opera—the circles of his years seemed to fuse into one as the net rose up, held there, as if it could stay suspended forever.

"Mommy!"

It landed on top of the brimming water, mullet bumping and pushing, heads like mallets hammering the weave.

"Mommy!" Roger was starting up the pier toward the parked cars.

Hank handed the cord of the net to Blue and followed close behind. No jumping into the bay this time.

The boy was loping now, faster, shouting "Mommy!" as a sky-blue SUV appeared at the top of the hill, motor purring, turning the curve down to the lot.

Then he stopped, stark still.

A willowy lady with a tall daughter and a baby got out.

Roger turned back around. Hank caught a flicker of despair move across the boy's face like the shadow of a wing. He wanted to scoop him up in a giant hug and never put him down.

"Gradee," Roger said, distracted again by the net plumped with fish that Blue had hauled up for them. Roger's little hand wrapped around Hank's thumb, and the child led the way.

PART II

15
LUPITA

THE CRACK OF THE ROCK against the roof of her trailer startled her awake. The shot came again, like a banging hammer. It was not the first time she'd been roused by what she thought was a falling branch or a horse chestnut hurled by the wind. She turned into her pillow, trying to calm the flutter, the twinge of nervousness she felt that someone was targeting her.

It was her morning off. Roger was with his father, Mr. Hank already in his law books if not at the pier. Lupita wondered what Julio was doing just then. Rising in his bunk at the jail, filing into the commissary, the common yard, the work detail, the cell? *"Enjaulado,"* she said aloud. Caged.

She got up and looked out the window—mist lifting over the fallow fields, like that morning days earlier when blue light had washed over her window and she'd jumped up to see a figure racing away. The running man had been indistinct, but she knew it was Julio. The blue light pulsed, there was the sharp knock on the door, a man's voice saying, "Sheriff's office."

Were they coming to deport her?

"We are looking for Julio Blanco."

"*¡No está!*"

"We need to speak with Julio Blanco."

"*¡Un momentito!*"

She'd found the shirt balled in a corner, soaked with blood—"*¡Qué horror!*"—stuffed it in the garbage, and opened the door to a uniformed officer, a second behind him keeping watch. "Is Julio OK?" she frantically asked.

The deputy showed his badge. "We need to question him. Do you speak English?"

"I understand a little."

"There has been an alleged homicide—a murder—a man found stabbed on the golf course."

"Terrible!"

"On the golf course at the Bay Resort Hotel. Mr. Blanco is a person of interest."

"I do not see my brother in two days."

She had not lied. Maybe it was another man, she told herself, who'd been flying across that field.

After they'd left she'd stepped out into the edge of the field to see if blood was tracked over the matted grass. She waited a half hour to see if he'd return, no matter that she'd be late at Mr. Hank's. When light strengthened she saw two boys chasing a ball across the field, recalling Julio and Paco as kids. Of course, it had been him. She grabbed the shirt out of the garbage and took it to scrub at Mr. Hank's. Whatever had befallen him she could take care of.

"*La protectora*"—the protector—that had been her role since childhood with her little brother. Though at 5' 7" he towered over her by five inches and was only a couple of years younger, he still had the look of a boy, the way he and Paco had hurtled over the packed dirt of the refugee camp vying for the soccer ball, buried his head in her chest at their father's funeral, cried when she'd been the first to go north for work.

She'd developed an interest in students with developmental challenges from helping a young cousin in Honduras who had Down syndrome, then assisting a special education teacher. She secured a work visa, hired by an agency in New Orleans serving special-needs kids, some from Spanish-speaking families. The city was vibrant with Hondurans, many with Temporary Protected Status in the US after Hurricane Mitch's devastation. Along Williams Boulevard in Kenner, she enjoyed the foods from home as if she were still there. She yearned for her own family, though.

That Julio would be able to join her in the US was a blessing, the God-given grace of resort work allowing him to flee the gangs. The money he could make and send home, along with Lupita's contributions, was vital to Mama, covering her expenses, assisting Abuelo in his final years, and enabling her to keep the gangs at bay.

Lupita's work visa was renewed. Julio's lapsed. But she believed he could help his future in the US become secure.

"Aprende algo importante," Lupita had told him. "Learn something important."

The English language and special education—those were her paths. After New Orleans she moved in with a family on Mobile Bay with an autistic daughter, realizing there was demand for nannies who could take care of special-needs children, not only in the schools. When that family moved north, she stayed put, renting an isolated house trailer next to a field, about ten miles out from Fairhope. Vanessa, hearing of Lupita from other parents in the disability community, reached out to her. She'd proved the right person for the job.

There was a vulnerability to Roger as he got older that she understood, a way he had of being hurt by the actions of others—a startling movement, a touch, even by his grandfather—when no harm was intended. When he struggled to make a word, she sensed what he felt, as if he were speaking a foreign language. He relaxed around her, let her coddle and calm him.

"I need you for my family," Vanessa had said and paid for her to take courses at the junior college. Climbing the ladder—associate's degree, BA, special education certification, bilingual fluency—would argue Lupita's case for remaining stateside forever. "That you're working toward it," Vanessa said, "helps us keep you secure." She had progressed slowly, but was determined.

She dreamed of a green card arriving in the mail with its lettering, "United States of America Permanent Resident" with her photo on one side, Lady Liberty with her crown peering from the cross-hatching of green on the other. In the lower right-hand corner her fingerprint, unique, inviolable, would claim this new country as her own.

She made her coffee, cleaned her house, turned on her small TV to the telenovelas and tried to lose herself in the romantic entanglements of the actors. She scrolled through texts that Vanessa had sent her, sweet words to pass along to Roger, photos of her making a funny face to share with him. **Mommy is still working,** she wrote. **Be a good boy for Gradee and Lupita. I love you!!!**

A new text appeared, from Paco. He was coming by later, on his way to the restaurant.

In her refrigerator she found two bottles of Salva Vida that he'd given her, his gift from the Mercado Latino that carried the Honduran beer and many others. She saved them until early afternoon when she took out one to open, set up a folding chair behind her house, and took a sip. Her grandfather's favorite.

Salva Vida. Lifesaver. On the label was a red and white float against a blue and white Honduran flag. Paco had given Julio a *salvavidas*, the ice chest that buoyed him up like God holding the world in his hands.

It was Abuelo who'd been a lifesaver, too, teaching her, with a Salva Vida in hand, how to savor, a sip at a time, its earthiness. *"No seas como esos borrachos,"* he'd warned, don't be like these drunks, pointing out the addicts stinking of *guaro*, the local spirits made with sugarcane, languishing in cantinas.

"Una borracha." That's what her Abuelo would call Vanessa. He would not care how educated she was.

The drinking would start as soon as Vanessa and Mack came home after a day at their offices. While Lupita gave Roger his dinner, they'd be lifting their glasses, downing their drinks, the fights erupting. When it happened, she'd take Roger in the other room and sing to him. Vanessa would come to find them, hold them both, weeping her apologies. She began to confide to Lupita about her husband's tantrums and attacks. Lupita's English had not yet been good enough to comprehend all, but she understood enough.

"¿Te gusta?" The voice came from the corner of her house. You like it?

"Ah, Paco." She nodded to her door. He went in and got the other bottle.

He asked her about Vanessa. She would be home soon, she told him, though she had no idea if it were true.

"And Mr. Hank?"

"Before long he will have Julio free." Another hopeful answer.

"Your mama?"

"We are still well and happy is all she knows."

She'd made sure the weekly money that Julio wired home did not vary; she even went to the same Moneygram counter at Mercado Latino. She texted from her phone: **Hola, Mamá, estoy con Lupita,** *todo esta bien. Te amo. Julio.* Hello, Mama, All's well. I love you. Julio.

A loud bang on her roof like before made her jump from the chair. Then another, like the crack of a gun. She saw the third rock sailing toward them from the field, this one landing against the wall near her chair, and Paco was up, running toward the horizon like Julio had done.

"Paco, no!" she shouted and followed, kicking off her jellies to go faster barefoot on the furrows before realizing she was still clutching her beer when a projectile smashed the bottle, cracking it in her grasp. Jagged glass dug into her palm, and her blood flowed.

She kept running, seeing Paco in the deepening dusk with a rangy boy he had by the shoulder. "What you do? What you do?" he yelled at him.

A second boy appeared, looking on from the edge, as if to dart for help.

"I seen you from my window that morning," the second boy said, pointing at Paco.

"Crazy boy," Paco shouted. "Look." He nodded to Lupita, who was wrapping a handkerchief around her hand. *"Llama la policía,"* he said to her. Call the police.

"Why you people here anyways!"

"Policía," Paco demanded. *"Llama la policía."*

"Speak English!" said the boy in Paco's grip.

"Police!" Paco said.

"No, Paco, no, Paco." Lupita kept on in Spanish: "Do you have all your papers? Who will they blame?"

A shout came from the distance. "Dinner!" sounded a mother's voice.

"Who's out there?" shouted a man's voice from the same direction. "What's going on?"

Lupita held up her bleeding hand. "We will say nothing, you will say nothing."

"Deal!" the first boy said as Paco let go and they bounded off like jackrabbits, calling back, "Mexican bitch."

16

THE CAPSTONE

"It's an outrage!" said Hank the next morning when Lupita appeared with her bandaged hand, admitting what had happened. "I know where those little bastards live."

"Please. No more trouble."

He pressed her on taking action, but her distress was palpable. He relented but insisted she see the doctor.

Rocks hurtling through the air—the image cut through time to find him again.

In one of his University of Alabama yearbooks, the Corolla, 1956, he found a news clip he'd stuck there:

> Tuscaloosa, Ala., Feb. 6, 1956. Showers of eggs, rocks, and mud today marked the third day of classes at the University of Alabama for the school's first Negro student. State highway patrolmen joined authorities to help keep order. Autherine J. Lucy, 26 years old, of Birmingham, was able to attend only two of her three College of Education classes today. She was finally spirited off the campus by police at 1:10 P.M.,

returning 50 miles to Birmingham while anti-Negro demonstrators were diverted pelting eggs on an elderly Negro who had driven her here.

Pinned to the *New York Times* report was a long-ago note: *"Dear cousin, If those crazy crackers in Dixie make you angry and frightened, come north. We've got a room for you in Brooklyn and there are plenty of good colleges here. Sammy."* He had written back, he recalled: *"Thanks, cousin, a tragic situation I experienced up close, but I'll stay put. This is my home. Somebody has to help make it better."*

He hadn't needed his New York relatives—his Selma father's side of the family—to tell him about the hatred and chaos that day. He'd been in his second year at the Capstone, as the university was called, when Autherine Lucy had enrolled for those three miserable, heartbreaking days.

He'd been heading to history class when he'd turned a corner to see the mob pushing close as she was led to her car. She walked erect, looking straight ahead, an outcast refusing to cower. It was the faces of the mob, shouting and taunting, that not only alarmed but fascinated him. The boy with his lips twisted in anger yelling indiscernibly; the woman, chin forward, neck straining, as she cried, "Get the hell gone." Behind them were a phalanx of others looking on, male students in white shirts and cardigans, women in skirts, bobby sox, and saddle shoes, indifferent, unmoved.

He'd seen those onlookers, too, outside the Joodsche Schouwburg, the men in coats and bowlers watching stone-faced, then accusingly, as families were led out of the detention center by Nazi guards, the street sweeper stepping forward, shouting, *"Joodsche honden,"* Jewish dogs, and shaking her fist. An elegant lady in feathered hat added her voice to the chorus.

Had the boys who'd thrown rocks at Lupita been raised in families like that, harboring contempt for those who were seen as outsiders, as different?

Could her brother get a fair trial in a place where many might rush to judgment who did not know him, or understand the deed he was accused of? He put the question in his mental folder, "State of Alabama versus Julio Blanco." He built his defenses like a novelist composing, a writer friend told him, beginning with anything that came to mind, then focusing in, paring away, until he arrived at the essential narrative.

After breakfast, with Roger up and dressed, they got in his truck, and he drove Lupita to Dr. Yonge's. They passed a construction site and slowed and Hank caught the unmistakable rhythms of Spanish.

"Can you teach me?" he asked Lupita.

"Sir?"

"Spanish. A lesson a day. I'll pay you"

"*¿Por que quieres aprender?*"

"Why do I want what? *Aprender?*"

"*Aprender.* To learn."

"So I can understand Julio's world better."

In addition to his native Dutch, he told her, he'd spent his first years hearing French, one of the languages of neighboring Belgium, and Yiddish, at home from his mother and father and grandparents.

"I had to get to Selma before I took Spanish. In high school."

"Then you know Español!"

"I learned *nada. Bupkis*, we say in Yiddish."

She smiled and pointed down a lane to a small store. "Mercado Latino," she said. "It's where I send money to *mi madre.*"

He'd driven past that lane before but had never noticed the store.

The first time he'd tried to speak to the lone Mexican in his first-year law class, Jaime Montero, born in Georgia to parents from

Oaxaca, he'd made the mistake of assuming Jaime's family were laborers and that Jaime, like the children of many Jewish immigrants, was working his way up to greater opportunity.

"My father," Jaime told him crisply, "is a diplomat at the Mexican consulate in Atlanta."

They soon became friends.

Studying together for constitutional law class Jaime had explained that the Fourteenth Amendment, granting birthright citizenship to anyone born in the US, did not apply to children of foreign diplomats. A lifelong Atlantan, he'd acquired his green card at age eighteen. At twenty-three his naturalization ceremony was scheduled for the next week.

Hank had driven with him from Tuscaloosa to Atlanta, and when the group of new Americans said the pledge of allegiance, he felt a stirring as deep as when he'd glimpsed the Statue of Liberty as a boy. The love of country was one they shared.

What puzzled him was how Latinos in Alabama could become one of the new scapegoats. His law school's most infamous alumnus, Governor George Wallace, had ridden his racism to national visibility, a tactic that other white Alabama politicos had used. In a state where nearly a third of the population was black, some white leaders continued to stoke white anxiety. Only four percent of the state was Latino, though, some well established, others in the shadows, but a candidate even for national office could gin up enough anxiety about them to gain traction in an election. Another Alabama law grad, the US attorney general, presided over a Department of Justice that inflamed the fear, whether immigrants, mostly Spanish-speaking, crossed the border in dead of night or presented themselves for asylum. When had the yearning to become an American citizen, even the chance to try, he wondered, become criminal?

One night earlier that year Hank had fallen asleep watching the news only to wake to the picture of a terrified six-year-old behind bars like a tiny felon. Or had he been dreaming? He had been that child, separated from his parents, isolated by the Germans in a day-care dormitory changed into a holding pen. Was he conflating the past with the present?

No, it was true, the image was a waking one he would see over and again. The family separation policy, spurred on by the nation's highest office, stripped minors from their parents, put them in cells or spun them out to far-flung foster care—a "deterrent," leaders argued, to families risking all to come north. The panic he'd felt when the soldiers wrested him from Mama and Papa was surely akin to what these children would experience. There was little deterrence, as if there should be, but plenty of scars. After these little ones were grown, even old and gray, that shock of being pulled away would haunt them.

After Hank dropped Lupita off at the medical building to see Dr. Yonge, he and Roger set off in the direction of Mercado Latino. He passed three trailers on blocks, a cluster of women outside talking and laughing. He saw a landscape company work truck, the crew boss holding a clip pad, calling out directions to a team of men clearing a building site. They hacked their way through the brush with machetes. He slowed, only to be watched warily now from the stoops of ramshackle houses, reminiscent of his drives through Dallas County in Alabama's Black Belt, where his presence, in a largely African American community, called attention to itself in a different way.

He arrived at Mercado Latino and, holding Roger's hand, walked in to survey the scene. The murmur of voices lowered; faces turned toward him. On the TV high in a corner a soccer game was underway.

"Gradee . . ."

"Here, Rog," he said, and picked up a bag of cookies—*Galletas de Mexico*, the wrapping read—and opened it to give him one.

Making their way to the checkout they passed counters with red pinto beans, black beans, strings of chiles, bananas and plantains, corn tortillas, canned goods with brand names from countries south.

When he'd first moved with Margery to lower Alabama to start his law practice, they'd shopped for Passover at Schwartz's deli in Mobile until it closed down after Zelda Schwartz, its ancient matriarch, had died. Now all that was left was the "ethnic" food aisle of supermarkets, where a few shelves with Manischewitz matza and macaroons stood next to Goya yellow rice and leche de coco. Jewish delis in the area were gone, but the Hispanic markets were in full flower.

ENVÍA DINERO—the sign for "Send Money" was an arrow above a row like another for CERVEZA. Four men stood in line before a counter where they pulled wads of cash from their pockets and handed them to a woman who wrote out a receipt, punched in the numbers, and sent funds on to *la familia* in villages south of the border.

Roger wrested loose and went up to the last man in line and reached out. The man looked down, smiled, and shook his hand. "Hola," he said.

"Gradee."

"C'mon, Rog," Hank said, "let's pay for the cookies."

As they proceeded to the cash register the room fell silent, only the TV soccer making a sound now. One by one the faces turned toward Hank—some lean, high-cheekboned men with crisp moustaches and dark eyes, others round like Julio's, youthful, soft-gazed.

"*El abogado*," one said.

"*Necesito ayuda tambien,*" said another. Help, he knew that word, just like Lupita had spoken at the pier.

He reached the counter, paid for the cookies, and turned to see the dozen men had taken off their sun hats and ball caps, nodding to him in respect.

He nodded back as they walked toward the door.

One youth still had his cap on and his father popped him on the back to remove it and said, "*Señor Hank. Está pasando.*"

Mr. Hank is passing.

17
TURNING SOUTH

SHE'D SPENT THE FIRST NIGHT in Baton Rouge, holed up at a cut-rate motel, the second night in Lafayette, only a couple of hours west, but her hangover left her with a pounding headache. On the third day, she crossed the Texas border, Interstate 10 like a gritty river carrying her along, angling down to Galveston Beach for the night. The days passed in a haze. She knew how long it took for alcohol to metabolize beyond detection in the body—up to twelve hours in the blood, twenty-four hours saliva, five days urine, ninety days hair. The last was subject to false positives—prolonged exposure to cleaning products could create that same effect in hair, she'd read, and she'd done her share of mopping and sanitizing at the Beacon—but the others were dead giveaways. Each time she took a drink, opening the munchkin-sized vodkas in hotel minibars, she started the calendar over, determined to return the requisite five days after resuming her sobriety.

She texted Hank the lie that she was sick and was recuperating in solitude. "Probably the stress," she said, "of what I've done. But I'll get back there soon." Maybe she was sick.

After angry responses for days he now just answered, "OK." Rather than indifference he was furious beyond words, she knew.

Her flip phone had no internet, so she bought a tablet with Wi-Fi access and when she booked a room in Austin she Facetimed with Roger, who said, "Mommy working," the cover-up Lupita had supplied.

"Yes, my precious boy, Mommy is working."

He reached out his little hand and laid it flat on the screen. She felt it against her cheek.

"Mommy kye."

Wiping at her face, she told him she loved him from here to the moon, then asked him to hand the phone back to Lupita, saying to her nodding, gentle visage that she had Julio in her prayers and knew her father would do right by him.

When the screen went blank she felt more alone than before and fought the impulse to drink. What had the counselor in the Beacon session called it, not the problem but the symptom? What void was she trying to fill?

She started an email to her close college friend, Cecile, long married to a vintner in California. A year had passed since they'd been in touch. She had a rash fantasy—drive straight through to visit her, curl up, and enumerate her transgressions like they both had to each other while at Vassar. Cecile would calm her, help her find the source of her recurring anger. "You mellow me out," she'd told Cecile. Feeling whole again, she'd write a confession to Betty, return home and accept her fate. Roger's fractured words, "Mommy kye," his word for "cry" like a kite with no tail, was all she could take. Even with a long detour it was nearing time to return.

In her email, she dissembled to Cecile that she was on a solo excursion, the road trip version of the *Eat Pray Love* fantasy they'd romanticized in college when the book was hot.

As soon as she sent it another note popped up in her inbox: "Where are you? I want to see you. xo, Douglas."

The next day he flew to the Texas capital.

Cozy friends, they strolled hand in hand past food trucks and Tex-Mex cafés to the Congress Street bridge, watching the bats swoop at dusk along the Colorado River like a vast, wind-hurtled streamer. "It's how I feel," she said, as streaks of black turned and twisted. "Chaotic."

"They seem wholly predictable to me," he said.

Driving to the Broken Spoke in his rental car they tried line dancing, moving in a slow circle around the hall, novices among the twirling cowpokes by night who worked in indie film or software development by day. "Have a tall one," he said, ordering them two soft drinks at the bar.

"You can drink, you know, I can drive us in my car," she said, secretive that she had touched liquor at all.

"I wouldn't want a Texas cop running my plates if I were you."

She drew back. "You had to remind me."

"Isn't that why you're hiding out?"

She joined him in his room at the Driskell, a far sight more sumptuous than her motel, reminding her of the night she'd climbed into his luxe coupe at Walmart. Appealingly uncomplicated, he enfolded her in his embrace.

That was Douglas to her now, the comfort of his arms, of his body—his runner's taut legs, his soft, white-collar-worker hands—his voice after they'd made love whispering to her, "Mack was a damn fool to let you go," and a stirring that made her wonder if they could make a life together, a house in the historic district with a small garden for tomatoes—how Roger would love that—normalcy.

"So what are they saying about me at the firm?" she asked.

"That you're crazy."

She laughed, and when she did so he brought her closer until she felt the movement of his breath, the rhythm of his heart. She had never been able to relax with Mack like this, so simple. Her quarter-back husband, after lovemaking, had always turned away, like he was going over the plays of a long-ago game in his head, the cheerleader forgotten.

"They're a bunch of uptight motherfuckers," Douglas said.

She nodded.

He was silent now until she wondered if he were sleeping, then he spoke gently, soothingly, "What if . . . have you ever thought . . . you could just . . ."

"What?"

"Look into it."

"Into what?"

"Whether . . . talking to somebody would help. A professional."

"You think I'm crazy, too?"

"No, but there are these things, these things that go on inside people's heads. They can't help it."

"I was just in these group sessions. God, enough of all that."

"I know a really good shrink."

"R and R is my therapy."

"It could help. With the firm, I mean. They're watching all this."

She sat up in bed and pulled the sheet up to her shoulders. "They sent you out here?"

"I came for you myself."

"Ah, I see now what you're up to. Get in a quick fuck while you're at it."

"Stop it, Vanessa. Just goddamn stop it. I came for you because we're friends and I like you and admire you and am sticking up for you. Yeah, we're great together, like this, but if you think I came all the way out here for . . ."

"Of course not. You're too much of an operator for that."

"They're going to fire your ass," he said, getting out of bed and slipping on a bathrobe.

"I'm on medical leave!"

"You were, until you left the clinic and climbed in a car and went low-rent Thelma and Louise on us. Joyriding across the South. You're the wrong kind of hometown celebrity. Clients don't want that. The partners sure don't want that."

"And you just came out to tell me all this in person, in your super fucking deluxe hotel room?"

"No, you're right. Pure self-interest." He reached for his phone on the side table and clicked on a moving image. "Recognize anyone?"

As he held it in front of her she saw the grainy image of a security camera video. A blue sports car rolled up to the front of a door that slid open. Vanessa appeared, furtive in the rain, disappearing into the car. It sped off, the license plate visible. "Not hard for a detective to find this, your debit card, cell you bought, time of purchase."

"I'm not a felon!"

"You're acting like one."

"Why didn't they just send somebody to my door to haul me in then?"

"Because I pleaded your case."

Her father prided himself on being able to read people's faces. She sometimes thought it was a disability of hers, though, not knowing whether someone was being ironic or straight, sincere or fake. "You have no bullshit detector," a college boyfriend had once told her. She thought she'd proved him wrong but fell for every tired line in the book when Mack romanced her. Was Douglas being genuine now, or manipulating her?

"Mack will get off your back, too," he said.

"Mack?"

"You know he'll come after you for custody if you don't make a turnaround."

"He's too much of a fuckup himself. He doesn't stand a chance."

Before her loomed an image of Roger at Mack's house, Mack's tawdry girlfriend of the hour tucking her sweet boy in at night. "Fine."

"Thank God," he returned, slipped off his robe and crawled back into bed alongside her. "What a relief." He nuzzled her shoulder. "This will all be a weird detour, a little walk on the wild side that'll soon be forgotten. Forgiven."

"What now?"

"We enjoy the room and I'll let them know, and they'll smooth it out with the rehab center, your father doesn't have to get involved, and you pick up where you left off."

He reached for the hotel phone, called the concierge and asked Vanessa what she wanted —"Shall I get two cowboy rib eyes, why not?" he asked—and she said, "Let me treat you," feeling not relieved at her decision to return home but, instead, even more trapped.

"No, no, the firm's got it covered," he told her, then spoke into the phone, "medium rare, OK?" He looked over at her.

"Are you kidding me?"

He completed the order with two bottles of Perrier, then turned back to her.

"You've bought me off with a piece of steak?"

"Don't be ludicrous. You've made a decision. A fresh start. We're celebrating."

"You're working me like a con."

"You realize I'm implicated now, too," he said, his voice rising. "Here, look at this again. My car." He found his phone and pushed it into her field of view and clicked. The blue sports car rolling up in front of Walmart, the rainy night, the dash into refuge.

She was up and into her clothes.

"Two DUIs and it's like you're in that movie *The Fugitive*," he said. "Do you realize how nuts that is?"

"That's me. A madwoman on the loose."

"I'm on your side!" He was hollering at her now—"Your side!"—as she slipped on her shoes and was to the door. "You're not going to turn me into 'that guy.'"

"You're all that guy."

The hotel door closed behind her now, her fingers on the car keys, her headlights in the Texas night.

18
GOAL!

IF HE COULD OUTRUN THE charges he would. Not over the fields and into his skiff and out to the vast and turbulent gulf, but in this jail yard where the soccer ball skittered across the packed dirt with the inmates chasing it in thirty minutes of rapid-breathing, elbow-swinging release, the dumb feet of those raised on American football—the carjacker from Ohio, the armed robber from Tennessee—no match for the agility of Julio and the other Latinos who commanded the white orb, finessing it, left right, into the air, head butt, toward the T-shirts marking the goal, point!

He could tell who was a smoker, a doper, by how they moved, struggling, panting to keep up, but this enclosure with its chain-link fence topped by barbed wire and guards just outside toting their assault rifles was their outlet now, the escape with no escape, and he was mad to go faster, traversing a mile in the space no bigger than the distance between his mother's house and Tio Juan's five doors down until his uncle had fled to Mexico.

The ball flew at him and he stuck out his chest like a bantam rooster, letting it rebound from him to his teammate, carjacker Luis from Panama, tall and balletic, who whirled it with his right foot to Red, an Alabama shrimper who'd nearly murdered his cousin, a towering fright in the cell block but out here a lumbering oaf.

Remarkably, Red passed it haphazardly back to Julio who spied the open corner between the T-shirts.

He'd seen the move before in Honduras, at the games of team Olimpia, with Abuelo, their biggest fan. In a half-pirouette he was up, spinning midair, his instep catching the ball and sending it hurtling toward the zone.

"Goal!"

He seemed to hang there, above the world, looking out over the barbed wire and guard tower, as far as that stadium where he'd rooted with Abuelo for the home team, the howling of Mitch and the cries of *Los Escorpiones* and the blood-and-whiskey drenched pleading of Beau Shepherd all dropping away, just this cool Alabama air that held him aloft, like the shoulders of his teammates as, finally, he came spinning to the ground.

But then he was on the ground, tasting the dirt in his mouth, and there was a familiar voice at his ear, not a man he knew but the accent and rhythm as Honduran as his own. "Arnold Peralta," the voice said.

He recognized the assailant as Ricardo, a recent addition to the jail from La Ceiba, on the coast, where his father had drowned. Ricardo spit out the name of the murdered soccer star again: "Peralta."

Julio twisted around and grabbed Ricardo around the neck and wrestled him down, and as he choked him he thought of Peralta, the Olimpia star, shot dead from eight rifle blasts in a store parking lot while on an outing with his wife and baby. The police believed that the Honduran gang La Banda de Rafa was responsible. But there had been no arrests.

As the other inmates stepped back and the guards came running, Ricardo threatened that if Julio's mother did not pay more blood money in Honduras, *"te matamos,"* we will kill you, *"y tu mamá."*

"If you touch my mama I will kill you!" he shouted back, beating his fist against Ricardo's skull. "I will kill you!"

Hauled off, handcuffed, put into isolation, Julio felt the surging in his chest. It beat there, wanting to let loose, until the next day Mr. Hank arrived to instruct him, "*Cálmate.*" Be calm.

"*No puedo.*" I cannot.

"You must. Your conduct here has to be perfect. *Perfecto.*"

The old man's voice enfolded him like a balm.

"*Abuelo.*"

"Your sister is teaching me Spanish. *Me llamo Hank Weinberg. Lo sabes.* You know that. But call me what you will."

He took a deep breath, nodded, and tried to still the monster he was accused of being that strained to come forward.

19

UNLIKELY SUSPECTS

THE CORRIDORS OF THE COURTHOUSE, his steps quickening as he headed through the heavy doors, the banging of the gavel like the start of a pulse, Judge Partridge resting his hands on his Santa Claus belly, the approach to the bench—the choreography of fifty years returned to him in times like these, on his back, 4 a.m., Roger's breathing a metronome to his insomnia.

"Hank?" Margery's voice. "Can't sleep, honey?"

"My thoughts are churning."

The jury pool was ten thousand faces that still flashed before him in a cavalcade of choices: a middle-aged white nurse with a high brow and straight yellow hair; an old black mechanic who leaned forward, attentive, slightly hard of hearing; a rehab veteran who had turned to Christ. In voir dire the information had been volunteered, all too readily by some. He'd had a gift, reading those faces, the watchfulness that had come from his boyhood: who could be trusted, how a story would be heard, interpreted. That a whole trade had grown up of jury pool consultants struck him as just one more sign that the profession had slid from the high standards of his beginnings. He had long prided himself in honing the art of reading people. He treasured the law and had always been critical of road-side billboards announcing divorce and personal injury attorneys, or television spots for 1-800-LAWYERS. His honorable calling was diminished by manipulative marketing.

"You'll do great," Margery whispered in his ear.

"We might do a plea. His only prayer."

"How old is he?"

"He'll be an old man, I know that, before he gets out."

"Turn a little. Go on."

He felt her push gently but with certainty on his shoulders. Her hands kneaded the tight muscles between his shoulder blades; then he turned over to see her not there. He closed his eyes and relished the ghost of her touch.

Savaged by a stroke at age seventy, Margery had slowly regained some of her faculties, and Hank, then nearly seventy-eight, had decided the time had come for him to devote every hour to her recovery. Saying farewell to the office and courthouse, he'd prayed—going to synagogue regularly again since the time they'd attended ritually as a family in Vanessa's teen years—that she'd be restored as best possible, they'd have the freedom to travel and, with the arrival of Roger, grandparent together. After she suffered a series of setbacks, she'd grown confused about who he was, if he was in the room or not. The most plaintive call he'd ever heard, when he was sitting next to her in a chair, was, "Hank, are you there? Honey, where are you?"

"I'm right here," he'd said. "Right here."

Even now he whispered it to the ceiling, the air, the vanishing touch of her, knowing she was not there but conjuring her. That she had lived long enough to hold Roger, their delicate grandson, cradling him gently but firmly as Vanessa sat close, lifted his heart.

As if catching Hank's vision Roger stirred, rolled over.

In the curl of his grandson's lip he saw Margery, her beloved feature winding its way down through the generations. Vanessa had her eyes.

"When you look at her don't you see me?" she asked.

"I do, and it breaks my heart."

"She needs you."

"She needs to be responsible."

"When you attack her, ridicule her, she hurts even more."

"She couldn't care less."

"Reach out to her. Do it for me."

He'd only texted Vanessa so far, anxious at the thought of a confrontation on the phone. Douglas had contacted him from Austin to say he'd just seen her, that she'd relented to returning home but had taken off again into the night.

When the sun rose and Lupita arrived he headed to the pier alone. He threw his net, his circles irregular, hauling up only groaning croakers and wriggling pogies that he kicked back into the water before the Brown brothers could grab them to cut up live as bait. At least the pelican on the railing, shifting webbed foot to foot, would swallow them whole, down to darkness, oblivion. Nature's way.

He situated himself on Margery's bench. He pulled up Vanessa's number, called. He waited, hopefully, for her not to answer, the phone going to voice mail, but she picked up and asked, "Is Roger OK?"

"Yes, I just wanted to check on you."

Silence. "Thank you," she said. "I'm fine."

He heard the thrumming of a car, the playing of a radio. "Are you still in Texas?"

"On the road."

Margery was at his shoulder, prompting him. "Do what you need," he said.

"That's a surprise."

"Well"—he tried to go on supportively—"I know you'll be home soon."

"Not yet. I'm so sorry, not yet."

He held in the impulse to tell her what he really thought. That she was ungrateful. Selfish. With a young son, an old father, thinking only of her own pain, whatever the hell that could be.

"I hear gulls," she said. "You on the pier?" She added: "I hope."

"Just a breather. I've got a mission now."

"Please don't overdo it. I worry about you, Daddy."

"You have a fine way of showing it." If Margery scowled at him, so be it.

"Does Julio even have a prayer?"

"Why don't you get back here and help me make sure he does."

"It's hardly my area of expertise."

"You did a stint with a public defender."

"That's why I'm in banking law."

"You'll have no expertise if you get suspended from the bar."

He heard her exhale in frustration.

"And, yes, he does have a prayer. No criminal record, no motive, one unreliable witness."

"He was at the scene of the crime, his DNA was all over Shepherd, and there's the blood match of Julio on the weapon, not a small thing."

The story had broken that week of a Labrador retriever finding the knife sheath in a ditch, bringing it to his master like a shot dove. Detectives located the knife close by. Local media were all over it.

"You're following it closely for someone who doesn't give a damn about anybody but yourself."

"Undocumented and Hispanic," she went on. "The new Jim Crow."

"He needs an alibi. Where he was ten minutes before."

"I know, reasonable doubt, it could have been somebody else. So who was it?"

"It's not my job to find out."

"You don't think your fishing buddies have a hunch?"

From Margery's bench he looked down the pier. Regulars were leaning on the railing, or squatting on folding chairs, poles like divining rods angled outwards, waiting for the downward pull. He saw Blue, with binoculars trained on the far horizon, as if waiting for his son to reappear.

"Well, they like to talk. But what do they know? *Bubbemeisters*," he said, using the Yiddish for old wives' tales.

"I've been out there with you. They've got something on every-body. It's like a Greek chorus."

As she spoke, he felt a shift inside: talking about Julio's crisis put them back on level ground. He remembered his delight when she was in law school and they could discuss her classes in property and torts and criminal procedure like any veteran and novice, the static electricity of father and daughter dropping away. After her summer internship with the DA and a stint after graduation with a public defender's office in New Jersey, she threw up her hands, said she was frustrated and exhausted, and was ready for financial reward. He'd given her his blessing to go into banking law—at least the shift would bring her back home, a great gift to Margery and him— but he'd wondered aloud if she wouldn't miss the one-on-one with clients who truly needed her, no matter their transgressions, often trapped in an underclass where opportunities were few. She'd called him an "old lefty," expressed her devotion to Mack, who knew that making money provided what he called "the only real opportunity," and said she'd never feel guilty again about "enjoying my life."

Only Margery could bridge the distance between them, and her spirit whispered, "I love you," in his ear and he repeated it to his daughter.

"Love you, too, Dad."

Then she was gone and he wondered if he'd been tough enough, honest enough, had made it clear how outraged he felt at her behavior. He waited for Margery to guide him but she was gone as well.

He sat alone, as if the entirety of the bay morning wrapped itself around him and kept him apart.

He saw a flash, the glint of sun against steel on a fishermen's hip. There were knives out here, folding, curved, smooth, serrated, for scaling, gutting, filleting—an arsenal of blades. Which one resembled the murder weapon? A coarse hand could plunge any one of them into a victim's pulpy chest.

He noticed Blue had turned and was looking at him through the binoculars. Hank waved. Blue motioned for him to come and pointed to a phalanx of pelicans emerging from the horizon.

20
PIÑATAS

SHE FELT ODD COMFORT BEING back on Highway 90, having skirted San Antonio to find herself on the same ribbon of asphalt heading west that had brought her out of Alabama, Mississippi and Louisiana, avoiding the interstate when she could. By RV parks and rural churches, deer processing plants, tattoo parlors, mesquite furniture makers and grain companies, she chased the setting sun before she turned south again toward Eagle Pass. It had been three nights since she'd walked out on Douglas, the impulsiveness returning, the urgency to bolt even as she tried to keep control. Had the offer of a gluttonous meal, compliments of the firm, been the linchpin? Or the image of herself dashing furtively into his car? Or just the notion, anathema to her, of being watched?

She'd wondered how she might have fared in Oma and Opa's world—the roundup of the Jews, the relocation to the Joodsche Schouwburg, the separating of the children to the school compound like her father, little Haim, the train to Westerbork, on to Germany, Poland. "I would not stand for any of it," she'd proclaimed to Daddy. "Not as a mother, not as child. I'd have fought back."

"Blaming the ones who died?" he asked sorrowfully. She'd waited for an outburst of anger, but he only grieved. "May you never know this kind of fear."

He'd brought her to him and held her close. "My American child, you don't know what you would have done."

As much as she bridled at Hank's criticisms of her, she longed for that touch too, the knowing father embracing the naive child. Reassuring. Protecting.

She pressed the gas pedal harder. Dusk lay across south Texas in darkening wreaths, striations of clouds circling the winking towns in the distance, Eagle Pass fifty miles away. Just beyond was another world, Piedras Negras. She'd been warned by the AA crowd that geography was not the key to sobriety, but she knew that just over that border she could free her body of alcohol for good, and her head. Cecile was south, too, her friend had answered, her husband having added a vineyard near San Miguel Allende to his holdings, cultivating the Malbec grape.

With the countryside plunged into darkness, her headlights cut a swath down the ribbon-straight highway with small garlands of lights beginning to rise from the blackness. A string of tiny stars, loops of red and green, a shimmering cross. Christmas decorations! And just November! "Good God!" Roger's birthday was fast approaching. "You will be home," she said to the night, "by then."

Twenty miles from the border she saw a gas station ablaze, pulled in, went inside to grab a food. There was a rack of T-shirts with local slogans: "Save a Horse Ride a Cowboy," "God Made, Jesus Saved, Texas Raised," "It's Texas Thang, Y'all." Next to it was a line of piñatas.

The big green frog at the end looked bizarrely familiar, googly eyes staring back at her. Next to a blue donkey and red chicken a frog was a genial member of the menagerie, saucer eyes pleading.

"I'll take that one," she said, and the clerk unhooked the frog from the line and she bought gummy bears and peppermint sticks and chocolate kisses to fill it. Thirty-two dollars later it was in the back seat of her car.

"You'll love meeting Roger," she said over her shoulder. In the rearview mirror she saw his googly eyes staring off to the nighttime. The border town came closer.

The rearview mirror again, the frog eyes. The recognition of them—Roger's fourth birthday last year, the plastic bat in his hands, the piñata dangling low from the ceiling—almost made her veer off the road.

"He's just a little boy!" Vanessa had said to Mack, who kept repeating, "hit it, hit it, Rog." Little Roger swung and swung, the green frog motionless. The other children pressed close, crying, "let me do it," "my turn," "let me hit it," but it was Roger's day.

Imperious, untouched, the frog flew above the crowd of children, Roger unable to make contact at all. *Whap!* He struck it once on the leg, the frog turning. *Slap!* He hit it again, in the eye, and it rocked back and forth.

"Now, the killer blow!" Mack said, the children jumping up and down excitedly.

Roger looked off to the side like a light had caught the corner of his eye and he twisted wildly—*whack!*—the bat popping Mack on the forearm.

"God dammit!" Mack yelled, grabbing Roger by the wrist and yanking him back, the bat falling to the floor. "Don't ever do that again."

"Get your hands off him!" Vanessa yelled.

The children fell silent. Roger let out great, heaving sobs.

"Oh, fuck," said Mack, grabbing up the bat and crashing it onto the back of the frog as the candy rained down.

"I hate you!" Vanessa yelled to the image of Mack in her head. She'd held back her blistering words that day, the bat slashing the piñata, the children falling to the spoils as Roger stood in the middle, bawling. "I hate you!" she let fly now.

She slowed to pull over at a rest stop and dispatch with the evil frog but thought better of it. *Conquer your fears*, Hank had always said. "This time, Roger, we'll wait until you smash it yourself." She kept on.

Eagle Pass City Limits.

The higgledy-piggeldy of gas stations, fast-food joints, and check cashing operations gave way to a boulevard with bilingual signage of pharmacy/farmacia, dentist/dentista, shoes/zapatos leading to Puente Internacional, International Bridge.

The cars were backed up a quarter mile waiting to reach the border, and she joined the caravan, inching forward, spinning the radio dial to hear the baleful guitar of outlaw country and gleeful accordion of Mexican norteña.

Flashing blue lights startled her, the pulsing color bathing the back of her vehicle, getting closer, a siren wailing. Each revolution of light was like a beat of her heart, her license plate the giveaway, as Douglas had reminded her. Another light joined it and a voice blasting through a speaker and then officers were running alongside her car. She had no time to react when the border patrol descended on a truck two spots ahead of her, surrounding the vehicle as the driver tried to jump out but was grabbed and put into an armlock, two others emerging from the passenger side with hands up. Along with the driver they were handcuffed and led away. Were they convicts breaking parole? Mules on their way for a shipment?

Red lights flashed and a tow truck rolled down the emergency lane, moving up the line of cars as Vanessa and others were directed to back away. She watched the tow operators hook up the truck, noticing the Arizona license plate as a couple of cars in front of her were turning around and heading back on the exit lane.

She opened the glove compartment looking for the registration. Wedged beneath the auto manual was a passport: Margery Weinberg. Her mother's expression, even in a photo booth, was elegant and endearing. She had the self-possessed look of a woman who'd been loved at every stage of life—growing up in Tuscaloosa, by friends in college, by a devoted husband her whole, intact life. She had kept the fragments of Hank intact, too. Vanessa leafed through the pages, seeing the stamps: Argentina, Italy, France.

Next she found her mother's old driver's license. The glove compartment was like a box holding the past, Hank keeping her travel documents there, as if Margery would need them for their next venture. All they needed was updating.

She found what she needed. Hank had renewed the registration, she recalled going with him to the DMV a year ago, Roger along.

It had expired by a few weeks.

Best to turn around.

But then a guard was motioning her into a new lane opening up and it was too late to change plans.

When she reached the gate the border agent spotted the dated registration, but as she began to fabricate a story—the DMV had been closed for a holiday, then she got sick—he typed the numbers into his tablet and said, "It's OK. Make sure you keep a copy in your car."

He waved her forward to Mexican customs. She moved a few feet ahead, waited her turn for the green light. It came on red.

Her scant belongings were taken from the trunk, the glove compartment emptied, a sweep was made beneath the upholstery. "I'm a lawyer," she explained. "On vacation."

A handler appeared with a black Lab. The dog roamed object to object, nose inquisitive, then stopped at the piñata.

"Where did you get this?" the agent asked.

"About twenty miles back, gas station."

The dog pushed his snout into the fat neck of the frog, stayed there.

A sick feeling coursed through her. What did they imagine she was transporting?

"Open it, please."

She undid the flap and the agent lifted it and turned it upside down, the goodies streaming out. With each item—candy canes, bubble gum, lemon drops—she felt rising dread. A festive gift for her innocent boy had become a suspicious package.

She became aware of eyes.

From just beyond the bridge, bathed in darkness, they peered at her—children no older than Roger, their mothers and fathers behind them. The footbridge was alongside the road and people waiting were backed up in a ragged line.

"May I?" The agent took a chocolate kiss and untwisted the foil.

"Take it all," she said.

"No, no," he said, popping it into his mouth, "you're good to go!" He poured the contents back in, sealed up the papier-mâché.

She got back in. The light turned green. As her car crept forward, down the ramp into Mexico, the families waiting by the bridge stretched as far as the church steeple at the square.

She stopped, took out the piñata. It would be Roger's gift to the children. As she set it down they ripped it to pieces, grabbing at the spoils.

21
MI HISTORIA

"I NEED TO UNDERSTAND YOUR whole story," Hank said as he sat across from Julio in a meeting room at the jail.

Julio looked at Hank's face, the crinkles at the corners of his eyes, the corona of white hair.

"What brought you here? To this country?"

"A contract," he said, "to work in the resort."

"Why did you want to come here at all? What led to that?"

"*La tormenta*," he said. The storm.

"That was when you were a little boy."

"Before the storm," the translator said as Julio spoke, "everything was happy."

"*Feliz*, yes," said Hank.

"My family, my friends, my school. I was a very little boy, and I lacked for nothing. One of the first words I learned, my mother tells me, was *Honduras*, and it's a place I've always loved. I am a Honduraño. A Honduran. But the hurricane took it all away."

"You moved to a shelter, didn't you?"

"It was a sport center, outside of Tegucigalpa. So many people, so much noise, we lived in the gymnasium. I remember how my

mother made a tent out of a blanket near the edge of the grandstands. She guarded it like a lioness. I used to dream about being
at our home in the mountainside, but then the nightmare, the
teacher ringing the school bell, the wind beating at the walls, the
window shattering, running outside and the ground giving way,
like a giant slide beneath us. As little boys we thought it was an
adventure, a carnival ride, crazy, getting faster, then we realized it
was the earth itself that was breaking and we were sliding down
with it. The houses, the animals, the trees, the mud. Everything
sliding faster, then hurtling down the mountainside, the hurricane
roaring. 'A monster,' they called it. Like they call me now. But I
did nothing."

"Tell me more about the shelter."

"Like the storm we thought at first it was fun. But it got dirty,
there was shit everywhere no matter how they cleaned, and you
could hear couples having sex at night, sometimes right next to you
under their blankets, and then, after being there two years, three—
the government had no money, there was not enough housing being
built—some of the boys started going with gangs. Little things.
Picking up money and running it to a drop, stealing from stores,
from lady's purses, running a bag across town, anything, to make
a few *soles*—they paid the boys little—and sometimes they didn't
come back. Eight years old, nine, ten, they'd be caught by the police,
or robbed by other gangs, even murdered, but the gang leaders, the
big boys, kept their hands clean.

"Maybe the drugs were there before Mitch, the gangs, the money,
the killings, but I was too small, I didn't know anything. At the hurricane camp we played so much soccer—the church groups brought
us balls and sports shoes, clothing, sunglasses, comic books, all kinds
of things—but soon it wasn't about different teams but gangs. My
friend Paco, you met him, he works in the fish restaurant, started

hanging with one group, his big brother was in it. I didn't want any part of it. They were mean to me."

"How were they mean to you?"

"To my sister."

"Lupita?"

"The church people built houses, and more houses, and finally we moved to the cinder-block village. There was no work there and Papi went to join Abuelo in La Ceiba where Abuelo worked for the fancy hotels, gardening, landscaping. He found a job for Papi in the restaurant, but my father wanted to be outside, free, not caged in like I am here. He signed up to work on a boat. The fishermen went so far out. They say Papi fell overboard and he could not swim.

"The day after Papi's funeral one of the gangs started coming to our house, asking for money. 'We have nothing,' Mama said. 'We protect you,' they said. 'We can protect ourselves.' 'If you don't buy protection from us you will suffer,' they said. 'There is nothing more you can take from me,' Mama said.

"'What do you mean?' I asked her but she said nothing. After Hurricane Mitch there were so many Hondurans in the US, everybody in San Pedro had an aunt or brother or cousin in Los Angeles or Houston or New Orleans, and when the military coup came in 2009 there was even more violence, it became more dangerous—my mother's brother, Tio Juan, left for Mexico at that time, he was very political—and Mama began to beg Lupita, 'It will be better for you in the US, safer there, you can make money.' She did not want to go.

"One day, one day . . . Paco . . ."

He hesitated. The swirl of images filled his head. The flash of a blade. Blood pouring onto the ground. Running.

"What happened?"

"They wanted to kill me."

"Who?"

"My mother paid more."

"Who?"

"Every week she paid. She had a kiosk, a window store, with candies and soft drinks, then she began to wash and iron for the rich people. And I tried to make money, too. Working in construction, carrying buckets of water for cement. We were moved to a little house in San Pedro, and Mama had another little store and Abuelo moved to be with us. Every day he would walk down the streets of the city with his clippers and garden knife and disappear through a door into the courtyard of a rich family. Then he asked me to go into the courtyards with him, and he taught me how to clip and prune, to get fertilizer when the gardens needed it, and how to read the soil, that is the expression he used.

"'You will have something now you can do to save yourself,' he said. 'I thought Abuelo was very wise."

"Yes," said Hank.

"But it led me here."

Julio waited for the old lawyer to say something more, to ask him another question, but like a seamed prophet he just stared back, a figure in a church window. Could he see into Julio's mind? Running down the dirt road with the pack of other youth behind him, the heat of them pressing forward, closer, his name spoken in a death sentence, the fierceness of his mother, her machete at the ready, holding them back, the extortion keeping them both alive.

"You fear for your life in Honduras."

"I did not want to leave my mother," he said. "My father was dead. It was my responsibility, to take care of her."

"She wanted you to be safe," Hank said.

"There is no place to hide."

"Is someone threatening you now?"

He glimpsed a man passing by the window. He looked away from Hank to the window again.

He watched Mr. Hank eye him inquisitively.

"Nobody." The window again. The man whisking by, looking in.

He told how Lupita had gotten a work visa to help in a school in New Orleans and how his mother cried when she left and he cried, too, but not in front of his sister. When his mother told him it was his turn to go north, too, he said, no, he had to stay close. It was "my duty."

"What made you change your mind?"

"She came in the door from church and said she'd prayed to the Our Lady of Suyapa, the protector of Honduras, and Our Lady had spoken to her and said, 'To save your son you must let him go. If he will not go you must send him away.'

He said he applied to an agency looking to place workers with a chain of resorts and was given a work permit, an H-2B visa, he explained, for nonagrarian workers, initially good for a year—renewals could be granted—and headed to Hilton Head, to a regal golf course and sprawling lodge looking out over the sea grass and dunes. He worked on the garden crew, feeling Abuelo in his forearms and hands as he pruned and pared and trimmed his way into a new life, the money flowing back to Mama. Next he was sent to a lodge on Sea Island, Georgia. His visa was extended for another year.

Mama had been right—seek a land where he could be safe, a future where he could breathe without looking over his shoulder. That Lupita was on the Gulf Coast made the offer to transfer to Bay Resort an even greater gift. The calls he made home, telling of his good fortune, and the dollars he sent, made his mother burst into tears.

"I waited to see if my papers were renewed again. I heard nothing. I feared my time was up," he said. "It was time for me to go home. 'I will go,' I said to Lupita. 'I will return to Mama.' 'You cannot return,' she said. 'You will be killed,' she said. I had become strong, I told her.

"When Abuelo died, I was determined to go home, I was ready, whatever happened. It was in the summer. The fireflies in the Alabama sky flashed like the stars when Abuelo and I stood outside in San Pedro and looked up at heaven, and I knew he was signaling to me, 'You must stay. You are with me already.' Like Our Lady of Suyapa who'd spoken to Mama, my Abuelo among the stars spoke to me: 'If you return you will never get back to the US.'

"I kept working. Nobody asked.

"There are other workers at hotels, restaurants, flower nurseries who have no papers. They've said to me how they have come here, stories of those who were caught at the border, one, a brother, who died in the Arizona desert after crossing there, in the heat of Hell, no water, his body not identified for many weeks. They told me of a cousin who was wanted by the gang—the Scorpions, *Los Escorpiones*—who tried to run away, climbing onto the iron monster, the train, and how he was dragged down and cut to pieces. I feared for Paco, like my brother, who had not gotten away, his mother, Paz, was killed, but had enough money from all his family to pay a smuggler who got him here a year ago, the *propinas,* the bribes, leaving him in debt to the smuggler now who gets money from him still.

"When I walked onto the golf course to help the man who had been cut like a dead man already I knew that God had forsaken me. I knew that wherever I go I had no protection. All the evilness of the world, hunting me. Born with a curse. That is what Abuelo said of some people. Wherever they go the storm finds them, and blows."

22
CASA VERDE

FROM PIEDRAS NEGRAS SOUTH TO San Miguel de Allende was a hypnotizing drive, a similar distance, in hours, from home to Charleston. Vanessa had made this trek once before, in college, when she and Cecile had traveled with two boys in a van a farther distance, overnight from Laredo to Mexico City, spelling each other at the wheel. She remembered wandering Colonia Roma with its art deco buildings and hipster cafés, picnicking in Chapultepec Park, and peering into the blank eyes of giant Olmec heads at the museum, but the city of 20 million inhabitants, sprawling far beyond, was exhausting with traffic and noise. When they'd looped back, returning north to San Miguel de Allende, she'd felt herself relax again, as she would now—Mom's wheels beating against the Mexican thruway—if she could stay awake. After one night at a roadside motel, she yearned for a true refreshment, vodka on the rocks with a twist of lime. She still had six hours to go, and Cecile, who said she had spotty reception in the hills over San Miguel, had not answered her email. No matter, she'd find her when she arrived. She'd saved a few gummy bears from the piñata and popped those to distract herself.

She took an exit and pulled into the parking lot of a *lavandería* to see if she could pick up a Wi-Fi signal outside the bustling laundromat. Nothing. She followed the local highway south, paralleling the thoroughfare. She passed through a small pueblo where a spray of balloons on a gate and a sign, ¡FELIZ CUMPLEAÑOS, CARMEN! caught her attention.

Near the main square, she found a strong signal, stopped, and went online.

She pulled up the website Big Bright Balloons. Yellow ones were Roger's favorite, and she chose one with a smiley face, ordered him a dozen, shiny Mylar that would stay inflated, and scheduled them to arrive at Hank's house the weekend before his birthday. They could celebrate all week long.

She scrolled through hometown news, little of interest but Alabama football and a rogue's gallery of alleged felons, just as Julio's thumbnail photo had looked back at fearful residents the day of his arrest. Sports, crime, and weather—it filled the anemic digital pages of what had once been an abundant regional daily.

She clicked on her messages: updates from the Vassar alumni association, group messages from friends. And then one that made her brace herself.

Mack15. She felt a shiver. **Hey, V, you've skipped town. I had Roger yesterday. He's really anxious, I could hardly keep him still. He kept repeating Mommy. I didn't give you any grief about our arrangement, you know that. I always felt you could care for him better than me. But now? I figured the clinic would do the trick, and your father to keep you on the straight and narrow. But what I'm seeing, and what I'm hearing, is exactly the opposite. Would Roger do better in my care? I'm set up for it now. Maybe he's too much for you in light of what you're going through. Do we need to go back to court on this? Mack. P.S. I'm teaching him to swing a** bat, not a plastic one this time. He'll damn sure hit the piñata this birthday. I've got one hanging in my den.

She typed: **Mack, DO NOT THREATEN ME. You're such a bully. I can feel it clear across the country into Mexico**—she deleted "into Mexico," why should she give up her whereabouts?—**and once again you want to shame our son. He's doing all he can, all he is capable of. I have not abandoned him. I just needed some time to straighten some things out, but I'm coming home soon. Why would you even mention court? To try and intimidate me? Really? Do what you want, just don't put Roger in the middle. We can't tolerate each other, that's true, but we have to be civil for our boy.**

She sent it zooming Mack's way then returned to the balloon order and changed the delivery date to the next morning. In a bright burst of color she would let Roger know, over and again, how much she loved him.

Back in the car she decided to drive as long as possible into the night. Mack's words jolted her like caffeine: *Go back to court.* "You sonuvabitch," she said. She reached a fork in the road and veered left, continuing south.

She inhaled deeply. *Calm,* she thought. *Concentrate on your breath*ing. Slowly she exhaled.

She headed another hour, then two, into darkness, people appearing on the side of the road in her headlights then vanishing, motorcyclists approaching then gone, a mule moseying up from the embankment as she swerved to avoid it. Earlier she'd seen signs for the distance to San Miguel but hadn't come upon the turnoff for it.

When a hillside pueblo appeared with a main street, a few stores, hotel and cantina, she pulled over and went in to book a room. Casa Verde's lobby was painted a pale green to go with its name—Green House—with pictures of brightly plumed birds behind the check-in desk. In Spanish and English were the schedule of bird-watching tours, March to October, and a large photograph of a group of tourists with binoculars around their necks with the words, *Southwest Ornithological Society.*

"*Buenas,*" said the clerk, a lean woman with her hair pulled back in a chignon.

"*Muchos pájaros,*" Vanessa said.

"Not so many now."

"How much for a room?"

"One thousand pesos. Fifty US."

Upstairs, in her olive-green room, the pillow was foam rubber with a threadbare cover and when she pulled back the covers she saw the sheets had washed-out splotches of blood, like redbirds on a misty field. She picked up the phone to call the desk but it was dead, went back downstairs, and a new clerk, a large man flipping through a magazine, looked up at her indifferently. He reached behind him and produced another key. Room 302. A voile curtain, blue as jays, hung before an open window. Music from a cantina across the street poured in. But the sheets were clean. After shutting the window and trying to sleep, she leapt up.

She entered the cantina as a lone performer sang a Spanish ballad at an electric piano and drum machine while two couples clutched each other turning slowly beneath the light of a *Dos Equis* sign.

To be a stranger suited her perfectly. No well-known father, no crabby ex-husband, no law firm, no pressure, expectation, guilt about wrongdoing, sense of failure. Valedictorian or dropout, law associate or parolee, it mattered here not a whit.

With as complete a freedom as if she had landed from another planet—she smiled at the realization that she had—she went to the bar, oblivious to the surmising looks of the men, and asked for a tequila and vodka cocktail. Mack had introduced her to the drink, a Mexitini, at a Cinco de Mayo wharf party on Mobile Bay and she'd taken to it with relish.

She had no intention of drinking it—she ordered a glass of *agua* to sip on—but she wanted its presence, a double-dog dare to herself to abstain.

What was the name of this pueblo anyway? It didn't really matter. It was away.

She imagined Roger getting the balloons, bounding with delight as the yellow orbs danced above him, repeating, "Mommy!" She slipped his photo out of her wallet.

"He's a cutie," said a woman taking a chair next to her.

"Do I know you?"

"As of five minutes ago. Janice. From Casa Verde. Front desk. My shift's done."

"Your English is really good."

"My dad's American. I was born in Dallas."

"So you're a US citizen?"

"Mexico, too. I prefer it here, though. So, what are you running from?"

"Excuse me? I'm heading to San Miguel, I mentioned that when I was checking in."

"The birders come here during the season. Off-season? Anybody else hiding out."

"I stopped here by chance."

"What his name?"

"Roger. He's with his grandfather."

"See," Janice said, "everybody here's got a story."

"And you?"

"My husband and I needed a fresh start. We wound up here and he used everything we had to buy Casa Verde. He was into curve-billed thrashers and vermilion flycatchers."

"Sounds colorful."

"And *putas*. He got one pregnant. What an idiot. Her brother said he'd kill him if he didn't pay up. So he sold the hotel. For less than he'd paid for it. But he got cash. Laid out enough to save his neck. Then took off back north."

"But you stayed."

"This is one goddamn place I know he won't be coming back." She thumped the side of Vanessa's untouched drink. "What does this mean? You must be trying to quit."

The brazen nosiness of this stranger intrigued her.

"Or," Janice added, "pregnant."

"Hah! Hardly!"

She felt a strange openness that had been hard to achieve at the Beacon after a month. She felt unexpectedly at ease.

The musician started an Eagles hit, mixing Spanish with the English, and Vanessa surprised herself by singing along, *Welcome to the Hotel California/such a lovely place, such a lovely face,* with Janice taking to the tiny dance floor by herself and swaying: *You can check out any time you like, But you can never leave.*

"Hey," Janice said coming back to the bar. "I know what you should try." She spoke to the bartender in Spanish. The glass clinked down in front of her. "Lime juice. Club soda. Vodka. Vampire Slayer. Too much like a sno-cone to be bad for you." She pushed it toward Vanessa and signaled one for herself too.

"Why not, I'm in Hell."

"You are one unhappy lady."

"My ex," Vanessa, said, as she sipped the Vampire Slayer before guzzling it down. "The way I left Roger, bolted from rehab, screwed up work. All my fuckups."

"Smart women, shitty choices. Isn't that a book title? A lot pass this way."

Vanessa picked up the Mexitini, finished it off.

"Want something stronger?"

"This is my last one. Ever."

"Not to drink." Janice nodded toward the door.

Dismayed at the thought of returning to her shabby room she followed Janice outside. The night sky swirled like tumbling birds. The main street opened up to shuttered market stalls on one side, shops on the other. Toward the end of the street Janice opened a door and waved her in.

The shelves of the bodega were filled with boxes of cereal and crackers and corn meal and potatoes, carrots, onions, bananas of every size and shade of green and yellow. Two coffeepots stood on the counter—"I'll be firing these up a daybreak," Janice said—and a glass case of *pan dulce,* the sugary breads staler by the hour. "It's my morning job," she said. She opened a door leading to a storeroom— motioned for Vanessa to stay back—and returned a moment later with a tiny sleeve of white powder. "This is the good stuff."

She hadn't snorted cocaine since visiting Mack from Vassar, doing a line with the pretty ladies and lads of the Mardi Gras court getting ready for Fat Tuesday. It had kept her up two whole nights, and when she did a bump she felt her body race, awake enough now to drive on to San Miguel, hell, all the way to Guatemala if she wanted.

The store around her took on a precision of detail, the potatoes and carrots and boxes of cereal rendered by an artist with a touch so exquisite as to heighten reality. Janice's face, with her hair pulled back and sad brown eyes looked like her mother's. She wanted to reach out and hold her.

A stick of a man holding a satchel appeared at the door, entered in silence and disappeared into the storeroom, reemerging with the satchel under his arm. His eyes bore into Vanessa, who offered a chipper *hola*, but he turned his gaze to Janice who assured him, *"Una amiga. Está bien."*

"That's Flaco," Janice said. "It means skinny."

When Flaco exited she heard a loud engine roaring off—she hadn't noticed its arrival—and said to Janice, "I think I'm going to drive on."

"If you change your mind find me here in the morning. Good luck, sister."

She embraced her new friend and started back to the hotel. Arriving at Casa Verde to check out only two hours after she'd arrived she saw Mama's blue SUV with the passenger door half open. The glove compartment had been rifled through and the hood looked ajar. She got in to make sure it started but turning the ignition gave a dead click. "God dammit!"

With its battery gone and the night clerk answering no bell she trudged up to her room and looked out the window, watching another car making its way to Janice's store.

She lay down, taking deep breaths, the blue wing of the curtain eventually carrying her off, the roosters starting up not long after.

23
ROGER

LUPITA OPENED THE FRONT DOOR to receive the delivery, exclaiming, "*¡Que bonita!*" and Roger stepped back, wary of the shiny yellow orbs with upturned lines for smiles and googly eyes like fish. "Look, Roger, for you!" she said, handing him the string but he stepped back, shaking his head like the balloons turning side to side, answering, "no," then reaching out nervously, clutching the string, growing calmer. He let go.

They floated toward the ceiling. He grabbed the string; they stopped. Let go. Up. The string wiggled like a cat's tail. The sparkly ovals bumped into the ceiling.

"Happy birthday, sweet boy," Lupita read the card, "I love you, Mommy."

"Mommy needs to come home," said Gradee, joining them in the room.

"Mommy working," said Roger.

They bobbed near the air-conditioning vent, one turning like Gradee gazing down at him when it was time to get out of bed, another like Daddy, frowning and fussing, another like Mommy, a big sunlight smile.

He'd seen the sun yellow like that, a bright balloon in the trees where the moon sometimes sat, and he wanted to take one of these, a special friend, outside to meet it.

He yanked at a strand and Gradee said, "Here you go," and plucked it free.

Arms around it, big and plump, he hugged his shiny new friend, squishy like Mommy but not soft like she was, close like Gradee but not stubbly, all his own like Lupita saying, "*Cuidado,* careful, not too tight." He grasped his paunchy friend tighter and squeezed.

The googly eye was right next to his and he put his finger over it like he did with the fish, and this time poked. The googly eye widened, stretched, got bigger and fatter. He dug in his fingernail until it exhaled in his ear—*whoosh!*—then it was limp in his arms like a yellow raincoat Mommy made him wear when it grumbled and spattered outside.

He pulled at it, trying to yank it apart, pushed it together to make it live again, let it slip to the floor and stomped it.

"Don't be mad," Lupita said.

He picked up the yellow peel and started toward the door to chase the sun in the trees but Gradee grabbed him up and laughing, said, "I've got you this time," and squeezed him like the balloon but he didn't go pop. Then Gradee was singing a happy sad song Roger had heard when he was with him at the synagogue and the stained glass windows with the long-bearded men looked down, and he was in his grandfather's arms and put his face into his scratchy neck and the notes rising in Gradee were rising in him too and he felt they were floating happy and sad with the balloons.

24
BLESSED MOTHER

IN HER POCKET LUPITA KEPT the prayer card with Our Lady of Suyapa, *La Morenita*, the brown-skinned Queen of Heaven who had delivered Jesus Christ out of her pure body. She'd first seen her at the church an hour south of the hurricane refugee camp, Mama leading her by the hand into the sanctuary, marking the cross on her forehead with holy water, genuflecting, and approaching the Virgin's gaze. "She will answer your prayers," Mama said.

"Blessed Mother," Lupita beseeched, touching the card as she walked near the bay with Roger, "look over my brother in his time of need, give him courage, give him strength. Let him know your spirit, even as he turns away from his Father in Heaven, fill him with your love so that he may remember the power and glory of your son, Jesus Christ."

She had worshipped in the Catholic Church near this bay vista, sat among the pious and kneeled, folding her hands together, repeating the Lord's Prayer, then rose to stand in line for communion. "Body of Christ," she heard the priest say as the wafer touched her tongue and the chalice came to her lips. When she closed her eyes she saw the Virgin of Suyapa, not the Madonna depicted before her on the altar. Her brown skin, flowing, colorful dress, her dark eyes seeing, knowing, encouraging her as Mama did.

This was the vision before her she saw now.

"Save my Julio," she implored. "Restore his hope, his faith."

On her last two visits she knew he was already changing, dropping far from the Julio she knew with his easy laugh and ready grin. When he'd come to after being rescued from the bay, he had a luminous quality, even in the hospital, like an angel had inhabited him and was shining through, but the spirit had vacated him. He'd whispered to her about the threat against him by another inmate. "I will tell!" she said.

"If you do," he said, "I will be killed."

"Can I tell Paco?"

"Leave him be."

"We are sending money to Mama every week. Paco is contributing too. To make up the difference."

"What have you told her?"

"Nothing. But she knows something is different. She prays for you every morning and night."

"Do you know who hears?"

"Oh, my brother."

"No one. The man on the roof is not there. Talk to the sky. It is all the same."

He needed space, light. As a boy he'd been antsy, eager to be up, out, moving around. In the hurricane camp he'd been hard pressed to sit more than fifteen minutes for his lessons in the makeshift school where the teachers tried to impart lessons as babies wailed and neighbors washed themselves at the cistern and men fought over scraps like bantam cocks.

When he could run outside, he brightened, though, recharged by a rush of sun.

"What can I do here," he asked her mournfully, "but wait?"

"Faith will give you strength," she told him, but he shook his head.

"Getting strong," he said, flexing his arms, "will give me strength."

"We are not alone, Julio."

"In here I am."

"Blessed Mother," she continued, seeing a cloud formation assembling like a pedestal with the shape of a woman in flowing cloak awash in red and gold rising above it, "open his heart. Let him not feel betrayed by the King of Heaven our mother raised us to know, nor have a heart turned to lead by disbelief.

"I pray for Roger too, to be a happy and normal little boy, and Vanessa to find her way out of the alcohol and the darkness and home to her treasured son, and for Mr. Hank to lead us through this wilderness."

That evening, before leaving for the day, she handed Hank the prayer card and asked him to make a copy for her. "For Julio," she said—and he made two. The first was a replica of the card's size. The second was a blowup, as large as a calendar photo. He made another of the larger one and handed her both.

"We need all the help we can get," he said.

Visiting Julio the next day she sat across from him through the window and spoke again through the microphone of her love of the Lord and how the Blessed Mother looked out for him. She was allowed to give him the picture. "Look into her eyes, Julio. She will look back at you."

25
CODE OF ALABAMA

HE HAD TRIED TO SELL the law books upon his retirement but now it seemed like *buena suerte,* he said to Lupita after their Spanish lesson, "good luck." The multiple volumes of the Code of Alabama had filled his office shelves for decades and were a steal, he realized, for what he was asking. After three months with no inquiries, he decided to offer them for free to a lucky young lawyer. Still, no takers. "Mr. Weinberg," a friend of Vanessa's told him, "everything's online now."

Margery had insisted there was no room at the house and encouraged him to talk to a decorator who inquired about them for a couple wanting "handsome book bindings to line their library shelves." "Tell them to learn how to read and get some damn books of their own," he'd responded. He'd filled six boxes with his precious friends—how often they'd helped him see the way through a defendant's predicament—and set them behind the forgotten stationary bike and water skis in the far recesses of the garage.

He needed them now. Blue pixels on a gray screen were insubstantial, evanescent. Around him was the weight of the law.

As he dug them out he recalled their smell. He took out one volume, ran his hand over the maroon binding, cracked it open, pressed his nose into the crevice, breathed in the paper and stitching. His office high up in the Alabama Trust Building opened around him, at its entrance Miss Matilda, his lifelong secretary, with her soft sole therapeutic shoes and blue sack dress and forbidding voice to those who might attack him.

He had pieces of paper stuck in the pages, marking old cases, charges, strategies, defendants, in his cryptic shorthand. *CapM—Man*—capital murder-manslaughter—*Greg Hills*. Hills had been a small-time boxer who killed a stevedore named Jerry in a bar fight by the docks. The men began a disagreement while drinking, started to "take it outside," as the bartender testified, when Jerry jumped Greg. "You sonuvabitch," Greg yelled, "I'll kill you," and punched Jerry twice in the face. Jerry fell to the floor, fatally cracking his skull. That Greg in the past had delivered fatal blows to two other men did not help the defense. Hank got him off the capital charge, though, with a reduced sentence for manslaughter, at least two jurors looking like they'd been in bar fights themselves.

Earl and Martha Stokes, ABF. Accomplice before the fact.

The Stokeses, who were black, had been charged with aiding the murder of a white man, Jack, whose neighbor, Mo, also white, said Jack had been sleeping with his girlfriend and blasted him with a shotgun loaned to him by the Stokeses. Martha had taken the shotgun to Mo's, as Mo's own shotgun was being repaired for a faulty firing pin. The prosecution argued that the Stokeses had a vow to take down Jack for their own reasons—they claimed he'd stolen their land. "A vendetta of three against one," the DA said. "They all knew what the shotgun was for. They were in it together." Hank's defense was that Martha kindly took the shotgun to Mo for hunting, innocent of further motives. "The Stokeses were just helping out a neighbor." Mo had been convicted, but the Stokeses got off thanks to a lone juror who was an avid squirrel hunter. A white defendant guilty, two defendants of color not guilty—the verdict caused quite a stir.

Making that connection between defendant and jury was critical.

He'd had many defendants whom the jury wanted to send away forever on even circumstantial evidence, especially if the accused was black, the Stokeses being an exception. No witnesses, no incontrovertible evidence, no telltale blood. He was able to plant a seed of doubt if the man standing before them had something they recognized in themselves. After the sin of segregation had given way to faces of color in the jury box, too, he felt he might find more connections still. But he realized again that what was familiar, what resonated between defendant and juror could be something deeper.

A man who fixed cars, an RN, a high school Spanish teacher, a churchgoer, a baseball fan, someone who'd lived abroad or grew up military, whatever characteristic they had, that would give a juror an avenue into the heart and soul of the poor sucker before them in prison blues, was a way in.

Young Julio? What would make him relatable? An undocumented Mexican in California was charged with shooting to death a teen, an incident, said his defense, that was a freak accident. A Syrian who'd come in before the 2016 travel ban on Muslim countries and overstayed his visa was indicted on arson charges in Minnesota, the defense claiming mistaken identity. It was enough for reasonable doubt. Garnering more than local coverage, these stories had become national news. Julio's was becoming that, too. Whether a defendant was undocumented, a green card holder or full-fledged citizen, should make no difference in guilt or innocence in a criminal trial. Immigration status as evidence was "generally inadmissible," a recent ruling stated, unless counsel could establish a compelling reason to raise the issue. Should Hank try to do so? The suspicion, the wariness, by those who sat in judgment had seeped into the culture, Hank believed. Wouldn't it be better for jurors to know Julio's whole story?

He took out his notepad and penciled: *exact time "witness" claimed he saw. Coroner time of death. Blood samples. DNA. Murder weapon. Number Hispanics in community where from, when. Deportation. Elections DA.* In big block letters he added *MOTIVE*, and circled it twice.

In the corner of the pad he printed "F E A R."

He jotted: "Julio fear of being deported? Community fear of outsiders?" He added "Amsterdam," but scratched over it. This was Julio's story, not his.

While Roger was still with Lupita, Hank took a breather out to the pier, settling onto Margery's bench, envisioning scenarios of that late afternoon on the golf course. Julio's version—a scared youth who'd sought refuge from violence in his home country, trying to help the victim of another act of violence but too late to save him, grabbing money in a reflex, then panicking and running. The DA's—a lawless foreigner preying on an unwitting victim, robbing and stabbing him to death, who then fled to elude capture.

A hand clapped his shoulder. "God's beauty out here," Pastor Blue said.

"Do you ever wonder what he sees?" Hank asked as Blue sat alongside.

"He sees all," said Blue.

"Like our friend," Hank said, motioning to the pelican who'd taken up his position on the railing and turned a sideways eye on them.

"But unlike our friend all knowing, too. We need a name for him, her, by the way."

"When I was a boy there was a woman who sang by the Prinsengracht canal. I looked down from my room every morning and she was there. She had a big cape and the wind lifted it like wings. Papa told me her name was Josie."

"For Josephine?" Blue said. "From Joseph."

"Jacob's son Joseph, with his coat of many colors."

"Jesus's earthly father, Joseph."

"Different Joseph."

The pelican stepped closer.

"Josie," said Hank. "Yes, that's your name."

"God is infinite," said Blue. "We are limited."

"Wouldn't you like to be all seeing? Know what happened exactly in that mountain jungle in Africa?"

"Beau Shepherd knew because he was there."

"And God knew as well," Hank said.

"So many congregants came to me over the years. The loss of a spouse, the death of a child, a catastrophic illness or fatal accident taking all away. 'How could God let this happen?' 'God has a plan,' I said. 'Cry, rage, grieve, mourn, that is human, that is an expression of the love we felt, and the depth of loss. But trust in God.' Then it happened to me. If God did see, if he does intervene, how could he let that happen to Zach?" Blue hung his head and pressed his palms against his eyes, as if to blot away the images.

Hank put his arm around his friend's shoulder.

"God can't stop a bad man from doing wrong," Blue said, lifting his head and sitting up straight again. "That's why we have justice."

"Every accused has a chance to be heard, though."

"It was Beau Shepherd who was punished for doing wrong. But I don't think it was your man who carried out the sentence."

"Then who?"

"Damnation, y'all!" came from nearby where Cooter's son, hooking a catfish big as a mailbox, tugged it up onto the pier and stood over it lying there, whiskery and mean. "Left my tackle box with daddy," said the boy, careful to avoid the fin as he tried to pull out the hook with his fingers but the fish had swallowed it.

Blue was at his side, having no luck with pliers, producing a serrated knife from his blue jeans pocket, digging the hook from the writhing bottom-feeder.

"Only God knows," Blue said over to Hank, wiping the blade on his denim and slipping it away.

26
CALL-AND-RESPONSE

THE ROOSTERS BEGAN BEFORE FIRST light seeped through the curtain, her fifth morning at Casa Verde while her car brought new problems daily—a bad replacement battery, a flat tire and bad spare, a mechanic who didn't show—until she knew the raucous serenades, at first from the farmhouse over the far hill, next from a nearby pen, another from a barn behind the hotel, yet another right below her window, all crowing, *fuera de aqui*, get out of here.

Each morning, with San Miguel still in her sights, she had started by going to Janice's store. If she'd not been so hungover every day, she might have found it all pretty in a way, scenic and removed—the small road leading by the *taqueria* and hardware store, the braying of donkeys in counterpoint to the roosters, the starting up of motorbikes and banging of skillets, baby cries, Spanish streaming around her. But it was yet another prison she was making for herself, she began to realize.

As Janice fired up the big pots for coffee that she mixed with boiled milk for customers, set out *pan dulce* for the men who crowded in wearing huaraches or work boots, the young mothers who came in with babies in back slings to pick up packaged goods, Vanessa positioned herself on a counter stool and confessed. That Janice was only half listening, and no one else understood English, made it easier:

She told of growing up in Alabama, the long shadow of the Holocaust, her Dutch grandparents lost in hell, her embracing but crushing father, her tender and understanding mother gone too soon, her sports hero husband with his controlling temper and hateful disappointment over their struggling son, her beautiful boy needing her most and here she was locked away inside of herself in a strange place getting nowhere.

"And I've had every opportunity," she said. "My father gets furious with me. All this privilege, and so much anxiety, so much distress."

"You feel *enjaulado*," Janice said. "'Caged.' Why is that?"

"I don't know!"

"You have money?" Janice said.

"I work as a lawyer."

"You're rich!"

"I don't get the big fees."

"*Yo soy enjaulado*, I am caged," emphasized Janice. "Because I have no money. Why do you think I work three jobs?"

"Casa Verde, this bodega, that's two," Vanessa said.

"And . . ." Janice nodded toward the back room.

"Ah, that . . ."

She caught a faint shake of Janice's head. The man from the first night with the briefcase —Flaco, she recalled his name—had walked in. He took a stool next to Vanessa. "Americana?" he asked.

"Yes."

"Long way from home," Flaco said in a studied English.

"Tourist."

"You come back in spring. Many birds."

"*Muchos pajaros,*" she said.

"Very good! You teacher?"

"Lawyer. Abogado."

He nodded without saying anything but somehow his attitude had shifted. He seemed wary, glancing over his shoulder.

She wanted to continue with Janice, telling how she felt the familiar lowering of those bars now, needing to flee, like from the Austin hotel room with Douglas. The sensation never went away. "*Enjaulado.*" The Spanish got down in her bones.

"Your friend," Flaco said. "Here, I take photo." He waved her toward Janice.

She watched Janice grow tense and address him in Spanish.

An uneasiness settled over her like a harsh cloak and she stood to leave but saw him quickly capture her image with his phone camera then start out.

"*Esta nadie,*" Janice called to him but others began to leave, too.

Nadie. She was nobody.

An engine roared close and a Humvee came to a stop outside the door. Flaco disappeared behind its tinted windows.

"Why do you stay here?" Vanessa asked. "You can find a job in the US."

"You need to leave."

"My car."

"They think you're more than a tourist. Do whatever you need to do, but head home."

When she arrived back at the hotel, ready to make good on Janice's directive, to pay whatever it took to get the repairs, her mother's sky-blue SUV was nowhere to be seen.

27
ROGER'S MOON

HE KNEW GRADEE WAS MAD, huffing and puffing, shouting, "I can't believe my daughter! In Mexico! Car stolen!" They were words Roger did not understand, except *car*, and he said, "Mommy, pa-cakes," but Mommy was not there to take him to get pancakes. His balloons seemed angry, too, faces long and sagging, wanting to blow him a kiss but agitated like Gradee, and they started moving around like they wanted to be outdoors and fly around, cooped up in this house long enough with the shiny breeze out in the yard and up in the trees.

One of them, unloosed from the others, turned its eyes toward the door and when the daylight was gone and Lupita was fixing supper Roger opened the door and pushed at the screen and it flew out. He stepped outside to catch it.

The moon, not the sun, was in the branches and the balloon kept going, bumped along by the wind, and he raced to keep up.

He heard his name behind him, Lupita's shout, Gradee's shout, like nets the fishermen threw, opening in circles to catch him like he wanted to catch the balloon, but he went faster.

"Roger! Where are you?"

It felt like a game.

"Gradee," he said, his breath faster. "Lupe." But only the moon could hear.

He arrived at a clearing where the moonlight bathed the ground like milk he'd knocked over on a table and a hungry smell grabbed him: fish on a skillet. There was a square of light in a blank box on the edge of the clearing. A house. A window. He moved there, saw a man in the kitchen, went close, stood on his tippy toes, looking right into the eye of the fish sizzling on the stove, vibrating like it wanted to jump off the pan and fly away, too. Then it leapt! Right off the burning surface into the air over the pan and it was Gradee's mullet flopping up at him and he screamed and was off, a screen door banging behind him and the man yelling, "Who's there? I'll fix your ass!"

And the milky path drew him, showed him the way as he heard the hollering and felt lifted up like he'd gone flying off the pier, and he went tumbling down a gully, the taste of clay like he'd grabbed a fistful and jammed it in his mouth.

"Gradee!" he yelled and his grandaddy stumbled and fell into the pit of clay, shouting, "Roger! Roger! Are you hurt?" and Lupita next, calling them both, the balloon like a ragged face melting away as he tried to reach up for it and the eyes blinked at him and he blinked back and the night wrapped him around.

28
LA PROTECTORA

IN THE SMALL WORKOUT ROOM with a guard in the corner, Julio curled the barbell, up, down, watching the muscles of his forearms grow taut, the veins moving like snakes in the grass, his biceps bulging, arms growing hot.

On his cell wall the eyes of Our Lady of Suyapa looked back at him, saying, "I am of no use to you, not here," and he pledged to do what God, or his minions, could not. Not the wise Jew, not his sister, and surely not his mother nor her divine overseers provided any help for him here, though they tried, and wept, and prayed. Only he could protect himself.

Ricardo, who'd attacked him on the basketball court, had done a plea deal and was moved on to the state prison. But another man with gang connections, known as El Silencioso, had arrived. It had been his image passing by the window of the room where he'd sat with Mr. Hank. His presence loomed—*"el silencioso,"* the silent one—hovering near the edge of the outdoor pen where they scorched the soccer ball with their inside kicks and back heels and headbutts, as fierce as rivals in the World Cup. Lupita's words burned in his ears—the Scorpions had come to Mama's door saying, more money. *"No tengo,"* she had said. "I don't have."

El Silencioso, wherever he went—the commissary, the infirmary, the TV room—looked on. Even in the morning, when the alarm went off at 5:30 a.m. and they stood to be counted, the guard going down the rows shouting like a kid doing arithmetic, El Silencioso watched him from across the common area.

In the weight room the lean, quiet Honduran entered and took his place next to Julio, picked up two dumb bells and began to work them. El Silencioso started pumping harder, faster, and Julio did, too. His arms ached, he started to tremble, but he kept on.

He heard a voice, like whispering in his ear, saying, *"Necesitamos que hagas algo."* We need you do to something.

Had El Silencioso even moved his lips?

"There's a Salvadoran who's just arrived here. Elias. Short, bald, a dog. You know what happens to dogs."

Putting down the barbell, Julio moved to the bench press. An inmate with washboard pecs walked over, offered to spot him. Julio lay down, grabbed the bell, nodded, and the spotter hovered over him as Julio pushed upward, let the weights come down, one repetition, a second. He felt the oxygen rush into his lungs, the blood pump through his chest and course through his limbs.

At the top of the fourth rep he felt the barbell waver. He lowered it, gathered his strength, and pushed again.

"You spot our friend, the Salvadoran, when he comes in," El Silencioso said.

The voice made him lose his concentration and the barbell tilted backward, as though it were going to pull his arms down, the weight seeming to double, sweating harder, profusely now, to keep it from sinking down onto his chest.

The spotter reached down and grabbed the bar to steady him. "You're fucking workin' it, man, no problem," the spotter said. "I was like you when I started."

"Something," the voice said, "could happen."

"Why?"

"Don't you want to be our friend?"

"I'm getting out of here soon."

"You're going to Atmore," El Silencioso said. "To *La mamá amarilla*. Yellow mama," he added in English. It was the grim nickname for the electric chair.

The guard looked up. "If you're talking about the Yellow Mama, they don't use that no more." He made a gesture like putting a needle into his arm. "Lethal injection."

"I have a lawyer," Julio said to El Silencioso.

"They sell you out. Do a deal and you'll be an old man with your balls to the floor by the time you get home."

He had five minutes before he was to report back to his cell. He stood and toweled off. A stocky man accompanied by a guard and another inmate came in the door. The guard changed shifts and the new inmate said hello in Spanish to El Silencioso, who told him Julio was also Honduran, then goaded, "We're stronger."

"From El Salvador," the man said. "You spot me?"

Julio complied.

He added more weights than Julio had pressed, steadied himself and pushed upward. The barbell rose, wavered, and came down slowly. He started his second rep.

Julio saw right away that the weight was too much, the man's arms shaking, and it could come crashing down. He reached out to assist and as he gripped the bar alongside the weight lifter's hands he glimpsed El Silencioso giving the faintest nod. The barbell was directly over the Salvadoran's throat. He would secure protection from El Silencioso forever if he did his bidding.

He conjured it in a flash—the hurtling down of the weights, the barbell crushing the weight lifter's windpipe, the gargling cry— but instead held tighter and guided them back to their stand, the Salvadoran leaping up and clapping Julio on the back and calling him trusted friend. The silent one had left.

29
RECOGNITION

CAR STOLEN, CASH DWINDLING, CREDIT cards locked for fraud concerns, in desperation Vanessa called Cecile, who had still not responded. No answer, voice mail full. She phoned the San Miguel winery and was told Cecile had left with her husband on a trip to Mendoza, in Argentina's Malbec region.

How could she be so organized in her lawyerly round—calendar precise, documents filed, appointments verified—and run her personal life, the image pained her, like a drunk behind the wheel?

She had no choice but to call her father again, but he didn't respond. She texted Lupita, leaving messages with her location at the hotel, then rang Douglas, who began, "I'm so sorry about what happened to your dad."

His words were a vortex pulling her in.

He added, "Thank God your little boy's OK."

"*What?*"

"You didn't know? You really have fallen off the map."

He told her the story: Roger chasing a balloon into the night, Hank and Lupita running and shouting, a man startled by a face at his kitchen window, Roger tumbling headlong into a clay gully then Hank just behind, crashing downward, injuring his hip.

"Your dad's now out of the infirmary. Roger's fine, a few scratches. I talked to Mack, he's been really attentive."

"I've got to get there."

"Where the hell are you?"

"Mexico." The town, her route there, Casa Verde—she caught him up to date, saying nothing of the car.

"You've got wheels. Drive home."

"They're gone."

"For such a highly intelligent woman you are the dumbest fucking person I know."

"You're right."

"No, I can't help this time."

"I'm not asking you to. Please, Douglas, please just tell my father I called, that I'm on my way. Somehow."

Janice was not at the hotel today so she set out to find her, making her way to the store. Swallows turned loops against the darkening afternoon sky and music from the cantina started up. Through open windows in the mild dusk the sounds rose of voices and laughter, pots and pans, chairs pushed up to tables for the gathering of families.

She ached for her own family around her, at the long-ago Passover Seder at Bubbe's and Zayde's in Selma with the matzo ball soup flavorful and prayers resonant, at the bay after a swim enjoying speckled trout that Daddy had cooked on the grill, at the home she and Mack had made with Roger as they shared pizza and ice cream on a hot summer's evening with other young families joining them. So much happiness, her father had told her, just within her reach. Why could she not seize it?

Janice would understand, she knew, another outcast of her own making, the nation of the alienated, far-flung, yearning but apart. They were everywhere and found each other like friends in high school or college who formed their own clubs of the marginal, evaluating themselves as atop the heap. She'd disdained the women in rehab, but maybe the clients at the Beacon were her true clan. Janice would fit right in.

Her Casa Verde friend would help her.

She recognized the Humvee outside the store. The light was on but the door was closed. Voices were audible. "Janice," she said, knocking. "You in there?"

The voices fell silent.

"I need your help!"

A black sedan pulled up, two men got out, one with a suitcase, and without knocking went in, pushing the door behind them.

She thought better of knocking again, but the image of her father and Roger going pell-mell into a gully, the fright for Roger and the pain for her father pushed her forward. She rapped hard. "I need someone to give me a ride, my family's been hurt, to the bus or train, I can get money."

The word *money* was like a key and the door swung open and a hand reached out and grabbed her. Pulled into the room, the door locked again behind her, and she was between stacks of cash and bags of white powder.

"I'm sorry, I'll go," she said but the hand held her arm tightly. It was Flaco.

Janice regarded her coldly. "Don't you know a closed door when you see one? You fucked up again."

"You want money?" Flaco said. He nodded to the stack of bills. "*Pinche puta.*"

"Fucking whore is what he called you," Janice said.

"Tell them I'll never come in here again."

"You have money?" he said. "Give."

"I can get it. *Puedo.*"

"*Puedo*," he mocked. "*¿Cuándo?* When?"

"I'll make a call."

When she took out her phone he ripped it from her and hurled it against the wall and put a pistol against her head. "*¿Agente narcóticos?*"

"*Nadie.* I am nobody. *Nadie.*" The muzzle pressed into her temple, boring past her skin into her skull, her body whirring, otherworldly, sweat raining down her neck and shoulders.

The others huddled around the transactions with Janice, whose only comment was "*la mujer rica estúpida*" as Flaco forced her toward the back room. Stupid rich woman.

She was possessed by another spirit, Oma, corralled onto the train with Opa to Westerbork, then the transit to the concentration camp in Poland, a story Hank had recounted so many times that she stopped listening but now heard it in his voice and saw them too, Vida and Reuven, her grandmother hauled first into the windowless room with death waiting.

Suddenly Flaco kicked free a back door and pushed her out and she was hurrying across a vacant lot behind the store with Casa Verde in sight, through a broken chain link fence, fear electric around her—she convulsed at the crack of the pistol, imagining Flaco's bullet smashing into her back—but he had shot wide. Had he meant to hit her? Desperately she kept on.

She arrived at the rear of the building and raced around to the front door, bounded up the stairs, barred her door with a chair, drew the curtains.

Music from the cantina buzzed through the panes and a couple upstairs was pounding a mattress but she heard her own pulse and sensed the pistol against her skin. Her clothes were as drenched as from a storm. She started to strip them off, change, but stopped, went motionless. Footsteps heavy on the stairwell mounted toward her but kept on to the floor above. She turned off the lamp and lay down on the bed in her sweat, got back up and turned the light on—she did not want to be grabbed in the dark by an intruder. She peered out the curtains, saw Flaco angling down the street toward the hotel.

Or was it a trickery of shadows?

She reclined again on the bed, her body beginning to shake with the shock of mortality. One moment gave way to another in a tangle of images like the unraveling of a fever dream—storefront, gun barrel, stairwell, streetlamp like pale water through the curtains, and, rising up from the past, a woman and newborn so close she could hear their murmuring, stroke their skin. She envisioned Mom, in her last days, cradling baby Roger, in his first, holding him, no matter her final decline, with the tenderness and strength of a woman just starting out. Mom was gone, Daddy was old, Lupita wasn't blood, Mack was a disaster. There was only her between Roger and the world, and she was nowhere near him now. She wanted to sob but instead felt shame raking through her chest. She had failed to protect her young.

Then the first rooster was crowing and with the second one she was on her feet, packing her bag, readying to make her move.

A car door slammed and she looked out to spy a mustachioed man making his way through the dawn toward Casa Verde. This time the footsteps stopped on her hallway, closing in.

She grabbed the table lamp and stood away from the door. If he broke in she was ready.

The tapping was soft, insistent. Louder. "*Señora.*"

She clapped her hand over mouth to keep from making any utterance.

"*Soy el Tio Juan.*"

What?

"*El tio de Lupita.*"

It could be a ruse. Had Lupita mentioned an uncle named Juan, in Mexico? What had her father always told her? Don't act impulsively but don't hesitate yourself into a living hell either. As a boy in Amsterdam he'd made quick decisions—be silent when the Dutch Underground snatched him off the street, trust the clergy at Mozes en Aäronkerk, go with strangers to a farmhouse to hide. He'd sensed the right moves even as a child.

She closed her eyes, took a deep breath, and opened the door.

"Venga," he said, and waved her down the steps where there was no one at the front desk. She followed him to the car—*"Rápido,"* he urged—its tinted windows black on the outside, pale yellow from inside. Only the front windshield was clear.

Outside in a haze were the outlines of the pueblo with its shops blue and white phantasms, the brocade of churches squat against desiccated hills, the figures of children running through morning streets, shouts faint through the sealed confines of the car, and Juan's voice in elementary English telling how he'd worked in security for a government official in Honduras until the coup, then became a target of the new regime. With a heightened threat as well from the gangs in his San Pedro Sula neighborhood, Barrio Chamelecón, he had fled.

He told her that when Lupita had contacted him about Vanessa's plight, the details of her text, he knew the location, and the dread. He now worked in private security an hour from Casa Verde. "I'll go back to Honduras. One day. To watch out for others."

What he understood she could not tell but she told of how she had walked out of the rehab facility, breaking her sentencing, her fear of prison, her inability to reverse her downward spiral.

"And then," she went on, "I drove across the border."

"Why do you do all this?"

"Chance. Foolishness. Fear."

The villages were sliding away and she saw the rising forms of cactus like crazed men marching toward her.

She told of Janice, the storage room of cocaine, Flaco with the gun.

"Passport?" he asked.

She patted her pants pocket. "To the border it's six hours. *Seis*. Take me to a bus, *por favor.*"

"For you, now, not safe."

"It is too far!"

He pointed to a scar on his neck. "I run, too. But no more." He touched the edge of his eye and waved his finger. "You look. Everywhere."

"I don't want to put you in danger."

"*Cálmate.*" Take it easy. She'd heard Lupita use that expression to settle Roger. "Your padre *ayuda* Julio. I do anything, *cualquier cosa por la familia.*"

Juan avoided the major highway and kept to a back-road coursing by a stream. He became an angel ferrying her toward the far-off border.

She nodded, leaned back again in her seat, tried to relax.

Around a curve appeared a couple walking by the roadside. On their backs were sacks of belongings, the woman holding a baby in a front sling, the man cradling their toddler in his arms. Ahead of them was a cluster of three, another group of half dozen or more, moving raggedly by the asphalt, their hats tilted against the rising sun.

"*A los Estados Unidos,*" Juan said.

"Can we help them? *Ayuda?* A ride?"

Around the next bend scores stretched ahead, a cavalcade ambling northward, unstopping, tread steady.

"*Muchos,*" he said and shook his head.

Juan slowed to a creep as two children wandered into their path and a mother no older than twenty frantically brought them back to her side. The car rolled at a pedestrian's pace alongside and Vanessa pressed the window button. The dark rectangle came down. She found candies and cash in her purse and asking her name—"*¿Cómo te llamas?*"—reached out with it.

"*Milagros,*" the woman answered.

When the young mother received it she clasped Vanessa's hand—her palm so small and rough—and Vanessa saw herself in Milagros's eyes: affluent, coddled, crossing borders with ease, offering a pittance. Could this stranger sense all that Vanessa had thrown away? What Milagros herself, traipsing 1,500 miles seeking a better life for her children, might achieve with the same opportunities?

Vanessa tried to open the door. It stayed locked.

"Please," she said to Juan, "we need to give them a ride!"

He shook his finger no.

"We've got so much room!"

"Señora. It's not possible."

With Milagros still clutching her hand he began to roll the window up and the young woman let go. The face of the pilgrim – intense black eyes, wide brow, mouth flickering with a smile, or disdain, stayed with her as Juan said, "*Vámanos,*" and they sped on.

Late at night they arrived at the border where she got out and, alone in her US citizenship, walked the bridge to her country.

"Vanessa!" The familiar voice rang out. Mack appeared. "Thank God! I'm here to take you home."

30
LA TORMENTA

BACK IN THE SKIFF, NIGHT swirling, Julio dreamed, he grasped the gunwale, refusing to let the storm pitch him out this time. In the violent rain the stars were still visible, moving like a kaleidoscope, the waves reaching up to snatch them. Over and again they leapt, like wild dogs jumping to rip at men racing, arms flailing, to make it across the border. Down they fell, covering him in their cowl, slipping away.

He made out the Sand Island lighthouse, its black form against the vibrating sky, its Cyclops eye flashing and igniting his skiff, the ice chest, Paco's gift to him like a red channel marker saying this way lies catastrophe, but it seemed to guide him too, a great force shoving his vessel forward to the rocks at the base of the lighthouse promontory. In a moment of calm, as if a hand had stilled the water, he found his prow snug against a small boulder, clambered out and onto the land, pulling the boat up behind him. Shorebirds hidden in the lee of the lighthouse, startled by his arrival, lifted up, a pelican whirling by him like a kite ripped from a child, banking against the storm before returning to its perch close by. He watched it watching him.

The lighthouse door locked, he grabbed Paco's ice chest and crouched at the base of the tower, holding the cooler like protecting a child. He had escaped, the image of the dying golfer only a phantasm, the real assailant somewhere on the loose but not him. He opened the cooler, picked out a piece of grilled fish, wet and crumbling, but like manna as he fed himself hiding away from the pelican who stepped closer.

"*Aquí,*" he said, tossing a smidgen to his friend, who snapped it into his gullet.

He reached in again and felt a hard object, some kind of key or utensil? He lifted it out, a small cross, the size of a pendant, to hang on a chain. Had Paco dropped it in by accident? Or for him? He held it tightly as the wind roared around the lighthouse, then subsided. Before first light he took to his skiff again, the waters calmed, and headed west.

His motor hummed and bow sliced the currents, the air fresh after the tempest, the Mississippi coast and then the ragged delta of Louisiana soon appearing. That he should have enough gas to reach New Orleans was astonishing but the little motor propelled him still, toward the mouth of the Mississippi, the coursing paths of the bayou confounding at first—the cedars arcing against electric blue skies, the willows spreading their nets like the fishermen on Fairhope Pier—the stealing of moccasins and slithering of gators into the shallows making him want only to turn around. But where would he then have left to hide?

This way, the pelican above him showed, its wingspan a sacred canopy. By swamp camps and pirogues, under moss sweeping down like the widow veils from oaks on Bayfront Resort's seventeenth hole, coming into the wide stretch of the river where tugs pushed barges toward port, his tiny skiff holding its own, he moved toward freedom.

It came at the edges of the city, the beginnings of the French market at the bend in the river, the flow of people along the river walk, the small dock he came alongside, tying up, scampering out. He heralded the aroma of rice and beans and sausages and beer, sugary doughnuts and sweet pecan candies, melons and cane sold from carts and fortune tellers dealing out cards with pictures of jesters and devils, and old-timey jazz Abuelo listened to on the radio and the staccato of boys dancing tap on the corner and, in the distance, salsa calling.

Arriving at the club he lingered at the doorway watching couples pressing close, the conga catching him up, the blaring trumpets and thumping bass and accenting cowbell setting a rhythm in his limbs he had not felt in so long. He stepped in and a woman took his hand, pulling him toward her, and together they were lost in the surging crowd.

Oh my God, he thought, as she moved against him, the sensual splendor of it all, the months an illusion on the grounds crew of the hotel where the fortune-teller had laid down the skull card for him and he'd felt only the acrid embrace of the golfer with death gurgling in his chest, the heat from the blood gushing from the savage tear in his chest.

A phantasm too was the attacker in the night who'd opened the door of his cell left ajar by a guard, slamming a barbell against the back of his head, sending him into the void.

Only this woman's arms felt real, dancing with him, freeing him, across the pulsing room.

PART III

31

BLUE SNEAKERS

"I AM TOO OLD FOR this *mishugas*," Hank said, resting on Margery's bench at the pier, using his Selma grandmother's Yiddish word for foolishness. While *tsuris* meant trouble and woe—there was plenty of that with Vanessa now in Julia Tutwiler Prison for Women, Julio recovering from an attack in his cell, and his hip turning him into a slug—he felt more like the object of a cosmic joke than the victim of a tragedy. "I brought this all of myself," he said to Josie, who alighted on the railing, casting a squinty eye his way. "Whoever heard of trying to start over at age eighty-two?" In fact, he realized, he was now eighty-three.

The oldest person he knew as a boy was his paternal grandmother in Selma, ancient at eighty-one, a German Jew whose husband had died before Hank's arrival. As the refugee child from Amsterdam, Hank was the treasure of them all, and his grandmother would hug him singing in German, and when he was too big and wanted to squirm away would sit beside him on the porch swing. The march to the cemetery for her—she'd stopped stock still on the porch swing one day, the color run out of her face—was the first he knew of real death, a person he'd seen at the end. His parents and sister and brother had been whisked away in Amsterdam, like Blue's son, for-ever absent, not one minute older in his mind.

Mama and Daddy in Selma had both reached eighty, Mama going first, then Daddy. When he'd followed the hearse to the ceme-tery this time, the Alabama River winding through the city, the heavy oaks leaning down on the headstones, he realized, "I am orphaned twice now." Then Vanessa arrived, a mewling infant, her tiny, fiercely beating heart the hope of days to come. "I need that from you now," he said aloud to her, "a sense of the future. It cannot end with me."

Who am I, he thought, with sinewy arms and crabby hip, seamed face and bushy brows, to offer the promise of tomorrow?

He should have held fast when he'd first told Lupita this task was for a younger man. In fact, he'd decided that he must hand the case over. He would reach out to two up-and-coming defense lawyers soon enough. There was no money in defending Julio, but it could build a young hotshot's reputation. And some, as he'd tell Vanessa, even of her generation, really cared about the plight of the down-trodden. Maybe she wouldn't roll her eyes at that suggestion now that she was behind bars.

"Oh, Margery," he said. "I've been foolish. Time to let the hip mend itself and watch others throw their nets. *Basta. Finito.*" He wiped his hands together and hung his head low, feeling like a fish tossed up on the pier, gasping for air. "The end."

"Where's your buddy?"

Electric blue sneakers. They were planted before him like bright dahlias, spindly legs rising to calf-length blue shorts.

"Your little boy." Her accent was distinctly un-Southern. Great Lakes somewhere. Maybe Minnesota. "You're the famous lawyer, aren't you?"

"Who fell down the hole, yes."

"I didn't know anything about that. Are you OK?"

He nodded.

"I meant about taking up for the Honduran man."

"Not anymore."

"Why not? Oh my God"—she had startling blue eyes, like her shoes, and worry moved across them—"did something happen to him?"

"Do I know you?"

"I was out walking that morning you rescued him. I'm June," she said, extending her hand to shake. "Now you do."

"I didn't pull him in. That was my friend."

"You came to his rescue, the way you took charge. We were very impressed."

"I didn't do it for show. But thank you."

"Why aren't you defending him now?"

"June, there comes a moment in a man's life"—why was he going on to her like this?—"when it's time to let go."

"Don't," she said.

He looked at her quizzically. "You don't even know me."

"My husband stopped. Jerry had relished his work—he was an engineer; I sometimes think he loved bridges more than me. But he decided he was too old not to retire. He said, 'Let's get better at golf, let's go to the dance club more, let's be available for the grandkids,' and he came home and we did some of that, right at first, for sure, but then he just wanted to relax, and he sat and kept sitting and that was it. It's been two years since he passed."

"I'm sorry," he said. He patted the name on the bench. "Five for me."

"Margery? That was your wife? We always wondered about her story, her name here. What a beautiful memorial, a lucky woman. To be treasured like that."

"I was the lucky one."

He'd been roosting long enough. With great effort he struggled to get up, not wanting to reach for the walker Blue had loaned him.

June reached out and helped pull him onto his feet. When she gave him a quick hug he felt a frisson he had not experienced in years, a strange woman, lithe and airy, pressing close.

"Hope to see you again soon!" she chimed, and as he watched her clipping down the pier, blue sneakers shimmering, he waved and heard himself answer, out of earshot, "Me too."

32
LIT BY THE NIGHT

LUPITA WORKED LONGER HOURS HELPING with Roger since Hank's fall. She offered to bunk in over the garage, but Hank insisted she head home. He paid Paco to pick her up after his shift for a ride home.

The second night Paco gave her a six-pack of Honduran Port Royal, and third she invited him in to share some. She pried the caps off two cold bottles and they sat outdoors in the folding chairs but it started to drizzle. Inside, they sat next to each other on her small couch and said little, but she felt the air alive with expectation.

Please don't touch me, she thought. *You are like a little brother to me.*

He leaned in toward her and rested his head on her shoulder. She reached up and, without thinking, rubbed her hand over the top of his head. "*Estás cansado,*" she said. You are tired.

He nodded, then sat up and wiped his eyes.

"*¿Triste?*"

"I'm thinking about Julio," he said.

"The Virgin hears our prayers."

"Your mother's birthday is tomorrow, isn't it?"

"How did you remember?"

He reached in his pocket and pulled out two fifty-dollar bills. "Take this, to send to her."

"Keep your money!"

"Say it's a gift, from Julio."

"Ah, Paco, no."

"If my mother were still with us I would send it to her. But Doña Inez is like my mother now. Let her believe that her Julio is OK."

She remembered the story her mother had told her: Paco's mother, Paz, stepping outside of her house next door, the shoot-out between the gangs, the bullet in her neck, falling onto the road, crying out, "Paco!" But Paco had gone.

Mama had run to Paz and lifted her head, crying out at the warring factions, seeing the ones who extorted their monthly fee from her, who'd driven her own children north, her brother Juan to Mexico. But Mama would not leave Abuelo behind. And in her way she was the most defiant of all. When Paz died Mama went to the police to identify the shooters. They took a record of her statement. Nothing changed.

"¡Qué buen corazón! Paco," What a good heart you have. "Paz is looking down. She knows."

"We need to protect each other," he said.

"Yes," she said.

"I don't sleep. I think about my mother, I worry about Julio, our friends in San Pedro and Tegucigalpa, the people we know here looking over their shoulder. I worry about you."

"Shh, be calm."

"Soy nervioso," he said. "Tanto peligro." So much danger.

She cupped his face in her hands and said, "I need you to be strong."

"Fuerte," he said. "Sí. Contigo yo puedo." With you I can be.

When his warm brown eyes fixed on her she sensed an expression different than before—intimacy, yearning.

She stood up, took a final sip of beer, said, "It's late. Goodnight Paco. Thank you for being such a good friend to Julio, and to me."

But Paco went down on one knee.

"Lupe Vega Blanco," he began, taking her hand and bowing his head like a knight before a queen. "Will you"—he turned his face upward, worshipful—"marry me?"

"Paco!"

"Please, will you"—he held her hands tightly—"do me the honor of being my bride?"

The rocks that smacked the roof caused him to stand at first. They waited. There was only the patter of the rain.

"You're already like family to me," she began, as gently as possible, but in the next volley was a heavy stone like a sledgehammer beating down. Paco ripped open the door and plunged into the night.

"Paco!" Lupita yelled into the rain now streaming down. The small boulder that had smashed her roof had tumbled down near the steps. "Paco!"

She was answered by thunder rolling over the field, rattling her windows, lightning strikes moving closer illuminating no figure before curtaining the land again. Lights from far-off houses, one of them where the culprits surely hid again, were obliterated.

Then he was standing before her at the door as the sky ignited, a wild look in his eyes that had just been so tender, the scar in a slash over his neck glistening like a snake. Not from an operation, she knew.

"I'm staying here tonight to make sure they don't come back."

She waved him in and fetched him a towel.

He lay quietly, respectfully alongside her as they slept, and when she woke she found his arm slung over her, on his shoulder the faint outline of a former tattoo she'd never seen, "S-18" over scorpion claws, ghosting beneath the skin.

33

THE NIGHT OF BROKEN GLASS

WAS IT THE SAME HOOLIGAN who pitched rocks at Lupita's house that assaulted his, shattering his living room window? In his bathrobe, hip still wrinkling with pain, he trundled out to the yard and found the rock with the note rubber-banded around it: *"Dam Jew. You get the Mexcan off and it's your neck."*

He did not tell Lupita when she arrived, nor Blue who came by to drive him to the schools. It was not the scrawled words that made him tremble—he was used to the outrage of victims' families and friends—but the rock in the window. He'd only been a toddler in 1938 when upstanding Germans took to Jewish stores and synagogues with bricks and torches. But the tremors of Kristallnacht had found their way from the Rhineland into his Amsterdam home. He had an image of a couple who'd fled Cologne staying in their house, and of his mother, letting out a yell when his father accidentally knocked a wineglass off the table. Anne Frank's grandmother Hollander, he'd later find out, had left Frankfurt to join the Frank family in safe, secure Amsterdam. By 1940, as he'd tell students, the Nazis occupied the Netherlands. It had begun with broken windows.

Like closing the covers for good of his Code of Alabama—though he hadn't announced it—this school visit, he'd decided, was definitely his finale. Annually on Holocaust Remembrance Day he went from class to class, ending up at the synagogue by evening where he'd speak at an interfaith service.

He decided, this last Yom Hashoah, to carry the rock—and note—with him. He set it on a table before him.

"This stone before you has a story to tell," he began, departing from his usual presentation. "As ancient as the earth, it represents an ancient vice, too, a weakness. A sin known only to humankind. Hatred.

"On today, when we remember those who died in the Holocaust, murdered by Hitler and his henchmen, we ask ourselves, 'Why do people hate each other as they do?' 'Why do people act on that hatred through acts of violence?'

"In a moment I will tell you about my life as a small child in Amsterdam, and how I was taken from my parents, and survived because of their sacrifice. But"—he reached out and picked up the rock now and heard the gasp—"this came through my window this morning."

He read the note.

"What does it tell us?" he asked, studying the rock like it was a crystal ball. "That what happened in Hitler's world could happen in ours."

A boy raised his hand.

"I'll get to your questions in a few minutes," Hank said.

The boy stood now, short, red-faced, animated. "The way that Mexican stuck Uncle Beau and he bled out and all, it's a crime worse than any stupid letter you got through your window."

A teacher demanded the student exit the classroom but Hank halted him and said, "It's OK," then addressed him: "Mr. Shepherd's your uncle? I'm so sorry for your loss."

"He married my crazy aunt"—there was snickering but Hank silenced the students with a wave—"and he had Mexicans working for him, fixing up his yard, putting on his big parties. What did they have against him?"

"What happened to Beau Shepherd was terrible! A tragedy. I defend people accused of those terrible things, that's my job, but I do it for what this Holocaust Remembrance Day is about, too—the rights of every individual, the freedom for each and every one of us."

"The Mexican came here illegal."

"This is not about Julio Blanco's citizenship, who's from Honduras. And, for the record, he came here legally but overstayed his work contract." Why was he even letting himself get drawn into this debate?

"If he wasn't here he wouldn't have killed Uncle Beau."

"Don't you think he deserves the right to a defense?"

"Beau didn't have no defense. I wish he had. A gun would have saved his life. Your man would be dead in the ground instead of my uncle."

A girl called out, "Shut up!"

"You shut up."

"The man is trying to tell us what happened," she said, on her feet now. She was lanky, with a long braid of black hair. "He's trying to teach us something."

"Where you from?" the boy shot back.

"Ecuador."

"Figures."

"Stop, stop," Hank exhorted, "please all of you stop."

"You weirdo jerk," the girl lit into the boy, "my father's an engineer here."

"You're nasty," came another male voice.

When another boy jumped on this new one, Hank heard chairs tumble and crash, and somebody yelled, "Gun, gun," and students were falling over each other, desperate for exits, but when Blue jumped to the podium to hurry Hank away he refused, telling Blue to take cover but he was determined to do what he could. "Where is he?" he shouted. "The shooter. *Come for me, you bastard!*"

Security guards and police were streaming in but found no weapon. Parents and TV crews flocked to the perimeter as school was dismissed.

"I'm done" Hank said, as he and Blue drove away. "This isn't my world anymore."

34
A DAUGHTER'S HAND

"I'll help you," Vanessa told Hank on his first visit to Tutwiler when he revealed he was intending to bow out of Julio's case, his eyes older and sadder than ever.

"You're in banking!"

"You know my public defender's stint drove me crazy, but I learned a lot."

"It's irrelevant. I'm never going to court again."

"You've said that before."

"You were the one who told me I was too old to put up a decent defense in the first place, don't forget."

"That was then."

"When?"

"Before my journey."

As she'd worked her Tutwiler job helping in the kitchen and bussing tables, she had replayed that journey in her mind—growing up, college, Mack, Roger, the careening trip to Mexico, the young mother in the caravan, Milagros, who saw the self-involved, spoiled American woman in the imposing car who took privilege for granted. She could not help Milagros, however desperate for refuge.

But Roger and her father needed her, Lupita needed her, and Julio needed them all.

Realizations tumbled out as she tried to "be honest," as the instructor insisted in writing therapy, surprised by her own pen. When the class was directed to list five words that came to mind about their substance abuse, she put down: *Porch. Southern Comfort. Hug. Love. Auschwitz.*

When she expanded on that list she began to write of childhood summers with her Selma grandparents, the security and comfort as they sipped cocktails on the porch, how she never hugged anyone even today without thinking of her mom and dad, the sense that love had woven like a strong cord through the generations, but how the concentration camps had thrown stark shadows over her father's life, reaching as far as her own. "Does my drinking," she wrote, "help push back those shadows?"

Why had he been so hard on her, as she had been on him?

She composed:

I could never do enough to please him. He said he was proud, was always there with Mom on the first row of the school assemblies, applauding me when I was inducted into the National Honor Society and was valedictorian, and taking us three on a trip to France when I got a scholarship to Vassar, but never Holland, too many ghosts.

That my father had escaped the death camps never left his mind, his psyche. I felt it hovering over me, too. Here I was all through school, a regular Alabama kid, going to football games, swimming, going to the dances where the deejay played Queen and Kool and the Gang and Kenny Rogers, and I'd come home and he would have tears in his eyes.

"What's wrong, Daddy?" I said.

"I'm glad you're home safely."

"Why wouldn't I be? I was just out with my friends."

"I know."

"Why are you getting all upset then?"

"So much can happen in the world."

"It's not like we're in Europe!"

"Do you know what you're saying? That you could forget your Oma and Opa?"

"But Mimi and Papa are my grandparents."

"But you would not be here without Opa and Oma."

"Do you even remember them?" I said. "You were, like, six years old."

"Look." He pulled out his wallet and slipped out the crinkled black-and-white photo of a couple peering back, the woman's hair in a bun, her blouse buttoned high, eyes soulful, and the man, his lankiness visible even in the portrait—it was the long stretch of his neck—blazing eyes looking right into me.

"They were so young," I said.

"It's all I have of them."

"It's not my fault," I said.

I'll never forget his expression when I said that, not anger but a sadness so deep I had to look away. He started to say something, a flash of ire I'd call it—like he could have slapped me, which he'd never done—but then, just echoed, as if from far away, "Not your fault. You're right. Forgive me."

He was clutching the picture. In that moment I saw him crossing the street from the Jewish theater to the children's detention center, a lonesome little boy not knowing this was the last he'd see of his mother and father, brother and sister, anyone known to him in his whole world who would soon be deported to the camps, and in his face I saw the features of the photograph.

And in my face.

This is who I am, too.

35

BACK ON THE SCENE

HANK WAS GETTING AROUND BETTER—THE swelling from his hip
contusion going down, the pain subsiding after many weeks, the lingering soreness abating. He'd dispensed with the walker and extricated his father's antique cane from the closet to use around the
house, but not outdoors. His physical therapy was popping half a
codeine pill with morning coffee and summoning personal grit. He
could stand on his own two feet. He no longer wanted to make a
public show of his fragility.

He had not yet made a final decision about handing off the
case. In addition to Vanessa's exhortation about staying with Julio's
defense, he thought what Ruben Brown might say.

Hank had met Ruben, his late, great investigator, when they were
both in their forties, and he'd used the rumpled detective repeatedly
until his end. A former newspaper reporter with a restless streak,
Ruben was dogged and tireless. He'd been old school, using the city
directory, telephone, and shoe leather to find witnesses who were
reluctant to show their faces, turning up details of a crime following
leads the police thought they'd exhausted or were too stressed with
other demands to explore. He was computer savvy, but impatient

with the younger generation who did their sleuthing "peering into a glass box," as he put it. "The internet," he'd tell them, "is not the street."

"How do you do it?" Hank had asked Ruben after he'd turned up overlooked angles on a case.

Ruben had answered with a sly grin, like a guru revealing a mystical secret: "To start with I go out and nose around."

Hank could do that.

The story of the dog finding the knife sheath that led to the possible murder weapon had been widely reported in the news, along with every development in the case. The knife was now material evidence in the state's case. He studied a photograph of it in the discovery file. How distinctive was it?

He drove to gardening shops and sporting goods stores to nose around, familiarizing himself with the knives for sale, chatting up personnel to find out about different brands and uses. What was the exact kind said to be used by the assailant? How easy was it to get hold of? Did the grounds crew at the resort have others at their disposal?

In the manila folders packed into storage boxes next to his law books he'd pulled the files on other cases he'd handled involving a stabbing. He looked through photographs of coroner reports, his notes penciled in the margins. To what degree could you match a knife with an attack? The width of the blade, curve of the steel, length of the weapon—deep wounds suggested a kind of knife but there was no way to be exact, of course. How could the prosecution be sure the knife found in the ditch was Julio's? Even if there was telltale blood on the sheath, numerous workers checked out the gardening implements.

He'd walked the scene of the murder more than once, but this time borrowed a golf cart used by his late friend, Judge Nikos, and drove it the four miles along a back road to Bay Resort, rolling onto the golf course in the aftermath of a rain storm. The course was closed for thirty minutes after a lightning strike, and he had the soggy fairways to himself. He had never been on it all alone.

That "the street" in this case was also "the links" would have intrigued Ruben, a determined duffer who'd loved the game, "a crime-free zone," he'd quipped, "except for boozers, betters, and braggarts."

He rode the back nine, following the dogleg of the thirteenth, the long par five of the fourteenth, the short par three of the fif-teenth—a pond like a dangerous moat fronted it, an alligator hav-ing once crawled out there—and arrived at the sixteenth, imagining Ruben alongside him, showing the way. He imagined the witness, Cardenas, at his labors, raking the sand trap like a half moon along-side the green. He stopped the cart, stepped out. The sightline to the seventeenth green was straight ahead from where he stood. He took a step to the right; it was obscured by a hoary oak. He walked forward. How deep was the trap? He could see over the berm of the trap to the locale of the murder, but he was nearly 5' 11".

He stooped down a few inches. Only the top of the far-off pin was visible.

How tall was Cardenas?

He got back in the cart and saw other pins in the distance. "Damn," he thought, "this is visible from four vantage points."

Had there been anybody else on the course that late afternoon of the murder?

The rain began to pelt and he made his way to the pro shop. He went in and asked the young woman behind the counter how to reserve a tee time. "You want to play?" she asked.

"Just curious."

"Just ask, or call, and we'll put a time in the system."

"Do golfers ever play without signing in?"

"All these houses around here, all this acreage, some might jump on."

"Do people ever go out alone?"

"You're welcome to"—she eyed him skeptically—"but it's raining kind of hard now. Here." She handed him a towel. "We're still under a red alert, lightning strikes."

He heard rousing laughter from another room and looked in to see men drinking and playing cards, a big screen TV behind them with a football game going. "Hey, Mr. Weinberg," one said, waving at him. "I'm a friend of Vanessa's."

The other men gazed up at him, turned back to their game.

He imagined Beau at that table, a winner, a drinker, wandering out flush with cash onto the pastoral fields, golf clubs in tow, toward a violent confrontation.

Had he been alone?

The rain stopped and he rolled back home, knowing how Ruben would proceed. Ruben had been able to get anyone to talk to him. Before they did so on the record, Ruben explained, they needed to do so informally, often out of sight from prying eyes. He'd been able to communicate across languages and cultures, including the Vietnamese American fishing community in south Mobile County.

He'd have found out the name of Vanessa's friend, discovered where he worked, approached him as he was leaving his office for a cup of coffee. Maybe that young man had heard talk around the card table.

Or maybe that tactic would prove a dead end. "No matter," Ruben had said. "You might learn something you didn't realize at the time."

Hank began to seek out character witnesses.

With Lupita his impromptu translator, he talked to the men lingering by the Mercado Latino, those who knew Julio, played soccer with him on the field near the store. All spoke with affection, even admiration, of Julio, but none would come forward. They were, Lupita told him, afraid to walk into a court of law, whatever their citizenship status.

Even Paco, like a brother to Julio, said no.

They worried, Lupita said, that nothing good could come of it. "*El riesgo*," she said. "The risk."

Hank was definitely back on the case.

36
LA BIBLIA

AT THE EXHORTATION OF LUPITA, Julio began to attend jail prayer meetings. That he had not drowned and had now survived a savage blow to his head—no one willing to identify the attacker—was evidence enough, she said, that the Lord had covered him in grace. "Hold close our Lady of Suyapa," she beseeched. "She is protecting you."

Mr. Hank had secured a change of venue, arguing that Julio was no longer safe in the jail where first held, and that a fair trial was hard to assure in the county that had sent Beau Shepherd to the state legislature, and where the newspaper published continuous articles on the crime.

The new jail, in Mobile County near the seaport, was twice as large, with a view as narrow as a dungeon window onto the other side of the bay, bail bonds offices with garish signs lit up all night like casinos on a tawdry strip. The international presence was greater, too, with cruise workers and cargo ship deckhands afoul of the law during shore leave in Mobile waiting their court date, begging families back in the Philippines or Indonesia for money to pay their fines.

He came to realize that any activity available to inmates, from crafts to classes, was a welcome break from the tedium of a cell. He started going to prayer meetings in the same spirit of distraction.

The participants were varied: Javier, the son of a Honduran mother and American father, born in New Orleans, who was accused of knocking over a convenience store, putting a snub-nosed pistol to the cashier's temple; Jimbo, a black man, picked up in a stolen Grand Prix, on his way to the Florida Keys; Little Lee, disdained by them all, convicted of dropping his two-year old on the head while high on crack cocaine; Oscar, known as the "Big O" in on his second heroin charge.

There were those who joined for a week, a few days, and others, on interminable waits, who were as regular as their faith warranted.

The men took turns leading the circle, praying in a style like none he'd heard in his mother's church.

"Dear Lord Jesus," Javier began, "touch us with the wisdom of your word, fill us with the power of your spirit, forgive us our sins and let us be judged before you, the only judge who knows our true heart. With you we do not suffer but grow strong in our adversities.

"Know that we are sinners."

The group repeated the confession.

"But we are washed clean before you."

They echoed the words.

"We are fallen."

"We are fallen."

"But we will stand. Tall. Strong. Together."

The men clasped hands and chorused as one.

"Together."

He felt the coarse grip of the inmate to each side of him, the rough clutch of a little boy's father, a mother's child gone wrong. What crimes were these hands accused of?

He felt an odd stirring, a sense of camaraderie, the lot of them facing the long odds of any of them making it out, turning to a higher power for succor, as Mama did.

The first man, Skeeter, a longshoreman from Marion, told how his father had beat him as a child, how he'd first hit another kid in junior high—"knocked his fuckin' teeth out"—and spent three months in "juvie" before getting out only to floor a rival for his girl in high school, "bustin' his skull," in detention again. A few years later he was convicted as an adult of aggravated assault for a backyard brawl with a neighbor. His arrest this time was for violating a restraining order on his ex-wife, who claimed he had battered her.

The men prayed for Jesus to wash away his sins.

The next man, Enrique, had been arrested for possession of cocaine—"It wasn't me, and I didn't even know the motherfucker who was selling it"—but admitted he'd been an addict. "I'm clean now, praise Jesus."

"Praise Jesus," answered the group.

While some men asked a blessing for the victim of the wrongs they were accused of, no one confessed to the deed itself. They prayed for the power of Christ to heal, to restore.

All eyes turned to Julio.

When he recapped his charges everyone nodded – he had a kind of odd celebrity status at this new lockup, he realized—but to his own surprise he began to recount his dream about being back on the skiff, escaping to freedom. The boat tossed by the waves, the refuge at Sand Island lighthouse, the becalmed morning and motor with its endless gasoline purring as far as Louisiana, the pelican, wings spread, showing the way onto the unbounded streets of New Orleans—he recounted it, as if in a trance.

"Now," he said, "I realize." He took out the picture of the Our Lady of Suyapa that he'd been allowed to keep on him and touched the folds of her great cape. "*Como alas,*" he said.

"Like wings," Javier translated.

"*Ella me protege.*"

"She protected him," Javier said.

Julio nodded.

"But you don't need a statue," Enrique said first in Spanish then English. "Jesus is here, man. Not in the plaster figures. I came up in that, too. You ever heard of Cholula, in Mexico? It's where I'm from. So many churches, covered in gold and shit, saints out your ass, the fucking priests living like kings and the people poor as dogs, fighting over the scraps. That's not God to me."

"*Mi Mamá,*" Julio said.

"My mother, too," Enrique came back. "She's into all that fantasy. But put away your cartoon lady and feel this." He stepped toward Julio and slapped him in the chest, knocking him back. Julio started to jump back at him but Javier raised up his hand and said, "*Whoa, cálmate, hermano. ¿Que sientes?*"

What did Julio feel? His whole body was pulsating.

"That's the power of the Lord," Enrique said.

"Praise God," said Oscar, the others chiming in.

"What you feel," Javier said, "is God grabbing you. When he holds you tight, owns you, you are safe even if they fry your ass."

37

JUNE

Hank detected her at his back, just like he'd been able to sense Margery, stealing up behind him as he leaned against the pier railing, his net coiled in a bucket. He'd tossed the net just now and worried about his hip. He felt good enough to be out and about, looking further into Julio's case, but no more fishing for a while, he figured.

No more visits to schools, no more speeches.

And no more women, he told himself, feeling oddly smug, like he knew what this fair Midwesterner with her electric blue shoes— he glanced behind him, no, they were radiant orange today—was up to. He'd met so many of her age, as sympathetic friends in the aftermath of Margery's passing then, after a year had passed, as eager widows and divorcees. "I'm still married to my wife," he'd tell them, content to share lunch or a movie, but with the understanding they could only be friends.

He could hardly blame them for their desire, knowing the depth of loneliness that descended once he was home alone, or in grand-parenting Roger all by himself. He tried to play out what Margery might do—turn on music for the boy, envelop him with a bedtime story, letting him comprehend what he could. But he fell short as a solitary grandfather.

"I heard what happened at the school," June said. "The daughter of a friend of mine's the librarian there. I'm so sorry it turned into that."

"It's somebody else's turn."

"Kids don't appreciate what we have in this country. They need to hear these stories. They need to hear it, Hank, from you."

The pushy Minnesotan was annoying, but there was something about her flattery, and the way she said "Hank" that softened him.

"I hear Pastor Blue was with you," she said. "You're good friends, aren't you?"

"We joke I'm his rabbi, he's my preacher."

"We went to his church when we first retired here. A lovely man, very spiritual. Such a tragedy about his son. Jerry liked that church more than I did, he was even scheduled to go on that mission trip but got a summer cold. He caught it from an angel."

"Jerry sounds like such a nice man."

"You think that crash might have drawn Beau and Blue closer together," she went on. "But there was bad blood between them. I can see why."

Hank looked up the pier but did not see his friend.

"Can I try?" she asked. She pointed to his net.

The cockeyed request amused him.

"It's heavy," he said.

"And sloppy?"

"Very."

"Perfect. Give it to me."

What ploy was this?

"OK." He handed it over.

"What now?"

He came up behind, reaching around her and grabbing the loops. She was a good 5' 5", most likely having shortened an inch since her youth, as he had. He was accustomed to the squashing down. She scooched back—her brown hair whispered against his chin—and fit into the long curve of him.

As he draped his arms around her, the tingling coursing over his skin was unmistakable, the pressure of another human neither daughter nor grandson nor doctor—a vivacious eighty-year-old— sending a trill down his body.

"I used to fish with my 'vader,'" she said. "But never like this."

"You're Dutch?"

"My Papa was. From Rotterdam. I've never been there."

"I was born . . ."

"In Amsterdam, we all know that. Are you going to show me what to do or not?"

No matter the skirt of holes soaked with Mobile Bay sluicing down to his beaten work boots and her loud orange sneakers, they swayed as one, as if no one else on the pier mattered, the old couple on an island all their own letting loose of the net in an oblong throw that hung it up on the railing before it slipped over the side like a lumpy laundry bag, their laughter answered only by the riotous gulls.

38
SECRET CHURCHES

JULIO TOOK AN ENGLISH CLASS, and in the weight room, the cafeteria, or his cell, he read the newspaper, even if a few days old, sounding out each word like a first grader. It took him three days to get through the front page titled, "Hispanic Churches in Hiding," about undocumented workers gathering in secrecy to pray to the Lord.

In his prayer meetings he told of this outrage. Others in the circle reported what they had read, or heard from relatives—about a caravan of those fleeing Honduras walking hundreds of miles, stopped just short of the border and isolated in migrant camps where sickness took hold; children taken from parents and put in stark rooms behind bars worse than this jail, accused of no crime; those seeking asylum turned back, over and again, sent south to violent neighborhoods. As they told their stories and prayed, Julio knew some were violent figures themselves, with gang life still stalking them—there was no escape—but these were children of God, too, proud of heart.

It was an upside-down world, Julio knew, when those inside the jail could freely pray and those outside, the followers of Hispanic pastors, had to hide for fear of deportation. When ICE ramped up its pressures and workers without papers fled into the fields, they still congregated at "La Iglesia Metodista," or "La Luz Brillante Pentecostal," or "La Palabra de Jesús," often in mainstream churches giving use of their social halls or small chapels for the immigrant workers. There had been only one raid, but it was enough to send fear into the prayerful.

They began, said the article he slowly made sense of, to "go underground," meeting up in people's homes, often of church members who were citizens and offered dens and playrooms as sanctuaries. In the newspaper story a Honduran worker, Paco, identified by first name only—could it be his Paco?—said that people who condemned the undocumented for hiding out in sanctuaries in order to "break the law" were "Christian hypocrites. They have no compassion."

In the next day's newspaper he read a letter to the editor saying that "illegals are just that. It's un-Christian to break the law and they are by being here. Go home, I say to them. Respect our borders, obey our laws. That's Christian."

When Enrique was moved to Atmore after a plea deal, Julio began to lead the prayers, and when someone new arrived, uncertain of his faith, or in a fusty old religion like he'd been raised, believing God wanted them meek and regimented, it was his turn to slap them in the chest and say, "This is what you feel when he takes hold."

When nineteen-year-old Ollie, a behemoth football player charged with statutory rape, took Julio's punch he stood stock still and began to shake. "This here," the teen giant said, starting to weep, "is true church."

There was a story in the paper on Sunday and he kept it close at hand, about the naming of a bench on Fairhope Pier in memory of Beau Shepherd. With photos the piece recounted Shepherd's life, from his career in contracting, to his election to state office, to his work for the church that led him to the fateful mission trip in Africa, to his murder on the seventeenth hole of the Bay Resort Hotel. In the article Beau Shepherd seemed familiar, real, and Julio Blanco, described as "an illegal immigrant from Honduras with gang affiliations," a violent phantom.

Looking at the photos he felt Beau's macabre embrace, like Enrique grabbing his shoulders and slapping his chest. "El Buen Pastor," was the hymn his mother sang. The Good Shepherd.

Had God led Julio on that fairway to the seventeenth green? Was this his directive, to have trod that path? Had the Good Shepherd appeared in the guise of a drunken stranger?

He knelt and looked up at the divided sky through the barred window, a ray of light arrowing onto him, supplicant, waiting.

He felt himself lifted up into that light, a mission set before him pressing into his central nervous system. Its name he did not yet know.

In prayer circle the next day he spoke in a way he had not expected, as though his words were commanded from on high, that he wanted to preach, that if God should spare him from this ordeal he would give himself to others far beyond, and if not, carry his word to those with his fate.

"*Es mi camino*," he said.

My path.

39
DANCE OF MEMORY

ON HIS YELLOW LEGAL PAD Hank made a must-do list: whom to talk to, what to explore, where to nose around, Ruben's spirit guiding him.

- Get personnel reference, Julio, Bay Resort, model employee at work
- Get statement from pastor, Julio man of faith in jail prayer group
- Retest DNA and blood samples
- Double-check Beau Shepherd's fingerprints on cash in Julio's pockets

He heard the old energy in his voice when he spoke to Vanessa on the phone about the case, asking her to jot down the items, too, "to keep me on track."

A call from June beeped through.

"Talk to her," Vanessa said, "I'll hold."

He did, then returned to the call with Vanessa.

"She wants to take me to her dance club. I begged off, said my hip was acting up."

"Your hip is fine. Go!"

"But Margery . . ."

"It's OK to have a friend, Daddy."

He accepted the invitation to June's delight. "I'll drive," she said.

Getting ready on Saturday evening he gave himself a close shave, then put on cologne that had been in the cabinet so long he feared it had turned to alcohol. The musk scent bloomed around him. He got out his wingtip shoes and brushed off his powder blue sports jacket.

Waiting on June he started going over his list again.

Vanessa's friend, who'd hailed him from the card game in the lounge, was an attorney from Louisville, home visiting family. He said the big money wasn't gambled at the card tables but on the course itself. Hank took out his pencil, added to the list: "Talk to golfers, ask about betting." Then he set it aside. "It's Saturday night," he said to himself, "relax." He poured himself a scotch and sipped, for some reason thinking of his parents, their getting dressed to go out in Amsterdam. He'd loved the way his mother smelled, like the blooms in the flower market on the Singel Canal. He'd never found her particular fragrance again, no matter how he'd tried, wanting it for Margery.

As they headed down County Road 64 in June's Eldorado, he confessed he hadn't plodded around the floor trying to box step in more than a decade. He'd done his best for Margery at weddings and bar mitzvahs, but he could never find the rhythm when she coaxed him onto the floor.

"I'm no Ginger Rogers," June said, "I'd break my neck if I even tried to dance again in heels."

He laughed, pleased at the reference. Fred Astaire, Jimmy Durante, George and Gracie—they were the pop culture of his youth. Who did he have to remember them with now that Margery was gone?

"That's where it all happened," she said as they passed Bay Jubilation, an enormous red-brick edifice set back on a field.

"Life," he said. "So many twists and turns."

"Church politics, you mean. Blue would still be the preacher there if he hadn't been forced out."

"I thought he left on his own."

"Beau wrangled something. Jerry played golf with Beau a few times, said Beau must have been a golf hustler way back, before he became all churchy and political. Beau still loved to bet, he wouldn't admit it was gambling, might be a sin. Jerry lost three hundred dollars when Beau hammered him—it's a game where you challenge your opponent to double the bet after each shot—and Jerry went along with it, figuring he was ahead. Until he wasn't."

"Lots of betting in the game?" He thought of the cash spilling out of Beau's pockets, Julio grabbing it. How much was found on Julio? How much did Beau still have on him?

"Small wagers mostly, ten, twenty dollars," June said. "But heavy bets, too. Jerry used to say you can tell a lot about a man from the way he plays golf. You realize a shark like Beau would force out Pastor Blue from the church if he felt like it. He didn't want him anywhere around. By then, our pastor was a broken man.

"After Jerry died I went back to my roots, Methodism. We have a Passover meal on Maundy Thursday, the night before Good Friday, a seder. We love the traditions of your people."

The fascination with Jews. She meant well. Just as he had felt a lifetime of being looked at as apart, suffering for it, defined by it, he had felt the sense of intrigue, too. "Being a Jew," he had told Vanessa when she was a teenager, "is anything but neutral."

"Blue says the pier is now his church," Hank said.

"Maybe the dance club is mine."

The small ballroom was awash in pale blue light with a disco ball throwing off sparkles of white, and June took him by the hand as they entered, introducing him to friends. He downed his scotch and was content to watch the others swirling to the music. The combo—electric keyboardist-singer and a drummer—were finishing up a country swing when June led him onto the floor. The keyboardist changed to Sinatra—"Fly me to the moon," he sang—and Hank found himself in the familiar foxtrot. He could make a square on the floor, after all, and after another drink he felt himself loosening up. His hip was fine; he felt invincible.

During "It's Still Rock and Roll to Me," June took charge, bringing him to her, pushing him back—"rock step," she said—and they began an easy swing, taking him back to the Capstone. At Sigma Alpha Mu parties he'd seen the "Sammies" jitterbugging to high heaven, and finally felt like one of them. Old dog, new tricks.

June, agile and feathery, made him look suave, he thought, catching a glimpse in the dancehall mirror, adept at this number that asked he pretty much stand in place as June, grasping the tips of his fingers, leaned back, shook, shimmied, and turned.

A whistle blew.

"Change partners," she explained. "Don't forget you're mine."

Before he could say, "What?" a new woman grasped his hands, announcing, "I'm Alice."

They started a heavy-footed waltz.

"Hank."

"I know who you are. Your reputation precedes you."

"Good, I hope."

She flashed a big smile.

Her husband had been Arthur, having retired from the insurance business before a glide path to Fairhope Pier, succumbing to heart failure the very morning he caught a half-dozen white trout.

"I'm sorry I didn't know him," he said.

Edgar had been the husband of the next dancer, Carol, who said he'd been a bailiff at the courthouse—Hank remembered him in glimpses—but dementia had taken him away. Others danced and spoke to him like a confessor, and one said, "You poor boy, losing your mom and dad like that," and then said, "When I lost my George I didn't think I could go on, but here I am. And you've done that your whole life. No wonder you're taking up for that Spanish boy. I know Beau Shepherd's family. I told them why."

"*Why?*"

The whistle blew.

Before he saw June he felt her arms.

"They're pouring their hearts out to me," he said. "You've told them all about me, my childhood."

"One heard you give a talk in her church."

"It's not about me. I was only bearing witness to history."

"Inside of you today," she said tenderly, leaning her head on his chest, "is still you the little boy." She reached up and drew her hand across his cheek ever so gently.

His mother's palm in a whisper, touching him, her face vivid over him.

She had returned like this before, especially on his birthdays, when he would chart how old he was in relation to how long she'd lived, age thirty-six, holding her there forever: milky skin, onyx black eyes, curly dark hair, the beauty mark she was known for on her left cheek, the spot, said his father, where the Maker had touched his finger, pointing out how proud he was of his creation.

He was back home on Prinsengracht, flowers heaped along the sides of the canals, boats sliding by, laughter from the walk, in the parlor his parents dancing to the big Philco radio, holding each other as they moved to the music, Shayna and Benyamin joining them. He remembered turning circles, arms out, airborne, the music his wings. Had he been five years old? Nearly six? Just before the German soldiers came? When all was light and festive?

Why did this vision rise up to him now? The musician played a song that brought back an American girl crooning through the radio—*"ergens over de regenboog,"* his mother translated as they danced—and the keyboardist sang it now: "Somewhere over the rainbow."

June pressed close.

He was leaving his mother now, his father just behind, pulled from them by the guards, other children from their parents, even as they were saying, "We are right here, we will be together again soon," and he was hustled to the dormitory where the days and nights passed and nice women tried to comfort them and big trucks pulled up across the street and grown-ups were led away, then from the children's dorm, too, and he lost sight of Shayna and Benyamin, and strained to see Mama and Papa as the children were led for a walk around the block, once twice, the air brisker with the change of seasons. How close his home was on Prinsengracht, how far away.

He'd been the last in the row of children and suddenly the blanket covered him and the arms were tight and he felt himself lifted, thrown into that car, the noise of its motor, say your name is Hans, we are taking you to Mozes en Aäronkerk—he knew the church near the synagogue—don't speak, be silent, be brave.

Mama. Papa. They were locked away as he was spirited off. The church. The countryside. The abbey. The ship.

"You look sad," June said, leading him out for fresh air, and he put his face on her shoulder and felt her hand stroking his head and felt his mother's hand and began to sob.

40
NOT MOMMY

"Just four weeks and Mommy will be home," said Gradee, who kept his left hand on the steering wheel as they drove to Tutwiler and raised his right, holding up each finger—"One, two, three, four"—to show Roger.

"See Mommy."

"Yes. We're driving to see Mommy."

With Lupita sitting next to him, Roger leaned back and looked out the window at the Alabama fields rolling by, at the white farmhouses and red silos and green sheathed corn and cotton plants taking root in the spring. He imagined Mommy hugging him, her arms soft as teddy bears, her face against him like flowers, not starched shirts and newspapers like Gradee.

They passed horses with their tails always switching and cows with their mouths always chewing. Lupita opened a paper bag and brought out a sandwich for him and he chewed.

Gradee slowed and tooted the horn as a black hound bounded across the road.

Some roads were little with dogs and birds and others were big with trailers and trucks.

"I know you'll be a good boy when we get there," said Gradee. "She is so excited to see you."

"Roger is a good boy," Lupita said, and patted his head.

There were more shiny cars on the road, blue, red, and green, and he closed his eyes, feeling the weight on his eyelids. Gradee called it a nap, and when Roger opened his eyes again he was cuddled into Lupita and looked out to see they were pulling into a lot then getting out of the car, going through a creaky door where Gradee spoke to a guard and signed his name, and they all passed through a machine called a metal detector, even Roger.

"Shh," Lupita was whispering close to Roger's ear. "We will be so quiet, like fish, just talking with our eyes"—she made her eyes big and round like the mullet's—"so Mommy can hug you and she will be happy."

When they entered a bright room with strange people leaning close to each other, mouths moving like fish marooned on the pier, he was ready to leap up and fly. He'd heard the word *prison*, though he'd never said it, and that Mommy had told him that's where she was going to get well. He'd stuffed it in his brain but now it was flopping and flickering and he did not want to go to prison, too.

He was pushing up, standing, jumping as high as he could to reach the window right next to Gradee's head, wanting to slip through, out onto the gravel lot, on to the cottony fields and back home where he could see the bay and also smell it and hear it like Mommy's voice comforting him to sleep.

"Oh, no, chiquito," Lupita was saying, clamping down on his shoulder. "No flying away for you."

Then Mommy appeared in baggy white pants and shirt and hair pulled back like a pony's, and she was not Mommy but a lady from the other side of the wall it seemed who'd come in her place.

When she hurried to him he felt himself curl in to himself, leaning toward Lupita. "Roger," Lupita's voice was repeating, "Roger," and it was mixed with the voice of the woman who had taken the place of Mommy, and now Gradee's fierce whispering of his name, too, like a frantic beating, "*Rog*-er, *Rog*-er," but he clung to Lupita and wept, "Mommy, my Mommy."

"I'm your Mommy," said the stranger, and a lady in uniform and badge was asking them to quiet down or leave, and he heard shushing like the wind on the pier and he was taken outside with Lupita while Gradee stayed inside to talk to the lady he could see through the window, shaking her head, putting her hands over her face and crying, and it *was* his Mommy. He reached out to hug her but she could not see him and was led away.

41
RETURN TO MITCH

THEY WERE THE SAME AGE, from neighboring villages, and Samuel Suarez was awaiting trial, too, charged with being an accomplice to the armed robbery of a convenience store. He'd only been the driver, he said, but his partner had fired a shot at the clerk before hopping back into the car as Suarez hit the accelerator. They got no farther than a block before being surrounded. The bullet had missed the clerk, thank the Lord, he said. He'd prayed for the clerk to forgive him.

Suarez was an ordained minister in La Iglesia de la Luz y la Paz, the Church of Light and Peace, a small congregation that had met in a chapel of the Methodist church until, like others, it deemed it best to disappear from public view. At prayer circle Suarez had become the leader, recognizing Julio's passion for his newfound faith. They shared stories of Hurricane Mitch, the wind howling and rain crashing and mountainside roaring as home and school and church began to shake and shift and hurtle, their world a mudslide.

Mama had said that Jesus held them in his hands like robin eggs, cradling them in their fragility, and he'd scoffed at that. When Suarez said, *"Estuvimos protejidos en las manos de Dios,"* that they'd been protected in the hands of God, he felt it now. He knew the song: "He's got the whole world in his hands."

At the end of a prayer meeting when Suarez asked Julio to kneel, he did so and with the others encircling the pastor put his hands on Julio's head and asked, "Do you have a confession to make?" Feeling the anguish in his heart of letting the golfer die, Julio answered, *"Yo le maté."* I killed him. When Suarez forgave him, then pronounced, "You now have the blessing of the Lord to preach. You are the Reverend Julio Blanco, of La Iglesia de la Luz y la Paz," Julio felt the wind of the hurricane and the storm on the bay not crushing, wrecking, capsizing, drowning but renewing him body and soul.

42
TUTWILER LESSONS

WHAT I HAVE LEARNED AT TUTWILER
By Vanessa Weinberg Nelson

1.   I have learned there is nothing more painful than your own child watching you come out of lockup, seeing you like a stranger and wailing that he wants Mommy when I am right there. Nothing more hurtful than to have him pulled away from you. Or to see him know me suddenly, yelling out, "Mommy," as he was being carried out the door.

Locked away. That is how I felt more than ever in my life, and when I saw his beautiful little face twisted up in agony, first afraid then reaching out to me, I understood what it was like to be him, in his own head, in the crossed wires inside his own nervous system, locked away.

2.   I have learned that addiction has no limits and sobriety must be an absolute. When I was running from my demons in Mexico, feeling them bearing down on me, I was under an illusion. You cannot hide from yourself. A teenager should know that—a child should know that. How long did I have to take to grow up? There was a horrible

moment when I did face a demon, a real one, who was outside of me, who could have taken my life with the squeeze of a trigger. I had to run for real. At that moment there were monsters outside to fear and flee—my father always told me that—and inside ones to fear and conquer. Here I have been reminded that I know that. We have to be strong inside and out.

3. I am no better than the next person. If I may be more educated, more "accomplished" in some ways, in others I am at a deficit.

4. At the Beacon, before I took off, I had no patience with what I felt was the complaining, the whining, or what I believed was the forced spirituality of the other members in twelve-step. I was struggling with the attainment of humility, but did not realize it. In the program here I have learned to listen. I am no better than these other women. If anything, I look up to them. So many have not had the opportunities I've had. So many have gone much further, starting with far less.

5. I drank some in college and law school but it wasn't until I started seeing Mack and settled down South again that I started swimming in Grey Goose. It was my lubricant, my elixir. It made jokes funnier, laughter brighter, the tedium of my law practice more colorful. The liquor made me feel clever. It helped me feel like I fit it.

6. So I blamed Mack for my drinking because he liked to party, and that means, in the land of Mardi Gras and sunset cruises and happy hour just about any hour, cocktails, drinks with supper, what-can-I-fix-you-to-drink socialness. But the breakup of my marriage was not only Mack's fault. He didn't pour it down my throat. I chose to drink.

7. But drinking brought on the fighting. Then, when our precious boy was born, we blamed each other for how he was—how he should be, not how he could be.

"Maybe if you hadn't been drunk that would have never happened!" I can still hear his cruel accusation. I shrieked at him, accusing him of dropping our newborn too hard in the crib, unable to hold him he was so saturated with Jack Daniel's. There we were, the football star and the Phi Beta Kappa, savaging each other like cornered animals.

"You did nothing to cause this," the doctor assured us.

The circumstances my beloved child found himself in—a year behind developmentally, then two, then three—seemed impossible to understand. The delivery had gone smoothly, he seemed normal to us all. What was left then? Curse God?

"Who knows the answers," my father had said, embracing me while I hugged my baby boy, "for how we turn out as we do?"

8. I resented Mack, his obsession with perfection. He was the handsome one, the buff one, the guy in the letter sweater in high school who was the quarterback and frat president in college, then the golden boy stockbroker. Clients just like being in this presence. What he couldn't stand even when he was a mean drunk was falling short of excellence. Roger excellent? He could not even ride a tricycle without tipping over. But he was the bravest little boy every day.

9. But I did not help my husband understand our son either. Soon I didn't want Mack to even touch him, or me. We came from the same place but our cultures were so different. I realized that but only held that against him. I told him he needed to be gone, that he was the source of my alcohol abuse. The motivator. The enabler.

It was so bizarre that he came to Texas to pick me up at the border. It was his olive branch. On the ten-hour drive home we traveled straight through, talked about everything—but us. When he dropped me home we just waved goodbye.

10. I have learned what I knew already, but had to remember. My father loves despite all. My mother loved despite all. Do I have that capacity of loving? Of giving? And if I do can I do so, selflessly?

"We would give our lives to protect the child, who is ours." I can still hear my father's voice. "Oma and Opa, this is what they did. Margery and I, this is what we did. You and Mack, this is what you must do. Sacrifice. Protect. Nurture. Love."

I was far from here, in my selfish despair in a hotel in Mexico, when I understood how I'd failed to live up to this obligation. I had a memory, so clear I could feel it, Mom, in the last days of her life, weak and confused, barely aware if at all of where she was, who we were. I was reluctant to put my baby boy in her arms—what if she dropped him—but I did and sat right up next to her, keeping a hand on him at first in case I had to catch him. But I was amazed. She was assured, tender, in her loving. Her primal instinct, the ancient matriarchal figure, gently cradling the innocent. Her body knew what to do. Her heart knew what to do. And I realized, seeing her again in that memory—it was more like a vision—what I had not done.

"Sacrifice. Nurture. Protect. Love." Those were my father's words, they were my mother's actions, even in the depths of her decline.

I did not live up to this command.

I will do everything in my power to make up for it. To protect him, nurture him, love him through all.

11. What I have learned here so far is that if I can have a second chance others can too.

12. I have learned that if I help my father do his best to take up for a man who I believe is wrongly accused, I feel like I can make a contribution. It's a start. Now I know what Daddy meant when he would quote the line from the Talmud, "To save one life is to save the world."

43
WHAT JOSIE KNEW

OUT ON THE PIER HANK watched Josie on the railing shifting side to side. First light brought bounty and she would lift up swirling, plummeting, scooping her prey. She was not alone. A blue heron on the opposite rail—a new regular—posed, twitched, ready to dive.

Did they converse, he wondered? "What do you make of this ancient biped shambling toward us?" one asked. "Where is his little boy?" said the other.

"At home with his Mommy," Hank answered. "She's out free and behind me all the way."

Vanessa had decided to quit her firm, intent on helping him however she could. The trial date had not yet been set, but with Hank's determination, and Vanessa on his team, there was much work to do. His sojourn to the pier might be one of his last for a while when he'd have time to linger. He was back to making a difference.

Julio was now the Rev. Julio Blanco, Hank told Vanessa. That a defendant was a man of Christ had a potentially softening effect on a jury. Could a true follower have committed a heinous crime? A smidgen of doubt could prove the difference between a yea and a nay. Unless the pastor was a hypocrite. The defense would note his conversion, but not harp on it.

In the distance Hank saw the regulars, Blue at their heart. Was he preaching?

"What do you say, Josie?"

He caught a glint, an orbed reflection. Did she see all?

He stepped closer. Josie was motionless. Around her dark eye was a corona of yellow plumage, like her namesake in Amsterdam, the half-deranged woman with eyes over-made-up, her cloak like wings rising in the wind along the canals.

Josie rose, pinions beating once, taking her aloft. Catching a thermal she soared.

She did not plunge to the surface but kept on, performing, floating far out, flapping once, banking, back toward shore, acrobatic, continuing above the pines.

He hurried up the pier to the walk and saw her go farther, in the distance sailing as if summoning him. The light was rising in the town and he felt as if he too might fly.

In the gleam of her eye was the world below.

What did she see that late afternoon on the Bay Resort golf course? Pastor Blue seeking revenge on the man he believed had left his son to die in the African wilds? Or Julio robbing Beau then silencing him with a brutal attack? Or an unknown assailant in a long-simmering feud who made Beau pay the ultimate price? Or another golfer stinking of liquor and cash who argued with Beau and when tempers flared found a garden blade at the ready?

Did she look down and catch a glimpse of them all now? Roger burrowing deeper into Mommy's shoulder, Vanessa holding him like she'd never let him go, Julio leading prayers for the lost and condemned, Lupita heartsick about her brother, Hank gazing up at the billowing sky?

The leap of the mullet in a flash of silver, the shimmer of the sun in a cast net of gold, fishermen's voices ascending like heat rising around Blue, the bench with Margery's name waiting for Hank as he returned to the pier and took up his roost—in her acute vision she gathered in all.

Above him Josie reappeared, a cumbersome angel like he'd seen as a boy near Haarlem awaiting the transport to America. She had been white then, not brown, her embrace of the skies even wider, but maybe the years had played tricks with him and they were one in the same. The child who'd beheld her then, and the man she gazed down at now, were also the same.

Josie rounding was a reminder of how he had not yet made the perfect throw, not yet completed his own circle.

PART IV

44
MAY IT PLEASE THE COURT

As District Attorney Bridget O'Donnell, half Hank's age with chestnut hair and a driving voice, stepped forward to give her opening statement in State of Alabama vs. Julio Blanco, Hank felt the familiar electricity before he took the stage. Theater with a consequence, a law professor said of criminal litigation. After a nearly five-year absence from the courtroom he felt the butterflies of a beginner.

In the chair to his left Julio sat ramrod straight, a defendant on his best behavior, to his right Vanessa, in dark blue business suit, attentive with notepad and pen. The gallery was filled with Beau Shepherd's family and supporters to one side, Julio's, including Lupita and Paco and June, on the other, like a bizarre wedding with guests divided by victim and accused. Fairhope Pier regulars mixed in, their fishing duds dressed up with a random necktie or sport coat. Reporters, national and local, filled the back rows, with cameras outside the door. Telemundo and Hispanic News Service joined the array of English-speaking press.

On the bench was the Honorable Judson M. Stone, whose name was his fate, his chiseled face showing little expression. Reelected to the bench six times, he was now over seventy, so unable to run again. Stone's flinty demeanor masked an inquisitive spirit, a passion for nineteenth-century novels and opera. Having known him for forty years, Hank felt they were kindred spirits in the love of story, though Stone had ruled against him as often as not. At least Hank was not a wizened ancient in his eyes.

Two weeks before, the judge had granted Hank's pretrial motion, hashed out with the prosecution, to allow evidence of Julio's immigration status, with application to motive. Vanessa had been surprised that her father had wanted to insert citizenship into a criminal proceeding, rarely allowed in some states, as it had no bearing on culpability. "You've done your homework," he'd answered her. "But it's who Julio is."

O'Donnell forcefully laid out the case: Julio Blanco, a Honduran national then employed by Bay Resort Hotel and Golf Club, stalked Beau Shepherd, a contractor and former state legislator, targeting him on the golf course. That Shepherd was flush with cash—"he'd won large sums playing cards and golf and betting on the game"—made him a mark. That he'd been drinking—"he'd wrestled with alcoholism since surviving a plane crash on a mission trip in Africa"—made him vulnerable. The two men struggled and Julio used his advantage. The weapon used—"plunged beneath Shepherd's collar bone, puncturing his lung"—was a gardening knife in Blanco's possession. A witness, Reinaldo Cardenas, employed by Bay Resort, saw the attack and shouted at Blanco, and immediately called his supervisor. "As Shepherd was collapsing," she said, voice rising, "the young Honduran grabbed the money and ran. His DNA was on Shepherd's shirt, his own blood on the sheath of the knife later found in a ditch. The knife was located close by. A chase followed involving the sheriff, the police, and shore patrol. Blanco would be gone now, escaped to who knows where—a noncitizen, work permit expired, who'd be virtually untraceable—except a storm got hold of him on a skiff on Mobile Bay. Fate? The long reach of justice? Whatever your beliefs we know for sure on thing: the accused"— she pointed to Julio, and Hank saw him wince—"is here with us now, for your judgment.

"The evidence will show that Julio Blanco traveled two thousand miles to arrive here at our home, lived and worked here to reap what he could by whatever means possible, and took that ambition to its vicious max—preying on Beau Shepherd for cold, hard cash, taking him down with a savage knife wound when Shepherd resisted, leaving him to bleed out on the seventeenth green of a golf course in a miserable death. The physical evidence, the witness, the DNA evidence, the motive—it's all there. And Blanco's own words in Spanish, '*Yo le maté,*' 'I killed him,' were uttered in confession to the Reverend Samuel Suarez in a prayer meeting in jail.

"Julio Blanco is guilty of the heinous crime of homicide in the course of a robbery. Julio Blanco of San Pedro Sula, Honduras, like an invader come to sow mayhem right here in our hometown, robbed and stabbed to death Beau Shepherd. Julio Blanco may come from far away, but right here, in our home, he is guilty of capital murder."

As the DA walked back to her table Hank regarded the jury. Vanessa had found what she could through public records of their family origins. Who knows what he might touch on, adding grace notes to his composition? Tony Weaver, of the Mowa Choctaw Band of Indians, was from up the road. The four African Americans were descended from slaves brought from West Africa, Togo, and Barbados, and the lone Asian American from the Vietnamese boat people resettled on the coast. Five of the whites had forebears who'd left Ireland, Norway, Italy, Croatia, and Lithuania, seeking prosperity and freedom, the sixth, a yesteryear Mardi Gras queen, claimed lineage back to the French settlers.

"May it please the court," Hank's voice rang out, fuller and more resonant than he'd felt it in years.

"The defendant today, Julio Blanco, is a young man from Honduras who pursued the American dream, traveling to the United States lawfully, toiling hard, helping his family. On an unexpected evening at a golf course near Mobile Bay, he did what is all too rare in our selfish world—went to, no *ran* to, the aid of a man in critical need. To a golfer who cried out, 'Help me,' because he was profusely bleeding from the chest where he'd already been stabbed. Where a knife from an unknown assailant had gone in so deep that it punctured"—he slapped the lapel of his jacket—"his lung. That golfer, Beau Shepherd, was bleeding out, all alone, 'Help me!' Those were his words.

"Julio Blanco heard that plea.

"If Julio Blanco had done what all too many people might have, he'd have gone on about his business, not wanting to be involved, and would not be here today. If he'd hesitated because of the risk he faced of being picked up and detained or deported, he would not be here today.

"But Julio Blanco, a minister, I might add—he'd later be ordained a Holiness preacher—did unto others . . . you know the rest of the golden rule.

"And now he is standing trial for murder.

"The state's charges against Mr. Blanco turn on a lone witness, Reinaldo Cardenas, who says he observed a homicide on the seventeenth green of the golf course of Bay Resort Hotel. Cardenas, a groundskeeper for Bay Resort, said he was in the sand trap of the sixteenth hole, smoothing out sand for tee-offs the next morning. What Cardenas claims he saw, all the way on the seventeenth hole, was Mr. Blanco stabbing Beau Shepherd in the chest, stealing his money, and running away. The state's prosecution leans heavily on that account. But Cardenas was three hundred feet away in the declivity of the sand trap, the evidence will show, with a thick leafy oak tree between them.

"The district attorney told you that the weapon was a gardening knife used by Mr. Blanco, but the defense will show that the grounds crew had a dozen knives like that at its disposal. Called a *hori-hori*, its name in Japanese, for 'dig-dig,' the knife has a serrated edge and is kept in a sheath. The resort hotel buys that knife by the box. DA O'Donnell reported that Mr. Blanco's DNA was found on Shepherd's shirt. There's no disputing that—because Mr. Blanco, a caring soul, a man of God, tried to help Shepherd as he was dying. The prosecution also said that the pastor confessed to the crime to another inmate. The so-called jailhouse confession was recounted by a man looking for leniency from the prosecution, and who cut a deal with the state.

"Mr. Blanco took money that Shepherd thrust at him, or that he picked up off the ground—and, yes, he ran. He threw the knife and its sheath into a ditch. A poor boy who'd labored for years to help support his mother in Honduras acted out of impulse, and fear. Let me tell you why.

"Born into a mountain village in Honduras, Julio and his family were devastated by Hurricane Mitch in October of 1998, a monster that killed eleven thousand Hondurans. In 1998 Julio was in kindergarten in a one-room schoolhouse. Then the ground gave way and everything around them was destroyed in a massive landslide. Entire villages buried in one terrifying morning.

"They moved to a temporary government shelter in a gym. Soon the shelter sprawled far beyond, jam-packed and squalid, and temporary became one year, two, three. They were relocated to a cinder-block village built by churches and nonprofits. Maybe a mission group from this area even lent a hand.

"Julio's mother, Sra. Inés, widowed, struggled to support her children with a candy kiosk. Gangs staked out their territory and extorted a 'war tax,' a fee to be safe, to be left alone. Julio, getting older, was a target for their recruitment. He stayed loyal to his mother, to his family. To those in need. When they moved again, to San Pedro Sula, the demons followed. Gangs, war tax, danger. Julio's older sister found a job in New Orleans and it was up to him to help out, and protect, his mother, his grandfather, his family.

"There was one other demon, too. Brutal poverty. One in five Hondurans earns less than two dollars a day—two dollars—and Julio's sister, and his mother, soon entreated him, 'Go to the USA.' Chased by the gangs, determined to do more for his mother and family, he did what people from around the world have done for generations—from Scandinavia, the Mediterranean, Eastern Europe, Asia, as Africans brought in bondage—he set out to make a new life. To provide. To help those in need.

"He'd learned gardening from his grandfather, and with a work visa from a resort hotel chain he made his journey. The visa was extended. In 2017 he waited for another extension but heard nothing. He worried it had expired, but he kept on. Working. A model employee. He'd been transferred here, to Bay Resort Hotel and Golf Club, rented a room in a bunkhouse, and visited with his sister, who'd moved from New Orleans. And kept working. Once a week he caught a ride to the Mercado Latino out County Road 181. He sent a MoneyGram to his mother in Honduras. For how much? Two out of every three dollars."

He noticed the slightest nod from juror number four. Making a mental note—she was a grandmother with a tender heart—he scanned to see who else might feel that tug. Impassive faces all.

"Nearly twenty years to the date in 1998 that Hurricane Mitch had destroyed his childhood, on an October evening in 2018 he was engulfed in another catastrophe. 'Help me.' Those words gave rise to a hurricane of their own.

"Mr. Blanco veered from his usual path by a beautiful camellia garden, climbed over the fence, and went to the man clutching his chest with one hand, holding out a fist of bills with the other, as if he needed to pay someone to give him aid.

"'I'll help you,' Mr. Blanco said not with words, but with actions. He approached the bleeding man who reached out and clutched him, pulled him close. It was a death grip. The last person on this earth Beau Shepherd would ever touch was Julio Blanco.

"To die alone is a terrible thing. Beau Shepherd met a cruel fate but alone, in his last moments, he was not. Julio Blanco—the Reverend Julio Blanco—was there."

Juror number eight leaned forward, the schoolteacher of Scottish descent, and Hank felt his momentum.

"But Mr. Blanco was scared. After his humane impulse to help came his reflex action to take what was handed to him from a dying man. Given the fear Mr. Blanco had learned to live with as a man whose only crime was to overstay his visa, he knew the consequences it could have. He lost his head. He ran. Yes, he ran.

"What would happen if he were found next to an admired member of our community bleeding to death on the ground, that blood on the sheath of his own knife? It would be exactly as it was when the Guatemalan greenskeeper pointed his accusing finger at him— he'd be guilty by circumstance. By being in the wrong place at the wrong time.

"And he was—in the wrong place at the wrong time.

"He would no longer be seen as a dependable resort worker but, in the eyes of others, a threatening alien. He'd join the litany of groups who'd come here, as he did, for freedom and protection, for hard work, often judged by their differences. Judged through the lens of being Irish or Italian or West African or Caribbean or Asian or black. Or even white European. Or Native American. Misjudged by somebody as other. An easy target for an accusation, for a criminal charge. For a transgression he did not commit.

"Beyond a reasonable doubt—that's the state's burden of proof in its charge against Mr. Blanco. Beyond a reasonable doubt when a so-called eyewitness observed the scene from a sand trap three hundred feet away. Beyond a reasonable doubt when Mr. Blanco's DNA on Beau Shepherd came about because he held the dying man. Beyond a reasonable doubt when he took money that Shepherd thrust at him and ran because of his immigration status, not because of his guilt at having stabbed a man to death.

"Beyond a reasonable doubt when he was at the wrong place at the wrong time.

"Beyond a reasonable doubt when Julio Blanco took to heart, 'Do unto others'—you know the rest—'as you would have them do unto you.'

"Whoever sent Beau Shepherd to his terrible fate should be reckoned with.

"But it was not Julio Blanco. Don't let him become a victim, too."

45
TE QUIERO

PACO APPEALED TO LUPITA AGAIN, and yet again—"*Cásate conmigo*"—and as she sat next to him through the start of the trial she felt herself opening up to him, and his words, *marry me*, like never before. Seeing Julio at the defendant's table and the lawyers staking out their opposing stories, she felt a shudder move through her. What if Julio were convicted? On her visits to him in jail, with Mr. Hank as his lawyer, she'd sensed that all would turn out well. After his conversion Julio's smile returned, too, and he seemed untroubled by the fate like a machete over his neck threatening to slash down. Prayer had accomplished what Lupita had hoped for. But now she felt the vertigo of uncertainty. The district attorney had told a story that, to those who did not know Julio, might rule the day.

During Mr. Hank's opening statement Paco had reached for her hand and squeezed it, and she'd thought, "All we have is each other."

At her house that night with Paco on the couch sharing Imperial beer she rubbed her hand up his arm to his shoulder and lingered there. "Tell me," she said, "what is this?"

He shrugged. What?

"Your tattoo."

"I had surgery. In Houston."

"It's still there. A whisper."

She moved her hand and he clutched his own shoulder and cursed the image that ghosted still, the past pressing forward.

"You were in a gang," she said. "You want me to marry you but you can't tell me?"

"I left it."

"They look for you wherever you are, you know that. Julio, in jail. Mama, in San Pedro. They know everyone, everywhere."

"I killed a man," he said. "Julio knows."

She felt a sense of vertigo, and she imagined it was Paco who'd felled the golfer, letting Julio take the rap—his shift at the Fish House didn't start until an hour after the time of the homicide—but weren't they brothers? Cain and Abel, Mama had said, is like us at war with each other, as she'd looked sorrowfully out the window one morning at a neighbor's son shot down by rivals. What did even brothers mean anymore?

She pushed Paco away.

"Listen," he implored.

When he was twelve years old, he told her, a few years out of the hurricane camp and in the cinder-block village, Paco's brother Evelio had been in a fight with another boy, Alejandro. The next day, Alejandro's uncle showed up with him to confront Evelio. When Evelio got home with a gash on his head a neighbor swore revenge on Evelio's behalf. That neighbor was "un Escorpión." Three Scorpions cornered the uncle one night as he was walking with Alejandro outside of a bodega. They left Alejandro alone—but gutted the uncle. The police called the crime "unsolved."

After what the Scorpions did for him, Evelio joined the gang. Looking up to his big brother, Paco soon joined, too. The black and red scorpion was tattooed on his arm.

To so many, he said, they were heroes. Why?

"Because of the protection we afforded to the weak, the sick, the elderly. We were not *criminales,* he said, but *protectores.* Protectors.

"But there was a boy, Pablo, who was different than other boys," he went on. "A friend of Julio's. And they made fun of Pablo, exaggerating his walk, mincing behind him like silly girls.

"'Leave me alone,'" Pablo said.

"'*Mariposa,*' they called him." Butterfly. Queer.

"Julio defended Pablo. The two of them, close friends, were smoking cigarettes on a bench behind the school, and two Scorpion gang members came up on them and Julio said, 'Go away,' but they came closer. Pablo said, 'I'll leave. It's me they don't like.'"

"'Don't move!' Julio said, but Pablo began to run and the Scorpions chased him, caught him. "*Horrible.*" Paco slapped his hand against the top of his chest. Where the knife entered, he said. Collapsing his lungs. To die like that is to gasp for air like a fish on the pier, in agony. Julio could do nothing.

The gang watched Julio after that, taunted him at school, mocked him.

"Late one night as a storm was rising, Julio was walking home from church, alone, holding a sheet of newspaper over his head as the rain began to splatter. From a doorway two Scorpions jumped him, one pulling him down, the other grabbing and tugging down his pants.

"I was just behind. I saw the knife in the Scorpion's hand and I was a Scorpion, too, yes, but I ran to help Julio. I grabbed the knife and sunk it into the Scorpion's gut. He was dead in minutes.

"I had saved Julio, my friend and brother, but I had killed another Scorpion, my gang brother. I was a walking dead man now. I left that night. But my mama. My mama!" he said.

The bullet in Paz's neck, Lupita's mother running to her in the street, cradling her head, the men with their gang tattoos and guns and knives freely roaming, terrorizing, following them even here, into a trailer in rural Alabama.

"Oh, Paco, *mi amor*."

"*Te quiero, te necesito.*" That he told her he loved her, needed her, and implored now, "*Cásate conmigo,*" turned her heart completely over.

"*Sí, sí está claro. Estaremos juntos.*" Yes, we will be together. "*Siempre.*"

"Always," Paco said in English.

The next morning before the trial resumed, they filled out an Alabama marriage certificate, had it notarized and filed it with probate, and asked Mr. Hank to pass on the news to Julio. In the front row of the gallery as the proceedings began, Lupita and Paco watched as Julio entered flanked by guards, looked right at them pressing his hands together in prayer, giving a nod and beatific smile before taking his chair, a blessing for Lupita greater than all the angels in heaven.

46
THE WAY BACK

THAT MACK, GENTLER AND MORE attentive, was taking care of Roger
as Vanessa went to court, and that Hank encouraged her to take part
in that day's cross-exam, made her feel as though she were slipping
into her old self again: the Vanessa who'd finished a day of classes
at NYU and strolled unencumbered through Greenwich Village, the
sense of possibility all around; the young woman who'd met a cute
investor jock down South and played with him for fun, then returned
to the gravitas of studies and probing dialogues with friends at East
Village bars; the law grad, after a stint with a public defender up North,
who'd taken a chance by moving back South with a regional firm. She
and Mack had been drunk when he proposed—Stoli on the rocks for
her, Maker's Mark neat, for him—and she wondered if she'd started
becoming someone else then. With all eyes on her in court, though,
she felt the buoyancy of the younger Vanessa who'd returned home
for romance and work, thinking to give the Deep South one more try.
Could she maintain that sense of possibility this go-round?

She'd cross-examined the coroner, pressing him to be definitive
that the wound in the victim's upper chest was consistent with the
blade of a garden knife.

"How long before Shepherd would have expired after the blow?"

"It depends on the angle of the blow, the depth."

"By your estimation?" she asked.

"Five to ten minutes, tops. In the victim's case he suffered a pneumothorax, which happens when air enters the space between the rib cage and one of the lungs. The air pushes on part or all of the lung, causing it to collapse. At the same time blood would gush from the wound."

"So someone who's suffered a stab wound in this way could still be standing, talking, after several minutes?"

"Objection. Speculation."

"Overruled."

"The lack of oxygen would create an extreme lightheadedness, thus confusion. But, yes, the person who'd sustained the blow could be on his feet still, and communicating—or trying to communicate—until he lost consciousness, fell and died."

"It's possible, then, that an assailant could have delivered the blow to Shepherd's chest and the defendant"—while looking at the coroner she pointed behind her to Julio, a tactic Hank sometimes used—"could have come upon him ten minutes later, by then gasping for breath, delirious."

"Objection! Leading the witness."

"Sustained," Judge Stone said.

She knew the question would bring an objection from the DA and be sustained, but as Hank had taught her, "you've planted a seed in the jury's mind."

Why she'd avoided the courtroom for banking law, the dull marshalling of numbers from money men who left her dazed with their prattle, eluded her now. The fates of financial institutions did not compel her like this contest of who was guilty, who not, of a terrifying crime. She had a flickering image of the gun held on her in the cantina, how long she felt its barrel bore into her, the target on her back. She'd felt it all the way to the border, and beyond.

The prosecution had laid out the scenario of armed robbery ending in a stabbing death. Not manslaughter but capital murder—that's what they were pressing. He'd set out that evening to steal from Beau Shepherd, weapon in hand, the prosecution had said, "knowing how the men gambled and drank. You'll hear testimony to that effect. He knew who was vulnerable. Why do so in plain view of anyone on an open fairway, on a green heightened by its being set up on a rise? The seventeenth green, Mr. Blanco knew well, was tucked away behind the grandeur of the oaks, a dogleg of a fairway nearly hidden in the shadows of late day."

In tag team with her father she'd asked the detective who'd worked the case how much money had been found still in Shepherd's billfold. She'd let the answer—"two hundred and six dollars, and two hundred and eighty in small bills in his pocket"—stand on its own. Julio had only run with a bloodstained half of that amount.

Hank told her, during break, that he sensed they were not yet winning the jury, though. "We haven't shaken their confidence in O'Donnell's story. They fear this young man too, imagining being preyed upon by Mexican hordes, Honduras be damned, it's all the same to them. Julio's the embodiment of the political mythology. You understand what that means. It goes far beyond an Alabama courtroom."

But what if Julio had, of his own volition, plunged that weapon into Beau Shepherd's chest? The nagging from her younger years came back to her—the game of criminal defense could be quickening, even stirring as she felt now, but morally suspect, too. Could she feel that they were helping to get off a man who'd done exactly what the prosecution—with its array of experts—had argued?

Back in her house in the evening, Mack was waiting for her. He'd spent the day with Roger, fed him dinner, and put him to bed. They agreed the house they'd shared provided more stability for Roger than Mack's apartment. In a rush she excitedly told him about the day.

"I've never seen you this fired up before," he said. "It's"—he reached out and brushed his finger over her cheek, and she did not pull back—"a different you."

"I sort of feel that about you, too," she said. Her own words surprised her.

She told him how alive she felt, "how I've needed this urgency, this sense of consequence. But then I wonder what if we're playing a game to win at all cost, but our defendant is the one."

"I thought you were all in with Hank."

"What's that supposed to mean?"

"He's all in with Julio. You're on the team."

"Nobody could be more loyal."

"Than who, you?"

She drew back. "It's always that, isn't it?"

"Just be supportive, don't question."

"I supported us."

"Is that what we're talking about?"

"I moved back here for you."

"You wanted to come home!"

"I *drank* because of you."

"Well, that's accepting responsibility for your actions, for sure."

She hesitated. "OK. Because of *us*."

"Well"—his tone softened—"that's not who you are now."

She fell silent. She felt the old ache up through her chest, throat, the vodka at her lips.

"You're becoming a damn fine criminal defense lawyer," he said.

"With much to learn."

"Come here."

In his arms she was in her apartment again in the East Village with the smell of curry curling in the window. She'd made her decision even then that this Southern quarterback with the strong shoulders, the tender eyes, the love of daiquiris and sunset on the bay, was somehow who she'd end up with. Only the bottle with its demons inside had come between them. But now they had both put it away.

"I want us to make a life together again," Mack said. "Our little family."

"Oh, wow. Mack, I've had a big day. And the next one will start . . ." She looked up at the clock.

"I'll be here for Roger first thing," he said.

"Thank you," she said, nearly inviting him to stay but ushering him out the door.

47
THE UNEXPECTED WORLD

THE WORLD OUTSIDE OF JAIL was illuminated with a kind of majesty. No matter, in his jail blues, he was flanked by cops, transported in a secure van to the courthouse, then led up a freight elevator in the back. He caught just a glimpse of strangers on the sidewalk, the oak trees in the square in their autumnal changes, the red brick of the cathedral, the couple picnicking in the green space near the courthouse, the river curling just at the edge of town with a coal barge pushed in by tugs—God's glory.

Even the face of the judge—hewn from granite—and the reddish brown hair of the prosecutor falling in waves over her blue suit, seemed lit by the divine. The story that spooled out about him seemed unreal, though, like the account in the newspaper, another Julio concealed in the late-day shadows, emerging with garden knife in hand, stalking the unwitting golfer whose only sin was too much bourbon and wagering and being alone and vulnerable at the witching hour. With Shepherd's money in his clutch, the dirt of Alabama on his shoes and the desperation of Honduras in his heart, he'd fled.

The prosecutor had the owner of the Mercado Latino tally up the money Julio had sent by wire to his mother in San Pedro, an amount substantially more than the wages Julio earned at the resort, calling into question his honesty. Was he a good son or a thief?

Hank showed that some of Julio's funds to his mother were amplified by contributions from his friend, Paco—Paco had made sworn testimony to that effect—after his own mother had been gunned down, elaborating on the street violence until Judge Stone directed him to stay within the scope of the cross-exam. Paco had wired funds to Sra. Inés on his own, Hank was able to demonstrate, after Julio was incarcerated.

The Guatemalan coworker next on the stand, Reinaldo Cardenas, with the use of a translator, told how he'd just arrived at the sixteenth hole, beginning to rake smooth the sand trap—part of his daily routine—when he heard a shout and looked up to see a golfer on the seventeenth green clutching the pin, blocked by another man in front of him. The two men began to struggle. He watched as the golfer fell to the ground and the second man bent down, then stood and, as Cardenas yelled out, started running away.

"What did you do at that point?" O'Donnell asked.

"I called my supervisor to tell him what I witnessed. He said to stay where I was, that security was on its way."

"We have a record of Cardenas's cell phone calls entered into evidence," the DA told the judge. "Exhibit D."

An image of the call log appeared on a large screen.

"Do you see the number that you called?"

"Yes." He repeated the number that was his supervisor's.

"And the time?"

"Five thirty-six."

"Your Honor," O'Donnell said to Judge Stone, "I have submitted documentation from NOAA, the federal weather agency, showing the time for sunset. I would ask that the court take judicial notice that the sunset that day was 6:08 p.m."

"That fact has been noted," Stone said, addressing the jury, "and must be accepted as true."

Julio knew that Cardenas had claimed he was the assailant, but his words first in Spanish, then translated to English, continued to reverberate in the courtroom. Cardenas's tone was shocked, even outraged, and Julio wondered if the Guatemalan had it out for him, hoping to take focus off his own border violations. He recalled how they'd chatted personably about tropical weather and its impact on the gardens and their families back home.

As Mr. Hank was standing now to do the cross-exam, Julio glanced behind him—where was Lupita?—and saw the family of the victim, Shepherd's sunken-down wife patting at the tears running beneath her dark glasses, Shepherd's children about his own age, and the scornful looks of their friends. Other observers, farther back, scribbled on notepads, newspaper jackals like the one who'd made him and Mr. Hank the target of hate mail.

A shudder went through him. Had Lupita given up on his cause?

He turned back to the front when he heard her voice in Spanish—why was she raising it in the courtroom?—and another, familiar but impossible, and knew he was imagining now. His mother's house, outside of San Pedro, the sound of her voice, close, urging him, insisting, he could not stay here any longer, that he was a marked man, that now was the time to go.

Judge Stone was banging his gavel and calling for order and Lupita was imploring, *"Silencio Mamá, por favor silencio,"* and Mr. Hank asked to approach the bench and conferred with the DA and judge who granted a half-hour recess. As Julio was being led out for the break, he twisted around to see his mother, as if standing in the doorway in San Pedro Sula, reach out to him, look heavenward in prayer, then press her hands against her heart.

48
YOU FOUND ME

JUNE WAS BEHIND SRA. INÉS's arrival, Hank found out during the recess. She'd gotten her name and contact from Vanessa and, raising funds at church, paid for her tourist visa and plane ticket. They'd only made Lupita aware the day before, knowing she would protest, that the trip would be too burdensome, too emotional, for her mother.

Hank feared it might be.

After court was back in session Hank took up the cross-exam of Reinaldo Cardenas, pressing him on his line of sight from the sand trap—in the declivity, past a giant oak, through the late-day shadows—challenging his ability to discern action so far away.

"You said that the golfer, Beau Shepherd, was blocked by this figure who approached and struggled with him. Let me get a clear picture of where everyone was standing."

He dramatized as he spoke, turning away from the witness and pretending to reach out to an invisible man in front of him. He turned back. "Is that the correct view you had?"

"I knew it was Julio," Cardenas said.

"Because you saw his face?"

"I've worked with him. I know him."

"You testified that 'they struggled.'"

"Yes."

"Then you could see his hands?"

"Yes."

"But his back was to you?"

"He turned."

"Oh, he turned? Like this?" He rotated, his profile to Cardenas. "A little to the side?"

"Sort of."

"Yes?"

"I don't recall."

"But you say you could see that he had stabbed Shepherd?"

"Yes."

To each question—"Robbed Shepherd?" "Fought Shepherd?"—Cardenas answered yes.

"But you are unsure how he was standing?"

"He was standing so I could see him."

"You do not know exactly?"

"I do not remember."

"But you remember everything else?"

"Yes!"

"Do you know how long Shepherd had been there?"

"No."

"Bleeding and crying out?"

"No."

Hank pressed on. "Asking for help?"

"No."

"Did the tree at the edge of the sand trap obscure your view?"

He could tell when a witness was agitated, getting tangled up, annoyed.

"He is the murderer!" Cardenas exclaimed.

"*¡Ay, que no!*" said Sra. Inés.

Judge Stone banged his gavel. "Silence in the gallery."

"*Él no hizo nada mala.*"

That Sra. Inés yelled out, "He did nothing wrong" caused the judge to smack the gavel again and ask, "Please escort this woman from the courtroom," but Lupita was already getting her to stand and starting to usher her out when Hank said, "That is all, Your Honor," and court was adjourned until Monday.

He had no control over the press of cameras around the woman as they spilled out onto the front steps. With Lupita translating, Sra. Inés told how the gangs had terrorized her neighborhood, extorted money from her, threatened to kill Julio. She said she loved her home country, even though a hurricane, and refugee camp, and violence on the street, had made it a place so many wanted to flee.

"*Yo pido que mi país vuelva a ser un lugar de belleza y paz y comunidades fuertes, con un futuro para los niños*" and when Lupita translated that her mother said, "I pray that my country will be a place again of beauty and peace and strong communities, with a future for our children," Hank thought of the old men and women in the synagogue like him who'd lost who they loved, what they loved, in Poland and Romania and Czechoslovakia and Germany and France and Holland. He was solo now, the only one in his community who remembered still.

He felt a sense of admiration for Sra. Inés, for Julio, Lupita, Paco. They had turned to him for succor, but they were the resourceful ones. He saw a woman at the edge of the press gaggle who looked familiar: the dark, deep-set eyes, the kindness in her look.

She was like his own mother, returning again.

What was it about June that brought back images of his childhood? That her own father had been Dutch?

She would be there, yes, listening in on what Julio's mother had to tell, and doing what she could to help. She would understand.

"Did I do the right thing?" June asked as she approached him. "Bringing Julio's mother here like this?"

He nodded. "Yes. You're an amazing lady."

"Then you'll come over for a glass of wine when this is all done and we can relax together."

49
GOOD CATCH

THE WAVES ROLLED UP ON the beach and grabbed Roger's feet and when they did he yelped, Mommy laughing, Daddy, too, the three of them "a little family," Mommy said, words he understood because he was little and his family was Gradee and Lupe but they were not here and Mommy was and Daddy, too, lifting him high in the air and turning him, his green windbreaker billowing so he felt like Daddy was the boat and he was the sail.

From way up he could see the Gulf of Mexico with its crests like Gradee's white hair in the wind, it made Roger laugh, and the birds that laughed called gulls and Gradee's favorite, the pelicans, like he could ride one right now, and Mommy said, "How would you like it if Daddy came to live with us again?" and Roger said, "Gradee," and Mommy said, "Gradee can visit every day," and he said, "Lupe," and said, "Lupe will be with us too, just like now, but she is married to Paco and one day they'll have a little baby of their own."

Daddy set him down now, his feet squishing in the sand, and said, "I've got a present for you!" He reached into a bag and pulled out a brown oval ball with stitching on the top and said, "It's football season."

"Oh, Mack," Mommy said.

And Daddy said, "He's going long!" and held the ball up and stepped back and back again as the waves lapped Roger's feet. "He's in the clear!" Daddy said and lifted the spinning football up gently into the air, arcing it toward Roger, who watched it and laughed and held out his arms and, *plop*, it fell into them and stayed there, like a cozy brown puppy, and Daddy was cheering, "touchdown, touchdown! Roger's the star!"

50
ROUNDUP

WORD CAME SATURDAY EVENING WHEN Paco was on his shift at
the Fish House and Lupita was with her mother, watching TV at
her house. The 6 p.m. news opened with the headline, "Feds Grab
Illegals," and video of agents in blue "ICE police" jackets raiding
a construction site, a chicken processing plant, local restaurants.
The camera followed one officer entering the back door of the Fish
House and workers running out into the night.

"Answer me, Paco," Lupita said, calling his number, getting his
voicemail, texting him to no response, her phone lighting up from
a Salvadoran friend whose husband was taken into custody from a
furniture warehouse, handcuffed with zip ties, then from Vanessa
who was with Roger and Mack at a beach café where she witnessed
officers hustle workers out a kitchen door.

Her phone rang again: Mr. Hank.

"They took Paco," she said.

"Vanessa told me. If someone comes to your door asking to see
you do not even answer."

"They took Paco," she repeated in a daze.

"A show for the politicians," Hank said. "We'll get him an immigration lawyer. The best."

She peered out the window, imagining a vehicle roaring up, the law approaching like when they'd come looking for Julio.

A rap came at the door and Lupita, keeping her mother back, went to the door, holding her breath in silence.

"Lupita . . ."

"*¡Imposible!*"

When she realized Mr. Hank was still on the phone she fabricated, "It's a neighbor, it's OK," and opened it to Paco who dashed in.

He'd just left the Fish House kitchen, he told her, to go to a refrigerated unit out back to haul in more shrimp when he heard the voices of the ICE agents. He kept low, waiting them out, but then they were outside too, their flashlight beams ricocheting around the woods.

A voice he knew had called out to him, the restaurant manager saying, "Paco Jimenez, are you out there? We need you back in here," but he'd crouched low, like Julio had done in this same patch of scrub, until the van started to roll away, the faces of two coworkers from Honduras at the back window as it sped away beneath the street light.

"Stay here," Inés said to Paco, "the lawyer will protect you."

"I can't go back."

"They'll send him back," Lupita told her mother.

"Look," Paco said.

From his pocket he slipped a fake US passport, opened it to show his photo and the name, Myron Cortez, born in Minneapolis, Minnesota.

It was good for seven years.

"This man, Cortez, drowned in the sea," he said. "Swimming here."

"Is this real?" asked Lupita.

"I paid three hundred dollars."

"You can't."

"I have to go."

"Where?"

"I'll send for you."

Lupita's whole body shook as she went into the kitchen and laid bread and ham and cheese into a sack then into her bedroom to pack him clothes and heard Mama say, "I'm stepping outside," as Paco came in the bedroom behind her and shut the door.

He began to cover her with kisses, and though they had been intimate on the night she'd said "yes, I'll marry," she had been exhausted then, preoccupied with the images of the prosecutor assailing her brother and the coroner's grim report and the golfer with blood saturating his shirt and images of Paco protecting Julio by stabbing the gang member with a knife like the golfer had been stabbed. Was that why Paco was fleeing? Could he have done this crime? Why couldn't she block out that notion? But she wasn't thinking any of that now as he enveloped her this time.

There were only the two of them in a house trailer alongside an Alabama field and as they made love she had an uncanny sense that a child was taking root inside, her native born, and knew she would stay put no matter what befell her until Paco called for her to join him in their new life.

Then he was gone into the night and Inés was back inside, and they jumped when a rock smashed the roof and cried out when a cherry bomb exploded with a flash, rattling the tin drum of their habitation, sweat pouring off them in fear, but then the night was still and together they were strong.

51

PLEA

As the new week began, the state put on Samuel Suarez, who testified Julio confessed to him, before his ordination, *"Yo le maté,"* I killed him.

Hank had asked Vanessa to do the cross-exam. He'd always felt she had the grit of a defense attorney; he was there to guide her as needed.

She made clear that Suarez was desperate for favors from the state. When she asked him, "Isn't it true you were arrested and charged with being an accomplice to an armed robbery?"

"Yes, but . . ."

"Just answer the question," Judge Stone directed.

"Yes."

"Was this statement you've reported made during a prayer meeting in jail?"

"Yes."

"A time of high emotion?"

"A time of confession. Yes."

"Were you hoping for leniency from the state for reporting what you claim was Mr. Blanco's statement to you in that prayer circle?"

"No!"

"Did the state offer to resolve your case if you testified against Mr. Blanco?"

"They talked about it, but that's not why."

After her cross-exam, and the prosecution rested, O'Donnell offered a plea deal: twenty years on lesser charges with the chance for early parole. When Hank explained it to Julio, he added that, upon his release, the feds would surely deport him. "I'll be dead but you'll be in your forties," Hank said. "You'd still have a lot of years ahead of you. Otherwise? A conviction could mean life in prison, or, worse yet, death row."

If the proceedings played out, which way would the verdict go? Why didn't Hank yet know?

He'd begun to sense an engagement by the jury, a sense of connection to Julio's plight. He'd spent a lifetime knowing that facts mattered, but ordinary folks in the jury box still heard what they wanted. All he needed was one to resist the pack, and surely that's what it could be—the lone holdout making all the difference in the mob.

The prosecution had a murder weapon, blood, DNA, a coroner's report, a suspect in flight, a motive of robbery. And an atmosphere of anxiety about all the outsiders like Julio Blanco in their midst.

He believed passionately in the jury system, the better angels that would prevail in ordinary folks called to civic duty. Even so, they were bathed in the culture of the day. Innocent until proven guilty? He feared it was sometimes the inverse equation.

That the jury's decision could go either way flummoxed and pained him. Jury verdicts were not meant to be a guessing game—he was right nearly always as to the outcome. He could feel it in his *kishkes*, "in your guts," he had translated the Yiddish for Vanessa in her youth.

"I want to tell my story," Julio said.

"Absolutely not."

"I want to tell my story," Julio repeated.

"There's a big risk," Hank explained.

But he believed he truly had an innocent on his side—Julio had little of a murderer's heat about him, he was a gentle soul deep down, Jesus his rock and redeemer. Would his recounting his own story create that iota of doubt?

He knew how Julio's recitation would go: the fall afternoon heading home from work, the garden blade sheathed on his belt, the cry of the golfer, the rush to give him succor, the blood pouring from Shepherd, the money on the ground, the dying man's embrace, the fear that set Julio running, the blood on his own shirt and seeping into his pockets, throwing the blood-stained knife into the bushes, hiding out until drowning in the storm only to be saved for this trial, this test.

And he imagined the district attorney, in her cross-exam, turning the story upside down to show motive, concealing the evidence, evading capture.

When Judge Stone called the lawyers into his chambers, he asked them to take a seat, produced an envelope, and said it had come to him by registered mail at the courthouse. "What has transpired is a highly unusual occurrence," he said.

"My clerk, Ms. Rosemary Young, took possession of it and, it may or may not have relevance to the Julio Blanco case but we did a quick perusal to ascertain it was not a random crackpot. There is a letter enclosed from an attorney in New Orleans with a sworn statement from two college students who say they were playing golf at Bay Resort the day of the homicide and took a photograph and posted it on Instagram with a man they identify as the defendant.

"The letter states the students recognized the defendant from a newspaper account of the trial and contacted a local attorney. Needless to say, I have no opinion as to authenticity or veracity. I'm passing this on."

Stone set out the picture. Hank saw Julio, in the skewed angle of a selfie, leaning into a golf cart next to the two students, holding up his fingers in the "V" of a peace sign.

Julio had said nothing of this encounter. Hank felt ire begin to rise up through him. How could he defend a client effectively who did not tell him the whole story?

In the corner of the image were numbers. A time stamp: 5:24 p.m.

Hank felt his emotion shift the other way now, a lightness taking him over.

It had been 5:36 when Cardenas called his supervisor to report Julio in a death struggle with the golfer.

If it had taken Shepherd twelve minutes to bleed out, there was evidence, Hank believed, to corroborate Julio's story he was elsewhere when the stabbing took place.

52
A SPECIAL HOME

BEFORE AN EXPERT ON DIGITAL technology was called in, a personnel officer of the Bay Resort took the stand, with Vanessa questioning, to testify about Julio's record as an employee.

"Has Mr. Blanco ever been written up with any work violation, or called in on any personnel matter?"

"No."

"How would you describe Mr. Blanco as an employee?"

"A model employee."

"Thank you."

"But we thought he had his paperwork when he arrived from one of our other properties."

"Thank you, that is all," said Vanessa.

"The murder has been a terrible blight on our club. It's not who we are!"

Judge Stone interceded. "Sir, that will be all. Thank you."

At day's end, after the trial wound through the first witnesses for the defense, Vanessa walked out with Hank, next to them Lupita and Sra. Inés, arms locked like schoolgirls traversing a strange land.

She drove home, delighted to arrive where Mack and Roger would welcome her, dinner on the stove—Mack had returned to his culinary ways—an evening of domestic tranquility awaiting. Each evening when Mack left to go back to his place she felt closer to the life they'd started before all fell apart.

Their romance had coursed from her dorm in Poughkeepsie, to her East Village apartment in New York, to the room in her parents' house back south, to this home she made with Mack and Roger until it blew apart. Between the courthouse and reaching her front door she made a decision: I want my life restored.

She picked up the mail at her front walk, among the catalogs one with the faces of smiling children, a rolling lawn, and the words, in alphabet blocks: "Green Bright: A Special Place."

"Damn, how do they find us?" she said, cursing the direct mail service that located her address as one with a child with special needs. Did the pediatrician sell addresses of patients? She could sue the bastard for that.

She entered and dropped the mail on the counter and immediately felt Roger's big, warm hug, Mack just behind them.

"You're in a good mood!" he said.

"We had a better day. A wing and a prayer."

"Nice for a change. Bubbly?"

"Bubblyyy," Roger said, as Mack poured three flutes of sparkling apple cider.

"Mack?"

"Hmm, babe?"

"I think we can make it."

She'd set the mail on the counter and put her arms around him now. "I've been selfish," she said. "I've been wrong. It's taken me thirty-five years to know who I am, what I want. And that's you, that's us, our little family."

She felt him shift in her arms, a subtle turn, like this exchange was not the end point of a long battle between them but a pause, a regrouping. How could it be? My anxiety, she thought. My lack of faith in the heart.

When he said, "Look, Roger," she heard his tone, though, bright and suggestive, and he was pulling away from her, on to the next objective.

He reached to the countertop and picked up the Green Bright brochure. "Look at these children, Rog. Happy."

"Happy," Roger said.

"Did you ask for this?" Vanessa asked.

"You know Jasper at my office? He's got a kid who's a bit like Roger. He was asking why I was taking time off, then we started talking about what he and Jen, his wife, went through."

"This is a residential school, Mack. Are you serious? Our boy is five." She tried to contain the alarm in her voice.

"Our boy, yes, he is. Our boy"—he leaned down and kissed Roger's cheek—"will become a fine teen, a young man. I'm so proud of you, Roger."

She detected his forced tone.

"Lupita will be back after the trial, and I'm looking into a morning program for him."

"You and I don't have a minute for ourselves," Mack said. "To be us."

She was silent.

"This will be good for us, Vanessa. Good for Roger. Jasper said . . ."

"I'm not sending my son to a residential facility."

"We'll go see him all the time."

"Never."

"A fresh start."

"Never ever *ever*."

"Like new."

"We're a family. Us three. Together."

"He needs this," he said, clutching the brochure and handing it toward her. "We need this."

"No fucking way." She slapped his hand away.

"I don't exist when Roger's around. That's always been our problem."

"Get out."

And when he did she was ready, finally, she felt in how she trembled with anger and expectation, to start her life anew.

53

THAT FALL AFTERNOON

To SEE THE PHOTOGRAPH WITH the college boys projected large for the jury was, for Julio, to walk home again that fall afternoon. As Vanessa interrogated a professor of digital communications about the Instagram posting—"There is no indication that the image has been doctored," the expert witness analyzed—Julio felt the cool air on his face after a day of hauling dirt, edging walkways, digging out weeds with his garden knife. The young golfers had approached him to smoke a joint and he had complied. The flavor of the marijuana curling into his throat—it came back to him as he watched the DA do her cross-exam, getting the witness to acknowledge a "small margin of error" in determining if a digital image was altered. The time stamp on the picture was indisputable, though. It was twelve minutes before Cardenas had called to report him stabbing Beau Shepherd to death.

How long had the banshee of Hurricane Mitch taken to collapse his classroom, wreck his house, send the mountainside hurtling downward? Twelve minutes at its furious height? Abuelo had given him a watch when he started school and he treasured it, following the needle sweeping seconds and the skinny hand marking minutes and the fat hand galumphing the hours like a tortoise slow but sure. When Mitch arrived, the watch kept steady as the bell gonged and the wind revved and the walls became Abuelo's playing cards collapsing in a heap. He tried to focus on the *tick-tick* of time on his wrist, knowing all would be well.

But his arms were soon flailing and hands thrusting and the time shook like the earth giving way, sheep bleating donkeys braying cows lowing roosters crowing as blackness fell and rays of light whipped by the wind brought dawn over and again before midnight once more, and the sliding earth and flooding skies broke the moving hands of the watch and when he looked again, at the bottom of a ravine, only twelve minutes had passed. When the storm moved on it was tranquil again, but the hands had no life. In that snatch of time the world had changed. Then a streak of red from a thicket—a scarlet bird rising, soaring—set it in motion again. Hadn't he seen a slash of red in the woods after leaving the students with their swagger, their pot? It was not a bird, though, he recalled of the flash of color now.

When he took the witness stand and Mr. Hank stood before him he began the chronicle of that day, how he'd left Honduras after the hurricane, after the gangs, come to America to work, arrived in Alabama with the grounds crew, sent his mother money, overstayed his papers, could not return out of fear, went to work that fall day like any other, met the college boys who offered him marijuana, posed with them for the selfie, started on his way again when he heard, "Help me" from the fairway, then added what he had never said before: *"Lo vi en los arboles, un color rojo, pero no fue un pájaro, yo creo fue un hombre,"* and the translator said, "I saw in the trees the color red but it wasn't a bird, I think it was a man."

Astonishment—it was the expression on Mr. Hank's face. The lawyer started coughing.

Julio had been told that he was not to introduce any new material in his testimony, that it was a recitation of what he'd told already. And certainly no testimony that was misleading or false.

But now he saw the red color in a flash, like an Instagram posting, a man's visor.

"Judge," Hank said, "may I have a glass of water?"

The judge nodded. Hank took a sip.

"You thought," Hank's voice asked tentatively, "you saw someone?"

"Yes."

"Did you see his face?"

"No."

"You *imagined* you saw someone?"

"Objection! Counsel is leading the witness."

"I remember I saw someone."

The judge instructed, "Mr. Blanco, please do not answer unless a question has been asked. The jury will disregard Mr. Blanco's last statement."

He waited for Mr. Hank to dig further, ask again, let him tell what he remembered seeing, but Abuelo moved the story forward, putting Julio back on the path to the seventeenth hole.

"Could you describe the golfer when you came close to him?"

"He was bleeding, in the chest, his shirt was drenched with blood, he was beginning to sag down, 'Help me,' he said. He held out the money to me."

"He held the money out to you?"

"Yes."

"Did you take the money any other way?"

"I picked some up off the ground, but only after he handed a fist of money to me."

Julio noted the same expression as before—uncertainty, bafflement. He had never told the story in quite this way.

"What happened then?"

"The dying man said, 'Run.'"

Julio could hear gasps in the courtroom, sensed jury members leaning forward, as if to hear more clearly.

"Could you repeat that, please?"

"*Corre.*" The translator repeated: "Run."

"Had you ever had any exchanges with the golfer, Beau Shepherd, before?"

"No."

"So he was a complete stranger to you?"

"Objection, the witness has already answered the question."

"Let the witness proceed," said Judge Stone.

"I worked a party at his house once."

The silence that came over the courtroom was like the moment after the hurricane had passed. His mother's eyes were mournful, already grieving for her son. Lupita gazed upward like he was an icon in her church.

Mr. Hank started a question, hesitated, began again: "What do you mean you worked a party?" There was no going back, Julio could tell. He was off script, and Mr. Hank had no control.

"I served drinks, food, cleaned up."

"Did Beau Shepherd personally hire you?"

"No."

"Who did?"

"Someone who worked for him. I don't know his name."

"Did you meet Beau Shepherd?"

"I only saw him, at the party, around a lot of people."

"How much did you get paid?"

"I never got paid. He owed me money."

Julio had given the prosecution a motive, he realized it now. A revenge killing. Like the Scorpions, an eye for an eye.

"Mr. Blanco," Hank began, and he could sense himself leaping into the void, too. "Did you know the golfer you found on the seventeenth green was the man you had seen at the party?"

"Only now."

"What do you mean?"

"I see it now. Like the man with the red hat."

"Were you in a state of shock that afternoon?"

"Objection! Mental operation."

"Sustained."

"Let me return to the statement you've made about Beau Shepherd's telling you, 'Run.' This is new testimony. Are you remembering this only now?"

"No."

"But you are just telling the court this now?"

"I thought it was a voice in my head."

He watched as Hank paced a moment, figuring.

"But now you believe he spoke it aloud? Run?"

"Yes."

"Why do you believe he told you to run?"

"Because he was worried for my safety. That I might be next. The next victim."

"You were frightened?"

"Yes. I was scared all around. For what happened to the golfer. For what would happen to me if I was arrested."

"What would happen?"

"This. Today. Here I am."

By the time Bridget O'Donnell came at him, catching him up crossways for changing his account, contradicting earlier statements, speaking of a voice in his head, revealing the victim owed him money, he knew he was a dead man, too.

54
WHICH WAY THE STORY

HANK ENCOURAGED VANESSA DO THE closing argument, and when she balked, saying she did not have the confidence, he answered, "I feel sure you're ready."

Her criminal law clinic at NYU, her summer internship with the DA, her one year in a New Jersey public defender's office before feeling overwhelmed and discouraged and turning to banking law—it was a primer next to what she'd learned from her father over the years, sitting next to him in the den when she was a teenager as he constructed his defense, playing "jury" when he practiced a closing argument, gleaning from him how he martialed the facts, zeroed in on the reasonable doubt, brought his conclusion home with a common man's poetry. She blushed with embarrassment at how she'd spoken to him at the Southern Folks diner when he said he was taking Julio's case—"Haven't you played Atticus Finch enough by now?"—and hoped he would not remember. She knew he would never bring it up again, simply try to make her the Atticus.

Mack had shown up at her front door late the night before, asking to come in, at first angry then imploring, saying he understood how she felt about Roger, that they could try again as a little family.

They would keep on all three together, he promised, not send their precious boy off. But she'd caught the bourbon on his breath, and knew she could not go back there again. All she said was, "I'm sorry, Mack, you've been drinking again, goodbye," then brewed coffee and sat down to sketch out her argument. At 2 a.m., still going strong, her phone buzzed. It was Hank. "Go over it with me," he said. As she talked through her speech he edited, shaped, became the father he'd been since her childhood, involved and guiding. This time another life was at stake.

The next morning the DA summarized the state's case, decrying "the willful stalking, robbery, and mortal knife attack on Beau Shepherd, the cold-blooded murder by an invader at first from afar, then a resident in our midst in a quiet little Alabama town where he'd even worked a party for his victim.

"The evidence has shown," O'Donnell went on, "that Julio Blanco, the defendant who conveniently got religion in jail, the Honduran who sent money to his mama back home by breaking immigration laws here in the United States, the 'model' employee of the Bay Resort Hotel and Golf Club who smoked marijuana with resort guests, was the perpetrator. With a garden knife he'd used that very day to weed and cut, taking the path through the golf course where he smoked a joint with strangers—and took a selfie with them, too, so brazen, so cavalier—he found Beau Shepherd alone and helpless on an isolated green, approaching him to rob him, plunge a knife into his chest, then hightailed it out once a coworker witnessed the crime. The defense has argued that the photo with the college students proves he was elsewhere at the time the murder commenced, but the coroner said there is a margin of error, a question, about just how long it would take a man to die from a stab wound to the lungs. How long had Blanco been standing there, grappling with Shepherd, before Cardenas saw him? Long enough for Shepherd to expire. And the defense wants you to believe that a digital image is the fact upon which Blanco's innocence hangs. But the professor of digital communications told us that, in this case, there is a margin of error. There's a term, exculpatory evidence, meaning evidence that shows the innocence of the accused. This is exactly the opposite. The evidence in this case is damning.

"Blanco confessed the murder to another inmate, yet changed his original account for us in the courtroom yesterday, saying there was a man in the bushes watching, the dying victim offering him the money and telling him to run. The knife, the blood, the DNA, his footprints, his confession, the eyewitness—that's not speculation, not a last-minute fantasy spun out by a desperate manipulator thinking he can wring sympathy from us by claiming he was helping a dying man. There is no margin of error in these facts. 'Help me.' We'll never know if that's what Beau Shepherd said as Blanco was stabbing him to death. Perhaps he said, 'Help me, God!'"

"You, the jury, have the decision in your hands. Julio Blanco can tell you one version of the story, then another, and yet another. Beau Shepherd is dead. Julio Blanco, right here, is the man, without doubt, who robbed him, murdered him, left him to his maker on the seventeenth hole. And fled."

She thanked the jury for doing their civic duty, concluding, "Your final duty is to return the verdict that is undeniable, without question, without doubt. Guilty."

Hank leaned over and whispered to Vanessa, "See this man before you," patted her on the back, and she was on her feet, moving toward the jury, seeing them as she'd researched their backgrounds, the descendants of immigrants, refugees, enslaved peoples, a Native American, a single tableau of community judging life or death. She felt suffused by her father's presence, the resonance of his voice in her own: "May it please the court."

She turned to Julio and gestured toward him. "See this man before you," she began. "Julio Blanco of San Pedro Sula, Honduras, young, hardworking, loving our country—the risk he takes in being here, even without these false accusations against him—loving the Lord, loving his family. Behind him, in the gallery, is his mother, Sra. Inés, next to her, his sister, Lupita. The testimony you've heard today that Julio sent money to his mother every week, money earned here working on the grounds crew of the Bay Resort Hotel and Golf Club, is absolutely true. A devoted son, a loyal brother, a dependable worker, a man of faith—that's the portrait that's emerged, in this courtroom since these proceedings began. A newcomer to our shores. Somebody yearning, struggling, determined, to make our home his home, too, a journey many of us here understand in our very bones because it's part of who we are.

"But this is not a trial about character, is it? It's about a trial about an action. Whether the accused"—facing the jury straight on she moved closer—"is the cold-blooded murderer who took Beau Shepherd down. Plain and simple. See this man, this man before you? If you believe the evidence shows that, beyond a reasonable doubt, he is the one, well, you know what to do. But if you believe that there is doubt, there is question, there is uncertainty that Julio Blanco did what the prosecution alleges—then not guilty has to be your verdict.

"This community was shattered when Beau Shepherd met his sad fate. For his family, friends, colleagues, those who knew him from his political campaigns, there was shock, grief, communal loss. A harmless man out playing golf on a beautiful fall day—what could be more picturesque in our bayside town—who meets a violent and bloody fate. That doesn't happen here on our lovely shores. We were all assaulted that autumn afternoon. But not by Julio Blanco. See this man? No, not by him.

"It is not our work here, of course, to solve the crime but to make sure that the wrong man doesn't get put away for years on end or, God help us, end up on death row. It is our job, together, to ascertain the facts, to listen to the witnesses, to review the evidence, and make sure it's airtight—or not. Not just 'convincing,' but inarguable. Proof. Plain and simple. Has my esteemed colleague, the district attorney, given that proof?"

She paced toward the bench and, to give the jury a break from eye contact—don't make them feel badgered, Hank had said—spoke toward the courtroom before turning to face the jury again, delineating each point of the prosecution's argument and explaining why it was "uncertain," or "highly subjective," or "flaky." Or "just plain wrong," and why the Instagram post of Julio provided an alibi of where he was at the time of the knife attack.

"No doubt," she said, "there is an urgency for the state to put the blame on somebody in a high-profile case like this, at a time of national debate, and contentiousness, over immigrants, a pressure to haul in someone who plays to our fears and put him on trial, even a passerby who decides to get involved. But 'anyone will do' is not the guiding principle of our justice system. Innocent until proven guilty *beyond a reasonable doubt*—that's the rule we live by. Mr. Blanco fled a country where that rule is not always honored, he came to a country where it is. We will make sure—you will make sure—it is honored here today."

Before her, as she argued, she saw flash the face of the woman in the caravan in northern Mexico, clutching her baby, trudging mile after mile, the sorrow yet determination, in her dark, absorbing eyes. When Vanessa had reached out touching her hand she had seen herself in the eyes of that stranger, and she wondered if she had made it across the border, been turned back, or was hunkered down still waiting her family's chance for a new day.

"My Dutch grandparents died in the Holocaust," she said, "but their son, my father, grew up here blessed with the rights of an equitable justice system, each defendant judged equally, without bias, without foregone conclusion. 'To save one life is to save the world,' he taught me, the words from a text in our religion. Julio Blanco tried to save a life—a stranger's. He would not be here today if he'd just kept walking.

"The life before you now—this man—is as sacred as all the world, the teaching means to me. Thank you, each and every one of you"— she scanned their faces slowly—"for your service to our community, to our criminal justice system. Your service to the highest good. To the golden rule we all commit to live in this country: Judge others as you would be judged. Innocent until proven guilty. You save the world when you save this life, the Reverend Julio Blanco, from an unjust verdict. I implore you to return, not with your hearts but your reason, the decision of not guilty."

55
AND IT CAME TO PASS

FOR SRA. INÉS THE DAY anticipating the jury's verdict began before sunrise, the prayer at her lips for Our Lady of Suyapa to enfold Julio in her robes, to give him the blessings of Jesus Christ Our Lord, just as she did at the Shrine of Suyapa, where she'd traveled time and again to pray for his safety. When she'd first walked into the Alabama courtroom, the scene had been just as she'd envisioned it at the feet of the Virgin, Julio falsely accused, needing her, as he needed her still. She tried to envision what the hours today might bring but could not, only that twelve men and women, strangers, would seal her son's fate.

For Lupita the day flowed from the night, her sleep fitful, imagining the two men in her life, Paco and Julio, like brothers since childhood, each in his isolation: in far-off Minnesota, and in the local jail, so far from each other after long being so close, chasing the soccer ball through the packed and sprawling hurricane shelter, taking up for each other, watching out for each other as gangs sought them still. Mr. Hank and Vanessa had defended Julio convincingly, she knew with the certainty of the cotton bolls out her window, but would the jury agree?

To Vanessa, who'd put her head on the pillow after the exhaustion of the closing argument, the morning came in a burst of sunlight, Roger next to her, his big eyes taking her in. She reached out and he snuggled into her shoulder. A friend of Lupita's, Sarita, a wisp of a girl from Uruguay, would arrive shortly to care for him. When the proceedings were done, she would start looking for a morning program for Roger in their bayside town. Even those few hours among new caretakers, other children, would be an adjustment for her, too. She had argued a capital case. She could do this now.

Julio woke secure, confident in his faith, not only Jesus walking by his side but also Lupita, Paco, Mr. Hank, Vanessa. He knew the verdict would be guilty—an appeal would follow, Mr. Hank said—but he was wrung out already with the process. He yearned for light, movement, the sea, Spanish all around. If they didn't believe him now why would they do so tomorrow, next year, at all? He'd heard the stories of men on death row, their appeals exhausted. He saw his own face there.

Hank's morning was like hundreds he'd known, waiting for a jury, rising early, drinking his coffee, thinking of his parents and brother and sister, feeling the air of an Amsterdam morning around him, realizing how one day could be the dividing line between sweetness and hell.

As long as he could be back by 8 a.m., shower and dress and be at the courthouse by 9 a.m., though, he'd be in good shape. He slipped into his fishing clothes, coiled the net into his red wagon, and started out. By the wild azaleas, by the marker for the founding of the town, on to the parking lot that by afternoon would be crowded with people heading down to herald the splendid sunset, he made his way. "Look there," he imagined saying to Roger as he got to the pier and saw a hurtling shadow of mullet—he missed having the boy with him—"it looks like a spirit breathing on the water."

He started to make up his net, throwing it over his arm, thinking not of Margery's dress now but June's—"forgive me," he whispered—nodding to Josie at her perch sidling closer, eyeing breakfast, when he saw Cooter approaching, crying out, "Did you hear? Did you hear!?"

"Hear what?"

"About Blue?"

"Blue?"

"They found his son. Over there in Africa, had a fever so bad he near 'bout died, pretty far from the plane crash, in a little village up in the jungle. In a coma, didn't know nothing when he come out of it, no ID, name, no nothing."

"Baruch shem," Hank said, stunned by the news. "Praise to God."

"Kind of funny if you ask me," Cooter said, "somebody out here said they saw somebody looked like little Zach Blue more'n a year ago."

"Maybe a haint," said T. Brown, using the slang for "haunt," a ghost.

A number of the pier regulars had started going to town to sit in on the trial at first but they'd returned to fish after a few days of snugging on neckties. The novelty was gone.

"What's happening with the Spanish kid?" Cooter asked.

"Jury's deliberating right now."

"Good luck to him," he said, the first words of warmth the grizzled old-timer had uttered in a thousand mornings.

"To you, too, Hank," the Browns chimed.

Had the pier jury changed its mind about Julio? "We should have presented our case out here," Hank said.

"Could be," said Cooter enigmatically.

"I need to talk to Blue," he said. "What a miracle!"

"Blue's gone," said B. Brown.

"Good and gone," said T. Brown.

"Where to?"

"Somewhere," Cooter said, "not here."

Josie's wings bellowed like a judge's robes. She looked grave, Solomonic.

The sun pushing up hit Hank in the eye and he sensed the hour had come to head home, get ready and head to court.

He tried to focus on the circus awaiting him—the gaggle of press and curiosity seekers and advocates, the friends and family, the prosecutors and law enforcement officers, the bailiff and Judge Stone, the guards leading Julio into the courtroom. In his mind, he saw Blue, leaning on the pier railing looking off for his son. Where had he been the last week of the trial? He'd not seen him at all.

When he was a boy he could size people up right away, know who to trust, how to survive. It had gotten him to America but he'd lost those instincts. He wouldn't survive now for a week, a day, in a concealing and deceptive world.

As soon as he approached the courthouse, saw the crowd, entered the corridors to the signal that the jury was returning, he felt the blood surge through him. Vanessa met him and they went in together. Julio was led to his place alongside them and the jury filed in.

When the forewoman stepped forward, he sensed what her conclusion would be. He could tell by her stoicism, the flinty tone of the syllables pulsing forward as she said: "We the jury find the defendant guilty as charged."

Sra. Inés cried out, Lupita's voice rose above hers. "No, no!" Julio bent over as if kicked in the stomach by fate. Vanessa sagged as if she might crumple, and the raucous joy from Beau Shepherd's supporters hung in the air only a moment before Judge Stone rapped his gavel and warned against outbursts of emotion.

Silence engulfed the courtroom.

Hank got to his feet. "The defense requests a polling of the jury."

The judge responded, "The court will poll the jury," and spoke to the twelve: "I will ask each of you in turn, individually, to affirm the verdict you have delivered. Answer clearly and succinctly, yes or no."

For Sra. Inés the answers came like the beat of the waves when her husband drowned:

"Is this your verdict?"

"Yes."

For Lupita like the rocks smashing her roof:

"Is this your verdict?"

"Yes."

For Vanessa the voice of Mack slapping her:

"Is this your verdict?"

"Yes."

For Julio the dumbbell smashing his head:

"Is this your verdict?"

"Yes."

For Hank the footsteps of his mother and father walking away, not turning back, gone, forever gone.

"Is this your verdict?"

"Yes."

"Yes."

"Yes."

"Yes."

"Yes."

"Yes."

"Yes."

"Maybe."

Hank felt a light rising inside of him, Josie taking them aloft.

"Tony Weaver?" Judge Stone addressed juror number twelve, the gentleman, Hank realized, who was Mowa Choctaw.

"You must give a yes or no answer."

"I just don't go along with it, Your Honor. They ganged up on me."

"Mr. Weaver," the judge pressed. "The jury has delivered a verdict of guilty. Is this your verdict?"

He shook his head. "Could be wasn't him."

"I will ask you one final time: Is this your verdict?"

A calm, certain look spread across the juror's face. "No."

Judge Stone glowered at the assembled, hand on his gavel, as if ready to call order. No one moved.

Hank held his breath, waiting to see if he would send the jury back for further deliberations.

"I declare a mistrial."

56
THE MAN INSIDE

Lᴜᴘɪᴛᴀ ɪᴍᴀɢɪɴᴇᴅ ʜᴇʀ ʜᴏᴜsᴇ ꜰɪʟʟᴇᴅ with camellias that Paco had snipped. She envisioned Mr. Hank and June and Vanessa and Roger arriving with sweet potato casserole and pecan pie and green beans and cornbread dressing, Mama in charge of the turkey roasting in the oven, the tablecloth embroidered with bright birds flung over the table for their Thanksgiving feast. She fantasized that Julio, scrubbed and smiling, had a young woman, a *novia*, at his side, *una americana*, his rogue walk over a grim lawn to a bleeding man a nightmare long behind. In her fantasy, Julio handed her a bottle of chilled champagne, then knelt to little Julio, Paco's and her baby boy, teetering, tottering, in his first steps, *un americano pequeño. Sin pregunta.* A little American. Without question.

Only three days had passed since the victorious mistrial and, with Julio remanded to jail, they waited for an update about a retrial. She waited for word from Mr. Hank, tried to be patient for word from Paco, looked forward to taking care of Roger again. Sarita was scheduled to fill in for one more day. She tried to put out of her mind that Mama would have to depart when her tourist visa expired. The news of Julio had filled the papers in San Pedro; a correspondent for a Latin American wire service filed stories. Back home her brother, she knew, would be a mark.

She took a deep breath like Vanessa had shown her from yoga class, exhaled slowly. Mama rested on the couch; the diamond-starred night pressed at the window.

Why did she smell turkey burning in the oven? Hadn't that image been in her dream?

She opened her front door and saw the flickers of red at the bottom of the steps, jumping to the side of the house, flames wavering, spreading.

"¡*Fuego!*"

Mama was already up running water, dunking the bedsheets in the sink, helping her lay the drenched fabric against the flames. The fire smoked through, sending up the noxious fumes, and a voice yelled out from the fields, "Your murderer got off free!"

"You're the murderer," Lupita shouted back then went inside to push a blanket into the sink, come back out and throw it over a lick skittering toward the rooftop.

The field resounded: "Law fucking breakers!"

She hollered: "We are not afraid of you!"

Red lights flashed and a siren screamed and the volunteer fire department trained the hoses on the walls and the streams rocketed inside, blasting the chairs and couch, the bed and chest of drawers, smoke and water, ruin.

After the fire was extinguished and the sheriff took Lupita's statement, she phoned Vanessa, who insisted, "I'm coming to get you two," and within the hour, their soggy, smoky clothes in trash bags, they were in the luxurious quiet of her friend's house.

Early morning her phone vibrated with the text from Paco: his address in Minnesota and the words: *"Ahora es seguro."* Now it is safe.

"Estaremos allí pronto." We will be there soon.

On the move—it was her life, still.

Vanessa did not ask, nor Mr. Hank, what their destination would be, secure in knowing Paco would be waiting. "We will put five months' severance in your account," he said. *"Gracias, mi amiga, por todas."*

"¡Todos!" she corrected.

"Sí, por supuesto, mi maestra," he said, and she grinned. My teacher.

Vanessa and Roger drove them to see Julio first, then on to the bus station. Before they boarded, Roger wrapped his arms around her. "No, Lupe."

"I will come back to see you."

"No go."

"Do not be sad."

"Do not," he said slowly, "be sad," and she yearned to know that how he'd spoken—clear, whole words like dance steps one in front of the other—were more than repetition.

This was her prayer to Our Lady of Suyapa, too, and she felt his arms hold tight as Mama pulled at her gently to break away as the bus driver was saying, "All aboard," and she gazed into Roger's soft brown eyes and believed that inside was a young man like any other who'd one day stand tall, her name on his lips, rhythmic and distinct.

"I pray for you always, Roger. I love you."

"Bye, Lupe. I love you. Bye."

PART V

57
THE MOUNTAINSIDE

HE WAS A MARKED MAN but a free one, walking the streets on the outskirts of San Pedro Sula, in his backpack his essential belongings. He breathed in *platanos fritos y carne asada, tortillas de maize y pan dulce*—plaintain fritters, grilled steak, corn tortillas, sweet bread— the aromas curling from the windows of houses he'd known since his teen years, stepping by one place abandoned, its front wall pockmarked by bullets, another at the end of the block, a charred hulk torched in a gang rivalry.

He might have one day to survive, a month, or year. He may have lived out his good fortune, but he was not afraid.

A second digital image had been sent anonymously to Mr. Hank, the DA, the judge, and a newspaper reporter, the message traced to a server in the Bay Resort business center, used by countless guests. The time stamp was 5:19, five minutes before the picture of Julio with the college boys. The photo showed the walkway under the oaks by the golf course, close to the seventeenth green. At a distance, striding away from the course, heading onto a thicket of scrub trees, was a lean figure, features indistinct. He was wearing a red visor.

Mr. Hank and Bridget O'Donnell met with the judge. With inconclusive evidence, the state dropped the charges against Julio.

When he'd gotten the word in lockup he felt a slap at his chest, like Enrique in the prayer meeting showing how the Lord struck. He felt the imprint of that hand, ecstatic and sustaining, when he'd been released, walking out with Mr. Hank. He did not cover his face like the men on their perp walks, led to jail, cameras following. Exiting he was indifferent to everything but the voluminous sky, the streaming sun, the other survivor, Mr. Hank, at his side. The last time he'd felt this expansiveness was on Mobile Bay, in the boat, pushed by the rising wind as the heavy weather rolled in.

This time he'd be ready for the storm. Two days after being released ICE agents came for him. He did not resist. Death threats had been made against him after the trial, and he felt eyes on him at the store, in the yard. He belonged nowhere. On the move—it was his life, still.

With the burning palm of God upon him, before the house that was Mama's already inhabited by ghosts, he stopped and knelt to the street where she had cradled Paz, collapsed with the bullet in her skull. "Paco, Paco!" she'd called for her far-off son, blood spreading at her temple, curdling onto the road. How his mother held her, rocking, smoothing her blood-matted hair, praying for her eternal soul.

"May Jesus our Lord keep you," he whispered, his prayer echoing Mama's. "And may he bless Paco and Lupita and the new life she carries. Your grandbaby, and Mama's."

He stood and said a prayer for his father and Abuelo, and for all those cut down by violence on these streets, in the country that he loved and that came up through him in its faces and voices and fields and coastlines. The sensation returned of a body sagging against him, the odor of whiskey and sweat, beefy arms around him, holding tight. Had God sent him into that labyrinth so that the seeming stranger, whose breath was on his neck even now two thousand miles away, would not die alone? "Beau Shepherd," he said. "I pray for your soul, too."

He had a distinct sensation of a man letting loose, stepping back, giving release.

A pack of boys rounded the corner, muscular and loping, a hydra-headed creature. They circled him, moved closer.

He backed up to Mama's entrance and pushed—the door swung open—and saw what they'd always kept there, at the ready. He reached in and grasped the machete, swung it to his side like he was on his way to hack clean the tangled, abandoned lots.

The five youths did not move.

"*Te reconocemos,*" said the leader, a scrawny teen. *"Páganos."* We recognize you. Pay us.

If he gave them what they wanted, he'd have no rest from their demands. He gripped the machete. The youngest looked no older than twelve.

He gave them 500 Lempiras. Twenty US dollars.

The leader nodded to the others. *"Volveremos."* We will be back.

As they roamed away, they turned as one to spot him, marking him for all time. Others who knew him better would come by soon. Those who'd remember how Paco had killed one of their own on his behalf. There would be no negotiations.

He wedged the machete into his backpack and felt the cash in his pocket raised by the denizens of Fairhope Pier. He'd exchanged currency at the airport. Now he took out 1,000 Lempiras.

"Ricardo!" he shouted at the house two doors down.

"Hombre!" said a wizened man, emerging, blinking at the light. "You're here."

"I want to hire you to take me to the mountains. It is a long way." He held out the money.

They first stopped at a market where Julio stocked his backpack with food, candles and matches, and a flashlight with extra batteries. Moments later in Ricardo's truck, they rolled by the banks and restaurants where armed guards stood sentinel, the church spires and office buildings and tourist hotels, the patches of dirt and benches where old men on plastic chairs gathered at dominos, embankments at the edge of town where the metal roofs of lean-to's caught the afternoon sun. The truck swept upward onto the highway, coursing through the scrub pine and a lone ceiba like Goliath standing out against the horizon. They jounced over higher and higher terrain over the next hour until Julio could look out the passenger window at the world falling away below.

With the small terrace farms and workhorses moseying in corrals and goats and sheep grazing, the vista took on an unreal glow, like a memory of home from his jail cell, the ordinary vista illuminated with majesty. The deepening incline—so quick to reveal itself, with lives clinging to its sides—was the landscape inside of him.

Was that a pelican below turning a slow circle, far from coastal La Ceiba, like it had in his dream? The first one he'd seen was on a trip to the Caribbean coast with Abuelo, the last on Mobile Bay when he and Paco, on a night off together when life was still sweet, cast their lines off Fairhope Pier, the water bird sidling close when Paco pulled up a croaker. He'd seen them through the high window of his jail cell, their V's arrowing past like a rebuke: you are jailed, we are free. He could soar now, too.

Ricardo downshifted, his truck climbing, wheels grinding their way up the curving road. A transport truck appeared in front, cages visible as they closed in: a delivery of hogs. They came within two car lengths, so that Julio could see the pink porcine flesh, the snouts snuffling at the wires, and Ricardo, forced to slow, shouted ahead, "¡Pendejo!" Soon they were nearly creeping and Ricardo cursed,

"*Chinga tu madre.*" He downshifted again and pushed his foot on the accelerator, gaining speed to pass. The road was visible only a short distance before it veered around the mountainside. They were alongside the hog truck when a red sedan approached from the opposite direction.

"*¡Cuidado, cuidado!*" Julio shouted.

"*No te preoccupes,*" Ricardo assured him, not to worry, and instead of slowing to tuck behind the hog truck again he jammed the accelerator to the floor, gaining on the transport inch by inch with the sedan speeding closer, no place for Ricardo to swerve away but the narrow edge of the mountain road then down into the ravine.

The large winged creature was joined by another, not pelicans, Julio realized, but vultures, their sooty black plumage and bare black heads tracking them as if sensing a feast. Julio could see Ricardo's truck in his mind slipping over the edge, hurtling downward, his newly free life crushed to carrion.

He heard a mashing of gears, a whirr, and the propulsion of the engine was like an old man renewed—why did Mr. Hank flash in front of him?—and Ricardo burst ahead of the hog transport, lurching in front as the sedan barreled past on its side of the road.

"*Gracias a Dios,*" Julio said, and Ricardo crossed himself and laughed at Julio's distress.

They turned onto a smaller road, bumped and jostled over stones, into declivities, pushing beyond any semblance of a road onto a tangled trail, then stopped. "*Ahora, basta,*" Ricardo said. He had driven as far as he could go.

As Julio said farewell and Ricardo rumbled away, he felt the stillness return.

Around him the quiet of the mountain rose, enveloping him, until in the silence he heard the distant chattering of starlings and a tree limb cracking and a brook making its music in a way he had forgotten existed outside the din of the jailhouse and the combative-ness of the courtroom and the reverberations of violence through the streets of his city, like the voice of the land speaking to him. His faith was still strong—"I'll never walk alone," he sang as he trod up the concealed path, the English words from the prayer group circling like a net cast inside his head—but he did not ache for Jesus as he had in his cell. Pastor Blanco he could have called himself returning here, but he felt strength in being just Julio.

"¡Qué hermoso este mundo, este lugar!" And as the recognition wove through him—how beautiful this world, this place—one word for him conjured it all. *Perfecto.* The question that had dogged him for months on end, "Why have I been punished?" now changed. "Why have I been spared?"

He pushed on until he could have closed his eyes and felt his way from the knowledge of boyhood. Where the henhouse once stood, splinters of boards were still embedded in the dirt, their white paint bleached away by twenty years' time. Two posts were all that remained from the small corral where Mama had kept her cow. A mule appeared from the bushes, surely belonging to someone on a random plot where a new generation struggled for subsistence. Abuelo had once told him he had a deed for their hardscrabble acre-age, and the fact the top of it had sheared off in the landslide did not affect title. The plot was still theirs.

The only way he could figure out its perimeters, though, was to start where he had last sat with his teacher and other students when the maelstrom changed all and draw a bead from there. The building and the trees he remembered being by the windows were gone. And young trees and saplings sprouted everywhere. He tried to figure where the classroom had been. He walked in the general direction of a large piece of tin half-buried and corroded and saw an item glinting white in the sun beside it. He knelt and dug and felt hard, smooth bits of a substance. He pulled it up. Bone.

Children swinging their legs at their desks, the scratching of pencils, a spitball fired, the bell ringing not for recess but the incoming storm, the roof collapsing as they tried to flee. He had never looked back until now. He went to the edge of the clearing and hacked saplings to make a cross tied with a vine. He interred the bones in a shallow grave. "Bless this child."

He went back to the siding of tin, extricated it and leaned it against a sapling, reclining beneath it, eating and falling asleep.

When he woke the next morning to whispers and chatter, he reached for his machete out of instinct but opened his eyes to see three little children standing at the edge of his metal lean-to. A fourth joined them and together, silent now, they looked back in puzzlement. He sat up. They jumped back.

"*¿Quiénes sois?*" Who are you, he asked?

They recited their names and he told them his.

"*¿Es tu casa?*" one asked.

He shook his head, no, it was not his house. "*Es mi escuela,*" he said. "School."

"*¿Usted es el maestro?*"

He hesitated. "*Sí, soy el maestro.*" He added in English: "Teacher."

"Tea - cher," they repeated slowly.

"*Mi escuela,*" he said.

The group—one more, now another—ran up, and in unison they sat down cross- legged. Waiting.

"*La escuela,*" he said again, patting the ground.

"School!" they chimed.

"*Sí. Bueno.* School!"

And he began.

58
CIRCLING

THE LIGHT ON THE PRINSENGRACHT Canal looked like it had more than eighty years ago, in the last snapshot in Hank's mind of morning out his window—silvery-blue over the gable rooftops, the Dutch row houses stepping off into the distance, light swathing the canal boats like a silken scarf, gossamer over the pots of tulips lining the banks, the young couples strolling, bicycles whirring by. The family who owned the house now, a doctor and teacher and their three children, had welcomed him in when he knocked on the door announcing he had resided there as a boy. Could he just take a look?

His had been the window on the top floor, looking down just like now as he touched his fingers to the pane, seeing the lady with the cape passing, Josie, singing. Did he hear her now?

"Mijn kleine," he heard a voice. My little one.

"Moeder? Vader?"

"Scholen," a voice answered. Time for school.

But these youngsters bounding down the steps to the kitchen were not Shayna and Benyamin but the children of the doctor, and he was gripping the banister to steady himself as he descended.

I must write all this to June, he thought.

It surprised him how often he'd thought of her since arriving in Amsterdam for the January light festival. They'd only known each other several months. At each phase of the trial—from the opening arguments to the verdict, with its startling turnaround by the lone juror—she'd been there at day's end, walking with him to the pier. He couldn't bring himself to sit on Margery's bench with her, so he made sure they just walked. On the day the photo appeared of the red-capped stranger they were on a bay stroll and the pier regulars, looking at it, too, pronounced their verdict: "That's Blue's boy. I'd know his lanky self just by that way he stooped, played basketball until he tore his hamstring, used to hang out here some, couldn't fish worth a damn, hung over the pier looking for what, no idea. Guess he found it."

When the FBI ran the image through its database and turned up no match, the pier jury was unmoved, insisting, in a story more dramatic with each telling that Zach Blue, surviving the crash, had sustained a concussion, struggled to keep up with Beau until he collapsed, was nursed back to health by villagers, and vowed to get even with the man who'd turned his back on him. "Unlikely," Hank had said, but even June had a theory: Blue knew full well what his son was up to and was a coconspirator. "If it were Blue's son," Hank told her, "I feel sure Blue didn't know at the time. But what if he knows it now? Would you turn in your son?" Then another theory developed among the fishermen when a con man serving time in Louisiana for embezzlement claimed he knew the murderer, a hit man with ties to the old Dixie Mafia sent to exact revenge on the golfer for a titanic gambling debt. "What do you think?" they pressed Hank. "What I know," he told them, "is that the wrong man didn't hang on my watch."

With June at his side he'd watched as the ICE agents took Julio into custody to transport him to the flight for Miami then on to

San Pedro. *"Abuelo,"* Julio said, and no other words were needed. He prayed for Julio's safety on return, a new life, eluding old dangers. Hank took June's hand and said, "If Julio can face what might happen in his home, I can face what did happen in mine. It's time for me to visit." That night, they'd sunk back on the sofa, June nestling against his shoulder, and dozed off together.

"I must tell you everything," he imagined sharing with her, as he left his boyhood home and started to the old Jewish quarter.

"These are the cobblestones I walked. This is the corner where we stopped to get chocolate. This is the synagogue where we gathered on Friday night and Saturday morning."

It was a historic site with a museum display of Kiddush cups and Seder plates and photographs of Amsterdam's Jewish community before the Nazis came.

He hesitated to look. Who might he recognize? He heard the cantor's chant and looked around. The walls echoed of voices in prayer.

"Come," his parents said.

How could he be six when he was going on eighty-four? How could he journey the street coming to a small bridge named for Walter Süskind—the man who'd condemned then tried to save his fellow Jews, as he'd told students—when he could close his eyes and feel himself ambling with Roger to the bay at dawn, pointing at the pelicans wheeling and the mullet sweeping in like a divine exhalation?

He found himself in a leafy area he recognized from his walks with his father, the Plantage, with its botanic garden suffusing the air with the scent of vegetation, the historic greenhouse with its windows like a house of worship.

"Are we on a trip?" he had asked as the whole family, Mama, Papa, Benyamin, Shayna, suitcases in hand, walked by the greenhouse, other families ahead of them, turning onto the street where the trolley ran by majestic buildings, including the theater where his parents had once taken him to a musical show.

"Don't be afraid, Haim," his father said. "We are all together."

When they arrived at the ornate façade of the theater, with jackbooted guards in front waving them in, he saw the other children there beside grown-ups, and there was Reuben and Jacob and Meester Moishe, their teacher, too, but he did not reprimand them like at school as they ran boisterously through the courtyard but sat glumly on a crowded bench where other adults pressed their faces into their hands and an old man wept and Papa began talking in a loud voice to a guard who answered in German and jammed the butt of a truncheon into Papa's chest and pushed him backward. He watched Papa's face turn red and start to lunge at the guard but Meester Moishe and another man jumped up and held him back. Then Hank saw his father lean forward—he was in disbelief, even now remembering it—and spit at the guard. The guard drew a Luger and pointed it at Papa's head. Hank ran to hug his father at the knees.

The woolen pants and slender calves and soft, scholar's belly where Hank pressed his cheek, saying, "Don't hurt my Papa"— he felt it all. The guard laughed and with his free hand squeezed Hank's shoulder, saying in Dutch, "A brave boy. You will work for the Rhineland, too," and commanded his father, "Beg my forgiveness."

The moment stretched long, Hank clutching tighter, peering up at Papa whose hand pressed against his back, the look on his face as if he'd tasted something foul. He would not respond.

The guard waved the barrel toward the ground. Papa pushed Hank away—Mama reached out and swept him into her embrace— and the guard commanded, *Kus mijn laars.* Kiss my boot.

"The law will not tolerate this," Papa said.

"Wij zijn de wet." He cocked the Luger. We are the law.

"Reuven," Mama implored.

Papa sank to his knees. *"Vergeef me."* He touched his lips to the gleaming black leather.

The guard holstered his gun, Papa stood, and they were given their bedding and led to a room with other detainees. Hank tried to catch Papa's eye, but his father looked away.

Forgive me. The apology wove through the years to find him still, Papa's low, tremulous voice. "You were the brave one," Hank whispered.

He felt the familiar ire rise up in him, the image of Papa powerless, felt his shame. He thought of Julio dragged in from the bay, powerless, judged. *We are the law.* The outrage of those words, the arrogance.

In the night he'd awakened in the theater to whispering. Mama and Papa huddled in a corner talking with another man, and by morning he had looked for Shayna and Benyamin but couldn't find them. They'd been taken across the street to the daycare compound, where the youth were moved. "It is only for a night, two nights," Papa said. Three nights passed. Four.

During the days the detainees gathered in the courtyard—more Jews arrived—and names were called to join those in transport to Westerbork, then on to what they believed were labor camps in Germany. Rumors circulated. The work camps were death camps.

The nightly whisperings grew until he'd roll over to see a cluster of adults with Mama and Papa, and the hour came when his parents said to him, "You must join your brother and sister in the children's residence." *No* he wanted to shout, but he said, "Yes, Mama, yes, Papa," and then they were on the street holding him tightly and saying goodbye before they disappeared into the compound without turning around.

In the daycare, turned into a dormitory, were rows of cots like in the stories he'd heard about orphanages, the innocents crying out for their parents in the middle of the night, the teachers taking them out for a walk around the block once a day with a guard patrolling alongside, and a man in shiny black hat and black uniform with medals and red armband with black swastika double-checking their numbers when they returned: *"Eins, zwei, drei, vier, fünf, sechs, sieben."* All the way to fifteen. *"Fünfzehn!"*

Hank had been *"fünfzehn."*

He entered the former seminary now, in the process of being turned into a visitor center along with the theater across the street. There were brochures on racks, signage showing where the adjacent nursery and daycare had been, the dormitory and garden, the hallways that served as passageways for children to be desperately spirited from capture to freedom, until found out.

A young blonde woman at the desk asked him in Dutch if she could provide him information, and when he answered in English, "No, I have been here before," she smiled and said, "Just let me know."

He stopped before a framed photograph on the wall of children on rows of cots. Had the captors taken it to show the tidiness of the bedding? He searched for a familiar face. One little boy, head on his pillow, looked piercingly at the camera.

The receptionist walked to his side. "It tears at the heart, doesn't it?" she said. "I see this image every day. Who can imagine the terror those children felt? Taken from their parents, so close across the street, kept here knowing nothing. This one." She touched her index finger to the boy glaring back at the photographer. "The hurt in this expression."

"The anger," Hank said.

Was he looking into his own eyes?

"Yes, I see that," she said.

She explained how some of the youngest children were rescued, lifted over the garden wall, hiding in closets, waiting until dark to be passed among strangers, into cars, on to church basements. Others were saved when the teacher took them for a fitness walk and, turning a blind corner, the last child in line was kidnapped by the Dutch underground. In one strategy a child jumped from a window on the street to take his place. "The teacher put her life on the line. The count could not change."

"The fortunate ones," he said.

"The ones whose parents took the risk," she said.

"What do you mean?"

"The parents who gave secret word that they wanted their children to be abducted to freedom—at great peril. If their children were caught they'd be bludgeoned, shot. Some parents felt it was too dangerous, that the children would never be put on transports to the camps, that it was a matter of time before the children were let go, that the Nazis could not be that heartless."

"The parents never knew their fate," Hank said.

Mama and Papa, whispering in the night, passing on the secret word: do whatever you can, even in mortal danger, to rescue our boy.

"All the adults were deported and murdered." She kissed her palm and laid it gently over the photo, as if to soothe the little ones. "And all the children who were not rescued, every last one, disappeared onto the trains."

He thanked her and stepped outside and walked down the street. At the corner, under a window.

This place.

He looked up.

A brightness caught him and he blinked to see streaks of white against the sky, like a great bird enormously winged, the white pelican he had charted above him near Haarlem, a harbinger of the world to come. He wiped at the sunspots, and the creature was gone, and he was that little boy gazing furiously into the face of the oppressor, now the old man looking back over the injustices he had confronted, reaching up and pulling down the sky and proclaiming so Mama and Papa and the whole world would hear him: "I'm still here. Here I am."

*

ACKNOWLEDGMENTS

WHILE I WRITE ALONE ON my Alabama porch, my literary community stretches far beyond. In this novel of the imagination, as in all my writing, that community is nurturing and vital.

It begins, as all else, with family: my wife, Nancy, listening to every iteration of my ideas, offering insights, affirmation, and love; our daughter, Meredith, a writer and immigration lawyer who closely read my manuscript and inspires me with her commitment to helping others; the home I grew up in with big sisters Sherrell, Becky, and Robbie, who celebrated books, music, and theater; and my parents, Evelyn, who taught me the joy of creativity, and Charley, whose vigorous legal practice, until age 97, showed his empathy, toughness, and passion for the law.

I owe thanks to my literary agent, Joelle Delbourgo, for her wise counsel and dedication; my insightful editor at Arcade, Lilly Golden; Skyhorse Group Editorial Director, Mark Gompertz; book jacket designer, Erin Seaward-Hiatt; and Fairhope artist JD Crowe, for his evocative cover photo of Mobile Bay.

I'm grateful to Sena Jeter Naslund and Karen Mann for inviting me twenty years ago to teach in Spalding University's low-residency MFA program, now, wonderfully, the Naslund-Mann Graduate School of Writing. They offered invaluable responses to this manuscript. I've gained insights from faculty colleagues, among them Elaine Neil Orr, Kenny Cook, John Pipkin, Julie Brickman, Dianne Aprile, Jeanie Thompson, Debra Kang Dean, Helena Kriel, Charlie Schulman, Kathleen Driskell, Lynnell Edwards, Ellyn Lichvar, and Katy Yocom.

Charles Salzberg and Karl Hein, New York friends, gave me expert first readings, along with Lynn and Cori Yonge in Fairhope, Frye Gaillard and Billie Goodloe in Mobile, and Andy Antippas in New Orleans.

Friends in the legal profession have offered key advice about my story, including Michael Gerhardt, Rosemary Chambers, Carrie and Ted Fiorito, and the dear, late David Weiner. Former Mobile Police detective Mark Johnson, a writer, helped me with details of law enforcement. Ann Harmon, a lifelong friend in Madrid, aided me with Spanish.

Others have been supportive, among them Lee Smith, Don Noble, John Sledge, Bill Pangburn and Renee Magnanti, Eli Evans, Richard Goodman, Doug Garr, William Oppenheimer, Barry Silverman, Howell and Krystyna Raines, Judy Culbreth and Walter Kirkland, Bob and Teen Siener, Champ and Anne Meyercord, Mimi and Steve Johnson, Rickie and Larry Voit, Rex and Marty Leatherbury, Dewey English, Jennifer Paddock, Jake Reiss, Tom Lowenburg, Walter Edgar, Mallory McDuff, Stephan Zguta, Bill Ferris and Marcie Cohen Ferris, Lezlee Peterzell-Bellanich, and all my book-loving extended family.

Historian and journalist Rodolfo Pastor, of Honduras, a New Orleans neighbor when we were at Tulane, welcomed me twice to Honduras: after college graduation, and twenty-five years later, when I was reporting on Hurricane Mitch. I felt deeply imprinted by those journeys.

Many sojourns have nurtured this book: walking miles of Amsterdam streets; interviewing Holocaust survivors in Alabama;

reporting on religion, criminal trials, and the diverse cultures of the South; the countless, precious hours with my dad, hearing his stories about his legal work; the stories my daughter Meredith told me as she reported on immigration, and co-produced a 2017 documentary, *Los Retornados*, about Hondurans seeking US asylum sent back home.